PRAISE FOR WHISPER HOUSE PRESS

Editor Capone has done a masterful job, as this multifaceted collection offers something for everybody. [...] This is a gripping compendium to curl up with on a spooky night or a haunted holiday.

KIRKUS REVIEWS — DREAD MONDAYS

A well done, page-turning anthology of stories about home being where the horror is.

KIRKUS REVIEWS — COSTS OF LIVING

Horror has often explored precisely what's terrifying about particular places. The frightening solitude of the woods, the crushing loneliness of an urban crowd, the eerie uniformity of the suburbs. [...] *Costs of Living* is the first collection that I know of which encompasses all of these extremes of experience across a wide swath of space. City, country, and suburb are all explored as terrifying places, proving that there's no place which is safe. With editor Steve Capone's first anthology, Whisper House has announced itself (by scream!) as one of the most promising small horror presses today, and *Costs of Living* proves itself to be an anthology that's very much of the moment and will promise to frighten the ever-living hell out of you—wherever you live.

ED SIMON, PUBLIC HUMANITIES SPECIAL FACULTY AT CARNEGIE MELLON AND AUTHOR OF *DEVIL'S CONTRACT: THE HISTORY OF THE FAUSTIAN BARGAIN* AND *PANDEMONIUM: A VISUAL HISTORY OF DEMONOLOGY*

While I devoured every bit of this anthology, I could barely look away [...]. *Costs of Living* is a riveting horror anthology that speaks to our sense of security and comfort.

CHRISTINA PERSAUD AT *ARTICLES OF HORROR*

Whatever your path in life, whatever your story is, there will be tales in this book that will hit you.

BOOKS FOR DECAYING MILLENNIALS — COSTS OF LIVING

DREAD MONDAYS

DREAD MONDAYS

A WHISPER HOUSE PRESS HORROR ANTHOLOGY

Dread Mondays: A Whisper House Press Horror Anthology

Copyright © 2025 Whisper House Press

For copyright information, contact the publisher at editor@whisperhousepress.com.

ISBN, Trade Paper: 979-8-9893919-6-7

ISBN, Ebook: 979-8-9893919-7-4

Cover Design by JD&W

Interior Design & Editing by Whisper House Press

CONTENTS

FROM THE EDITOR'S DESK

About halfway through my work on *Costs of Living*, I knew I couldn't stop with one anthology. I love the work. Putting together these books has been both the most complex and the easiest thing I've ever done. I find a great joy in collaborative production and plan to do more of it.

As soon as contributing authors completed reviews of our galley proofs of *Costs of Living* in August of 2024, an impulsive (and also compulsive) thought struck: I should do another one. And you know what else? September 1st would be a great day to launch a new project.

Why did I feel so compelled? The reasons were many and auspicious, indeed. Let's see...

For starters, *one* is a prime number. September 1st was a good day to start a project.

And if I kept the call open for two months, the close would fall on October 31st—the spookiest day of the year! (We ended up holding an extended deadline for limited demographics, but the original intent of a Halloween deadline held.) *And* we could close this anthology's call exactly one year before launching the book—September

1st's *Costs of Living* launch and October 31st's* *Dread Mondays* pub date were nicely separated while still landing close together enough on the calendar that marketing for each could pull double-duty in service of its complement.

There's the serendipity of starting a new project as we put a bow on the first one.

AND we'd be launching the second call exactly one year to the day away from the release of the first anthology, *Costs of Living*.

And beyond all this, I came up with the perfect name: *Dread Mondays*.

All the stars had aligned, and I determined (irreligious and unsuperstitious though I am) the universe had issued a command. I was therefore in no position to disobey.

My family and friends asked: Aren't you just finishing up the first one? Don't you need a break? No, dammit. I do not need a break. I need to *keep swimming*.

Costs of Living hadn't drained me of energy. Rather, that experience had jolted me as though I'd been asleep. My work with thirty-five authors on that project taught me a lot (see the "behind the scenes" / "from the editor's desk" notes on WHP's website), but the most important lesson of the bunch has been that this—curating, editing, interior designing, marketing, and publishing—is something I can do, and that makes me happy.

I can do it, I'm good at it, and I love the work. So why not a second anthology? And maybe a third... and a fourth...? As long as I can afford the costs, financial and otherwise, I am going to keep moving forward.

On that note, and as of my writing this editor's note, Whisper House Press has passed its first birthday without a print publication to its name. This has all gone as planned, but I hadn't foreseen the pressures that would conspire against continuing a publishing busi-

---

* We have since shifted the pub date to October 25th, 2025 to line up with some Utah Book Festival events.

ness that would cost a lot of money and even more time operating over eighteen months before offering any product to a market we have no idea if we can reach. It's all been costs and unknowns, multiplying and then compounding.

Except for the stuff that has really mattered most to me. These are: the connections I've made with authors, the pleasure of reading submissions (over 900 in the past year!), conversing with writers for interviews I've posted on our YouTube channel, and of course editing this work in partnership with the oh-so-high-spirited-and-kind contributors.

In February of 2025, we held a successful Kickstarter to raise a portion of my expenditures on that first book. That outcome was somewhat motivating, but if there's a football analogy that works here, it's "the best defense is a good offense," so I kept at it and got to work on editing *Dread Mondays*.

The *Dread Mondays* call had garnered over 600 submissions, of which I was able to accept thirty-six shorts. They vary in length—from ten words (Bénédicte Kusendila's poem) to Gallegos and Darkish's joint effort "Cutting Room," which clocks in at 3,899. Just under 72,000 words in all and a 2,000-words-per-story perfect average (another sign?). This is starting to look like a *The Number 23* situation...

As I edited, the *Dread Mondays* collection brought many a smile to these parched lips. I was tickled by Bert Piedmont's second entry into the Whisper House Press annals of teacup raptor tales, was grossed out at the aforementioned, no-holds-barred "Cutting Room," was inspired by Lisa Morton's support and her excellent submission —a delight of cosmic workplace horror. I was honored to again receive submissions from other leaders of small presses, among these M. Glass, Jonathan Reddoch, Elizabeth Suggs, and C.R. Langille. And although I didn't create a perfect weighting of different workplace stories, an additional wish for cosmic balance, I'm proud of how this anthology has turned out.

In the end, I am enamored of this whole editing and publishing thing. I've said it before: Storytelling in general and books in particular are humankind's greatest invention. That I get to participate in the creating of a few of these things... wowee and boy howdy.

If you're considering working on an anthology or starting a small press, please read my whisperhousepress.com posts to learn, step-by-step, how I worked through these first two anthologies. There you'll find everything from cost breakdowns to sample contracts and copies of emails I sent to contributing authors to keep them in the loop on production updates. I hope my efforts there are helpful to you. And if not, that's cool as well. Merely keeping the notes was a boon to my own think-aloud process.

I will continue writing about the day-to-day operations and lessons in starting a small publishing house (I do not dare to call it a "business" given that I haven't made a dollar from the venture, though it technically is).

For content disclaimers, **check the very back of the book**—but you may rest assured that in these pages the dog *will not* at any point die as a prop of emotional manipulation. This move is cheap and will never be something this press permits, dammit. While we're at it, in this aside, let us encourage you please to adopt a dog rather than supporting a breeder—our shelters are overcrowded to the point that dogs are dying in even our best-intentioned shelters because there aren't enough fosters and adopters out there. For more information, visit your local humane society—if you're in the Mountain West and want to help out some wolfish pups, check out Arctic Rescue.

I'm inclined to do another one of those neat ornamental breaks because I'm so tickled at the little spooky Whisper House Press crooked house. You know what? This is my show. Here comes another ornamental break.

Steve

May 2025

PART ONE
CORPORATE TERROR

Monday

monday rut—
black thoughts stir his tea
round round round

Bénédicte Kusendila

WHY YOU SHOULD ALWAYS BRING PIZZA TO MEETINGS

GEVERA BERT PIEDMONT

DIGITAL NEWS AMERICA LOCATED THE FOLLOWING AI-GENERATED meeting transcript on a Unieda Corporation hard drive. This discovery followed another massive internal cover-up of the deaths of several employees. An incident occurred several years ago in which industrial espionage allegedly caused experimental robots to malfunction and go on a killing spree.

Recording Begins

Dr. Lee: Good morning, Team Quetzalcoatl. After much thought, we have decided to concentrate for the time being on the small Teacup Raptors destined for the pet trade. The U.S. military has expressed interest in the large Alpha Raptors. And we still believe there will be an extended security market for the medium-sized Guard Raptors, especially among police, doomsday preppers, gangs, drug runners, and the like. It's best to iron out all the kinks in the smallest size first, like this cute little one here. Yes, Mystic?

Mystic: In light of what happened with Dr. Smythe and his children's birthday party, and when Richard brought a few home and the trucker convoy came to his neighborhood...

Dr. Lee: What are you saying, Mystic? Are you implying the Teacup Raptors are dangerous simply because two in-home tests didn't go quite as planned?

Mystic: *unintelligible*

Dr. Lee: Anyone else? Thurman?

Thurman: I'm working on silicone nail covers for their big hind claws. Like those soft paws things you put on your cat instead of declawing it, but obviously much larger. Here, look. (noises) I anticipate selling them in many colors at a great mark-up to coordinate with the blinged-up collars and leashes since we are going for the "ladies-with-purse-dogs demographic" with these Teacup Raptors. Anyway, come here, you little beast... Simply apply a few drops of heavy-duty glue—

grunts
parrot-like trills

—and then slide the silicone sleeve over the large slashing nail. Ow! Well, they gotta get used to wearing them. Watch me do it again on the other foot...

parrot squawks

Hey, hold this thing, would you, Manfred?

parrot screeches

grunts

Anyway, these particular silicone covers are just the prototypes. They could be reusable, I hope. Hey, come back here! Fucker's getting away.

laughter
parrot chirps

Mystic: How about their teeth, though? Are you going to make matching silicone muzzles? How about we alter the DNA again to remove the teeth and revert back to a bird's beak? They are really cute, though, except for the teeth. Hey, little guy—

Dr. Lee: It turns out we need the sharp teeth gene for other things as well, so we can't remove them.

papers rustle
chirps

Must that creature be running around on the table during the meeting?

Teacup Raptor: Hi!

Manfred: My god, is this one of the talking ones?

Dr. Lee: Hmm, yes. It seems more and more of them are learning to speak, which only increases their desirability as pets. We are searching for a specialist in avian communication to start working with a select few to see how much is simple mimicry and how much they understand. For the Alpha and Guard versions, speaking and understanding would be a great boon. And since we engineer those types from different base stock, such as cassowaries rather than turkeys and chickens, they will have much greater intelligence as well.

Thurman: I'm not sure how much I could scale up these claw covers—

Teacup Raptor: No!

[human] groans

Manfred: I guess it doesn't like having its feet touched.

Thurman: Fucker bit me!

Mystic: Muzzles, like I said.

door opens

Unknown Speaker: Dr. Lee, I brought the other Teacup Raptors, as requested.

parrot squawks, chirps, and whistles
door closes

Manfred: They are so cute, though. Look at their little spiky feathered heads. Come here, sweeties.

kissies

Dr. Lee: These are the three Teacup Raptors that attended Dr. Smythe's party.

Teacup Raptors: Hi, hi, hi.

claws scrabble on wood

Thurman: Um, I don't have claw covers for these others.

Dr. Lee: Relax. These are pets, right? The children at the birthday party just loved them! They like getting their heads scratched. See?

creature hums

Mystic: That first one is already pulling off its claw covers. Look.

Thurman: Dammit.

stylus tapping tablet

I guess I need to source better glue. It's hard to find strong, non-toxic adhesive—and look at how those center claws are ripping up the rare wood inlay of the conference table. And that one underneath the table is tearing the Oriental carpet.

Manfred: Richard had said they did quite a bit of damage to his hard-wood floors.

Dr. Lee: We should start compiling a manual for pet owners. Someone take a note: "Limit their exposure to hardwood floors and carpet," "Keep them off tabletops," that sort of thing.

Mystic: (*snorts*) "Keep them away from other pets and small children." "Muzzle them."

Thurman: In tests, muzzling them has only made them more aggressive. And then they can't speak. I thought we wanted them to talk and be cute? If they are muzzled—

Teacup Raptor: No.

Mystic: Is it possible to keep their nails clipped to blunt them? C'mere, sweetheart, let me see your—*ouch*!

Teacup Raptor: No.

Mystic: (*makes sucking noise*) They are certainly strong-willed. Are you sure they can't understand what we say, Dr. Lee?

Dr. Lee: We're not sure at all. That's why we're looking for a bird specialist.

Mystic: I guess it would have to be a bird specialist since there aren't any dino—

Dr. Lee: We don't use that word here. You know that.

Mystic: *grunts*

Dr. Lee: While we're in this meeting, we also have a large batch of assorted raptors in the robot arena, which we repurposed for a while as a testing ground. They are going through their paces with dog trainers, being recorded for our new avian behaviorists to go over later—

Manfred: These aren't dogs, though. They are nothing like dogs! Using behavioral methods that work for dogs won't work with these creatures. They are dino—

Dr. Lee: Stop using that word. These cute little guys are Teacup Raptors, part of the Quetzalcoatl trials. And they are being tested today in the battle arena.

Manfred: One of these not-dinosaurs is chewing on my ankle. Its teeth are wicked sharp. Ow! Get off me.

thud

Mystic: I think we need an entire list of warnings about these creatures. I don't like how they look at us. Their eyes are creepy.

Thurman: Someone taught one of the Alphas to use keys to unlock padlocks.

scrabbling

Hey, get away.

Dr. Lee: What? Who taught them that? Shoo.

clapping

Thurman: *unintelligible*

Dr. Lee: One of the guys who pilots the robot spidogs, I bet. They are shifty. Scoot, you. Away!

bang!

Manfred: No, those pilot guys are afraid of the raptors. Besides, they think the raptors will take their robots' jobs.

pained, grunting pause

Please, stop biting me.

Dr. Lee: I envision the spidog robots and the Alpha raptors eventually working side by side. No one else can offer this type of functionality to the military. No one. Unieda will be at the top of the industrial-military complex—

klaxons blare

[both human and Teacup Raptor] overlapping voices
door opening
unrecognized noises from outside the room

Dr. Lee (*muted*): What the hell is going on in the arena? It's not the damn spidogs going mad again, is it? Because that was industrial espionage—fine, I'll look.

screaming from far away, continued alarms
Teacup Raptor noises
door closes

Manfred: Okay, he's gone. What's going on? Stop staring at me, you feathered weirdo.

background: muffled screams and alarms continue

Thurman: Let's see if we can bring up any of the security feeds.

buttons clicking, stylus scratching on tablet

Mystic: Do you guys have security clearance for that? Hey! Off my leg.

stomping

These things are cute, I guess, but they're annoying as hell. No way would I have one in my house or let any kids around them. These three fuckers ate children, you know. They killed cops.

Manfred: Those claims must have been highly exaggerated. These raptors are based mostly on chicken DNA. That's why we called them "teacup" raptors, right? But their teeth are sharp, and those enormous claws sure are deadly, huh?

grunts

Mystic: Manfred. They killed Dr. Smythe's wife over a meat-lover's pizza. *A pizza.*

squawking, feathers rustling

Teacup Raptors (several): Pizza! Pizza!

Mystic: I don't have any pizza. Don't climb me. Ow!

Teacup Raptor: Pizza!

Mystic: Ow! Stop!

thud

Thurman: The security hacks I know are hitting a brick wall—hey, Mystic, are you okay?

Teacup Raptor: Pizza!

Thurman: Get off her! Mystic!

thud

Mystic: *screams*

Thurman: Manfred, help!

thudding
wet, juicy sounds

Teacup Raptors (several): Pizza, pizza, pizza!

Manfred: *screaming*

Thurman: *screaming*

wet, slicing sounds
eating

Teacup Raptor: Pizza?

eating
door opens

Dr. Lee: Oh, fuck. Not again.

Teacup Raptor: Hi. Hi. Hi. Pizza?

Recording Ends

THE GHOULS
BARRY CHARMAN

The two old men knelt to pray, elbow to elbow. Above them the crucifix recorded everything. They felt its grace. The atmosphere in the facility was unsettled at times, so it was important to pause. To reflect. When finished, they rose as one and left the chapel to return to their stations. There were calls to be made.

An intern passed them in the corridor and nodded. "Great work with the shooter." His eagerness was cloying.

The first old man smiled politely. "Kind of you to say."

They watched the intern leave.

"Bit fresh of him," the second old man grumbled. "Addressing us."

"Quite. Enjoys it too much, you can tell. We'll let him go. Give him a modest package."

They continued to their black cubicles. A phone was ringing. One of the men answered: "Winston here. Yes, your honor. Another school? Anywhere in particular? You want him to be a liberal or just a loner?" He listened, then put down the phone. "Just a prod job." He switched on his computer, looking bored. In no time he found a self-confessed incel online and began his work, goading the young man. Six sock puppets later, he sat back, chuckling.

"Got him?" asked his colleague.

"He's this close to snapping. The twisted media. Liberals. Immigrants. They're all closing in on him." He started typing his report. "Yours?"

The other man sat at his desk, thinking. "Congressman's son. Daddy needs to be distracted. The boy's easily nudged. Women are to blame for his faults. He should take his power back from them. He should make a statement that can't be ignored."

And he would.

They always did. A nudge here. A whisper there. Everyone was so blindly angry. It was easy to make them see anything. The operator just hoped he didn't kill *himself* first. He hated when the punks did that. It made all the work so pointless.

When misinformation is a banquet, nobody knows they're starving. In a cubicle full of laughter and pornography sat a blond man with shrewd eyes. A placard hanging above his desk reads, "No one knows they do not know." A second, "Their ignorance is bliss," was one of his many amusing mottos.

The sound of furious typing came from his corner.

The blond man's was one of many cubicles. Peals of laughter rang out from them intermittently.

A passing supervisor paused to praise the conformity of Christ.

The blond man gave him an automatic response, without looking up: "Carpenters use what blacksmiths make."

"Praise the nail, not the cross."

They shared knowing smiles. The blond man's duties were simple. He told people what and whom to fear. He deflected blame from the wealthy to the desperate. He stoked fires, proudly calling himself a stoker. A glib little nickname, but there were no penalties for being glib.

His fingers danced. His many alts screamed and vented, often to each other. Today his quota was ten immigrants killed. He got thirteen. There was a bonus in the offing, and hate was easy money. If they weren't guilty, then why were they targeted? If they were innocent, then why were they hated? If they weren't running, then why were they here? The blond man smiled as he added layers.

Confusion was the currency of the truly powerful.

ALL ROSE FROM THEIR SEATS AS THE CLOCK STRUCK FIVE. THEY walked in single file, chatting amiably. The brothel was upstairs, the chapel downstairs. There was a company picnic on Sundays. Wives and whores were tolerated. There was a home-brew bingo based on current events, often causing fits of hysterical laughter.

The newest intern joined the line of people, chatting idly like a disturbed bed of flies. He had felt uneasy since stepping on the station floor.

One of the older men patted his arm. "Bit green, lad? First day? Come with me, I'll show you around. You'll see what satisfaction looks like. A good day's work gets you a good night's rest, and the Lord has prepared many light hearts to come between."

The intern offered a faint smile, and the man took his hand. Behind them, two other men were talking animatedly about a little war they'd got going.

"Old gods and a bit of land. All it takes."

"Stir and wait."

"If only they had perspective."

"Oh, quite. Can you imagine?"

"They'll never not be confused nor grasp the source of their confusion."

"Deft. Very deft."

One of the two grinned then stretched. He winced. "We need better chairs—you know I sent a memo?"

That got a laugh. "They don't care about our comfort, only results."

The intern listened, oddly chilled. His grey tie felt rather tight. He supposed everyone felt like this on their first day. They all turned out all right, though.

DON'T BE COWED BY PROGRESS read the legend above the front desk, the first thing he'd seen upon arriving. That message would make sense soon, he thought. That would make sense soon.

CUTE AGRESSION
EMILY FLYNN-JONES

A RABBIT IS THE BANE OF MY EXISTENCE. ALL DAY, BELLA Bunny stares at me with her too-wide eyes, adorable button nose, puffball tail, stubby limbs, and blank space where a mouth should be. Strange that a character who represents important causes like food poverty, animal rescue centers, clean water initiatives, and youth mental health awareness would have no mouth to put a voice to the issues. All of these were my ideas to reinforce the wholesome image of the cute creature.

That's my job: boosting the profile of a charming cartoon. I've come up with hundreds of moralistic and educational stories for children aged two to five, secured crossovers with some of the biggest brands in the world, and put Bella's face on all manner of products.

Bella Bunny stationary, for you to engage in the archaic art of letter writing; purses of all shapes, styles and sizes; reusable water bottles because we're so about saving the planet; a night light to keep the nightmares away; stackable blocks with incomprehensible directions; completely pointless ice cube trays. If there's a garment you can think of, she's on it—even a fucking toaster. People eat Bella's shit up and I've probably made millions for the company. She's everywhere:

haunting me at the mall, through my television, and on the streets. And it's all my fault.

It's worst at work, where her face adorns everything: the company's walls, screensavers, vending machine filler, mouse mats, sticky notes, monitors looping program episodes, and on every toilet seat, pen, binder, and clock. The rest of the office is strictly decorated in her official color palette. My work world is awash in pastels. It makes me want to puke. I've come close, excessive salivation and bile burn rising in my throat. I choke it down like my other feelings about my job.

Have you ever seen something so cute that you just want to punch it or squeeze it to death? That's how I feel about our little mascot. It's called *cute aggression*. When cuteness overwhelms to the point it conjures violent rather than sentimental or caring feelings. I feel this. All the time. If I could, I'd slap the cute off Bella Bunny's smug little face, kick her in her non-existent crotch, soak her in gasoline and set her ablaze, build and put her into an iron maiden, or volunteer her as the lure at the dog track. I seem to be the only one at the office who has this reaction. For those not so immune, her cuteness seems to be infectious. All my colleagues have this peppy, sunshine-and-fucking-rainbows affect I lack the energy to fake.

It's so stinking pleasant around here that people even smile as they pack up their desks after being made redundant. They cheerfully take scoldings delivered by management in sickly sweet speeches, to the point where it is impossible to tell what was done wrong. It's disconcerting to see so many adults self-infantilizing and taking the persona part of their job so seriously.

I must be the only sane person here, but the atmosphere is getting to me, chipping away at that sanity. It's physically painful, as though my brain is being slowly flayed, bit by bit. The mind mutilation must be starting with limbic system chunks—it's getting more and more difficult to control my emotions.

Today, I have to pitch next quarter's marketing plans. I've spent weeks racking what remains of my sensible mind to come up with some pretty uninspired shit: a limited edition T-shirt collection with a barely hip designer for the millennial parents, an educational puzzle series, a colorful boba tea selection, yet another plushy, a Bella Bunny portable speaker, and a bunch of other prosaic crap.

Standing there before the board, delivering this garbage list, I maintain the sham smile I've slapped on my face. They beam back. When I'm through, they speak words of disappointment in excited-sounding soprano tones. The contradiction kills me.

I find myself tuning out, focusing instead on the giant rabbit plushie in the corner. In my mind, it morphs into a drooling, snarling, rabid, razor-clawed beast. It opens the mouth it has acquired in my imagination to reveal rows of overlapping, jagged teeth that snap with a threatening hunger.

This job and Bella Bunny will be the death of me.

I return to my desk, and this new, hideous version of Bella stalks me. It feels so real, but no one else seems to notice. The smiling idiots flit about in their usual, jolly manner. The bunny-monster mocks me for the rest of the day, leering at me from every angle of the office. It is impossible to focus on my work while being hunted by a fucked up figment of my imagination. I can't afford the distraction because I'm on a serious deadline, now having to redo my entire proposal.

That night, I dream of mutant Bella. She's sharpening her claws on my wall, gouging ridges into the plaster, holding my gaze with a menacing stare. I dare to blink and, in that instant, she looms at my side. Her talons dig into the duvet inches from my body. They're stained the rusty red of dried blood. Her gaping maw growls intimi-dations directly into my face. She's too close, and I can both feel and smell her breath, foul from what must be a grotesque diet—of incred-ulous employees like me, I think. Her ravenous sputum drips onto my skin. Not satisfied with plaguing my nine-to-five, this dangerous demon version of the cuddly cartoon pervades my sleep. Hating her all the more for her nocturnal haunting, I force myself awake, finding myself in pools of sweat. I leave the light on and my burning eyes open for the rest of the night.

The terribly transformed bunny is at the office when I arrive, exhausted, the next day. She does not go away. I can't smile through the distress, after days of torment and my peers asking me in their perky timbre if I'm alright.

I'm convinced this visage is Bella Bunny's true form, and everyone else is brainwashed by her cutsie veneer. Frightening as it is to be menaced every minute, I find new purpose and begin work on what will be my greatest marketing pitch ever. Now that I see what she is, I know exactly how to position her and pinpoint the perfect partnerships to destroy her. The ideas are flowing and fueled by fear, but this is my sole recourse against the beast: I must burn her brand to the ground. There's only one way to skin this rabbit.

Doing away with the usual presentation templates, I arrange my ideas on a black background covered in blood splatter with severe red text. It represents her perfectly. I render the vision of Bella I see and position her on each disgusting slide. Flipping through the pitch, I have never been more pleased with myself and am convinced this will defeat my beast. Collecting my delightful, dreadful things, I head to the board room to deliver my death blow with a genuine smile on my face—my first in weeks.

I pitch hunting knives with Bella's silhouette as handles. I've confirmed the shape is ergonomic and suggest it will perform well with certain American demographics, leaving the notion that it could be used to kill bunnies as subtext.

Next is a series of sex toys because rabbits are notoriously libidinous, and I go into explicit detail as to how the ears and nose could be put to specific, pleasurable use. Note: I would never use these personally. I don't want to fuck the bunny. I want to fuck it up.

For my garment quotient, I have a collaborative collection with an up-and-coming, German, gothic designer specializing in depictions of the abominably anatomical. I share classy blouses and flowing gowns depicting the visceral, ugly interior of the real, horrid Bella purporting this will help us tap into the Alternative audience.

Next is cosmetics: I present a perfume made from rabbit urine to promote upcycling and sustainability as part of the corporate commitment.

Bella Bunny already has a video game, so I propose we license our most valuable asset to the most popular survival horror, first-person shooter on the market to be used as an enemy character. I pair this concept with modified gameplay footage of their precious rabbit taking a headshot, her skull exploding and blood spewing from her neck with extraordinary realism. I loop this scene for my own gratification while I explain how my FPS strategy will crack the elusive male teen market.

My next proffer is a musical collaboration with a Swedish Death Metal band famous for their blasphemy and depictions of dead animals in their music videos. I imagine the Bella beast as one of those carcasses or as a digitally rendered stand-in screaming lyrics about Satan and murder, contending that this approach will introduce us to the Nordic audience.

I pitch partnering with a household-name soup company for a hearty rabbit stew, pointing to the importance of nutrition to the parents of our target demographics.

When it comes to episode themes, I have numerous propositions: a true crime adaptation as a public service announcement about stranger danger; another PSA where she develops a tail fetish to tackle the subject of sex shaming.

Then I suggest a television episode in which a bite from another rabbit turns Bella into a blood-thirsty fiend every full moon. For me, this concept reflects her true nature, but I frame it as an opportunity to speak about being accepting of those who are different or as some sort of allegory for warning against the dangers of addiction.

For Veterans Day, I propose Bella goes into the trenches. Natural tunnel diggers, rabbits would be well-suited for such combat. On the front lines, our PSA sugarcoats none of the horrors and could be an anti-war parable.

I finish with the idea that the bunny has an argument with her best friend and decides to make a new one from pieces of other animals, selling the notion as a tale of the value of friendship.

When I'm done, I feel a sense of relief. The only way to destroy Bella is to kill her reputation. I'm satisfied I have achieved that and am sure everyone will see the side of Bella I see now. Instead, I am greeted with silence and stunned expressions on faces that I have only ever seen irritatingly cheerful. I look to the giant stuffed version of Bella Bunny. She has returned to her adorable old self. I can't believe it. The bunny bitch is messing with me. I scream.

Ranting now that Bella is a monster, I rush the huge plushie and begin to tear at its squishy, soft body. I succeed in ripping off an arm and fling it across the room. I pluck her shiny stone eyes and button nose from her wretched face. Removing a leg with force, I toss it to the ground and stomp. Her tail has to go, too. I tug it from her form, stuffing my face while mumbling of her monstrosity through a crowded mouth. I grapple with her cute little head.

The office rendition is better produced than the crap we kick out to the public, so it takes a minute. Eventually, I hear the stitching rupture. Applying all my strength, I am full of righteous satisfaction finding Bella finally decapitated. Exhilarated, I stand amid body parts and wadding heaped like intestines. It's not the beast with deadly claws, needle-like teeth, and an aura of terror I had known, but I have made her my own kind of monster.

The corporate cartoon-worshipping fools still do not see. I shout furiously about Bella Bunny's wickedness as I am escorted from the building.

SAY MY NAME
SAMANTHA BRYANT

"Now stare into your partner's eyes." The trainer's voice had taken on a dreamy, hypnotic sort of tone. "Imagine you can see into their very soul. Let the connection between you flow."

Adam rested his hands on the table and looked at the man seated across from him. Though they had worked together for several months, he realized he didn't even know the man's name. Will? Walter? Something W, he felt pretty sure. He looked steadily at the man but felt nothing. His coworker was a quiet, steady sort. Not particularly interesting.

These kinds of exercises were the new department head's favorite team-building activities. She was kind of flaky, to say the least. Adam missed the old boss, who'd favored good, old fashioned alcohol as a bonding element. Even if he didn't feel any closer to his colleagues at the end of the day, there had at least been some fun and laughter. Much better than all this earnest, touchy-feely shit.

Adam's attention wavered. He wished he had been partnered with Lisa. Hers was a pair of eyes he'd happily linger on—clear blue, sharp enough to cut you. But the only two women in the group had been assigned as each other's partners, probably in an attempt to avoid another debacle like the one warranting last year's sexual harassment training that had cost the old guy his position. Lisa had her diamond-sharp eyes trained on the new girl who just transferred from upstairs. That left Adam with Wilbur, or whoever he was.

He forced his attention back and registered the amusement in his partner's eyes. Adam's distraction must have been obvious. He shrugged apologetically and tried again to maintain focus on the activity at hand. He met the man's steady gaze and tried to feel... something.

The man whose name began with a W said, "It's Wilt, dumbass. My dad was a big basketball fan."

Adam blinked. He was sure he'd just heard his coworker speak, but the man's mouth hadn't so much as twitched. Adam broke eye contact and looked around. Everyone else was intent on their partner's faces. When Adam looked her way, the teamwork guru cleared her throat and arched an eyebrow at him.

When Adam looked back at Wilt, the man wasn't smiling anymore. His brown eyes had gone dark and cold, and Adam swore he felt a swirling hatred in the look. He couldn't imagine what reason the man had to hate him. They barely knew one another.

"You already forgot again?" His partner's voice was in Adam's head again.

At this, his throat began tightening. Adam gasped. Panic rose, and his eyes widened. The room grayed at the edges. Adam collapsed on the table. Everything went black.

In the darkness, he fought to regain consciousness, but he couldn't get his eyelids to flicker, let alone open. They might as well have belonged to someone else. A wave of panic drowned all thought for a long moment. A distant ringing filled his senses.

"Ms. Smith? I think there's something wrong with my partner," Adam heard Wilt say. Was it his imagination, or was the man fighting a bout of laughter? The voice was muffled as though Adam were listening through a thick blanket.

He heard the chairs scraping and everyone talking at once, but he couldn't move and couldn't see. Anger and panic swirled in his mind. This couldn't be happening.

Somebody pulled him out of his chair and laid him out on the floor.

"What's his name?" the trainer was shouting.

No one answered.

Adam, he thought. *It's Adam*. Then the blackness took over, and all was quiet.

OUTSIDE IN
CAMRYN CLAIR

CAMRYN CLAIR

It's my first day, and no one else seems to care that our office is windowless.

When I comment, my new coworker points to the plant and pictures of sunny landscapes adorning his cubicle. The corners of his mouth crease into a practiced smile. "Just gotta bring the outside in," he says.

I buy a matching plant, which takes only days to droop under the fluorescent lights. I try to coax it back to vibrancy with extra water. When I offer the same attention to my neighbor's, the droplets slide off plastic leaves.

Artificial. Like everything else.

I tell my plant stories of summer—when it was light before *and* after the workday. Now in winter, I sneak outside with increasing frequency to savor the sun. First, warnings request I limit breaks. Then an employee improvement plan demands it.

"Our workplace values keeping people happy *inside* the office," my boss says in the HR meeting.

I nod and flash an artificial smile. Employees who are happy *inside* the office can afford to keep roofs over their heads and food in their stomachs.

Things that crave sunlight are doomed here. Better to not need it at all.

I replace my live plant with a plastic one.

ON THE NEW EMPLOYEE'S FIRST DAY, SHE COMMENTS ON OUR windowless office.

I point to my plant and pictures of sunny landscapes with a practiced smile. "Just gotta bring the outside in."

WADE VS. ROE
M. GLASS

A TEAM OF WAITERS DELIVERED PLATES TO LUNCHTIME DINERS seated around the table. The mouthwatering scent of roasted meat filled the private dining room. One of the uniformed servers dropped a plate of salmon in front of Wade. He reared back in surprise at the sight of the bright pink fish filet.

"Uh, I didn't order—" Seeing the waiter, Wade's words died on his lips.

Sweat covered the man's ashen face.

Must be hot as hell in that kitchen.

Wade surveyed his colleagues. The boss, Burke, and his co-workers had cut into their beef Wellington entrees. If he sent the fish back, he'd have to wait while everyone around him ate. He would stand out like a sore thumb. The boss, with his instinctive sharp-eyed, sharp-tongued radar, would call out, "What's the matter, Koblinksy? Meat too bloody for you? Maybe you're not ready to swim with the sharks."

And this waiter looked none too healthy. The less contact Wade made with him, the better.

"Yeah, okay," Wade muttered.

"Blerg," the waiter said. He shambled away.

Wade glared at his back. *Nervy prick.*

So here he was—he and the salmon—while the majority of his co-workers dined on golden-crusted beef Wellington. And on Burke's tab. He wished he were sitting with Vasquez or Hicks. They both had salmon. Did they actually want it, or were they also hapless victims of a twit waiter?

Wade saved the pearls of salmon roe garnish for last, a reward for his earlier restraint. Lifting his caviar spoon, he anticipated the light salty tang of the sea within the delicate red-orange bubbles of decadence. He bit down. A bitter taste filled his mouth and something gritty sifted between his teeth.

What the hell?

He lifted his napkin, but before he could spit out the bite, a co-worker turned to speak to him. Wade swallowed and mumbled a response, reaching for his water glass.

BACK AT THEIR WALL STREET HIGH-RISE, WADE AND HIS CO-workers trudged into the conference room for Burke's weekly meeting. *The Big Snooze Fest.*

Taking his seat, Wade frowned. His lunch sat heavy in his belly. Maybe accepting the salmon had been a mistake.

Ten minutes later, he *knew* it had been a mistake.

The first sign of trouble started with a quiet rumble deep in his core. A sharp jab, the thrust of a tiny stiletto into his guts, spread fiery needles of pain throughout his abdomen. He froze in place. *Oh shit.*

Burke did not find frat boy antics of subordinates amusing and the thought of farting during one of these meetings sent Wade's heart racing.

Or was that the salmon? His thoughts flashed to the sweaty

waiter. *He did something to my food!* Wade discarded that idea for another: *He had the flu bug or somethin'.*

Burke's voice droned.

Wade turned the page of the acquisitions report languishing in front of him. Were Hicks or Vasquez experiencing the same discomfort at their desks down the hall? Were they making a mad dash for the relief the toilets promised as Wade suffered Burke's long-winded speech?

The numbers and charts on the page blurred. Light perspiration broke out along his thinning hairline. He swallowed hard, and another sharp blade stabbed his guts.

What had begun as slender slivers of pain intensified into a fiery ball. He hunched forward over the report, hiding his distress as best he could.

He took slow, deep breaths through his nose. Surely Burke couldn't go on much longer, and then Wade would escape to the toilets down the hall. Hell, based on the expanding bubble of pressure and the heaviness low in his intestines, he might find it wise to visit another floor. He could bomb the restroom of the Deloitte bastards down on twenty, then make his escape.

Wade imagined telling the story to Hicks later and the two of them laughing. His emerging grin morphed into a grimace. Something shifted hard in the depths of his bowels. *I won't even make it to the elevator.* Best stick to this floor and ride it out.

His forehead oozed sweat, and a drop rolled down the side of his nose to *plop!* onto Burke's pie chart. Wade's hands clenched into tight fists, and he suppressed a groan.

A large railroad spike drove itself into his brain. Colorful lights flashed behind his eyes, and he squeezed them shut. *No. Not now.* Nauseated, his stomach flip-flopped, sloshing dangerously.

Gonna puke. If there was one thing guaranteed to piss Burke off more than a stray fart, it would be vomit. Wade's brain provided a picture of the next two months of shitty referrals from Burke, his favored method of revenge on junior execs.

A shaky weakness washed over his entire body, pinning him to his chair. Now, it was too late to make a polite escape to be sick in private.

Wade's vision blackened, and a small panicked sound escaped him. Had anyone noticed?

Help me, he thought at his oblivious co-workers. *Am I having a stroke?* The thought triggered a rush of pure panic. His heart pounded, a drumbeat exploding in his inner ears. The armpits of his shirt were sweat-soaked. Still, he said nothing. His shirt felt cold and sticky against his skin.

Something on the inside of his skull began to itch. And then to squirm.

Maggots! Wade's mind gibbered. *Maggots squirming in my brain!* He could almost see them: Inside his head, a mass of wiggling white worms gnawed the pinkish-gray flesh of his brain, devouring tiny chunks of his mind, digesting his thoughts and turning them to larval shit.

A heavy stone expanded in his middle and with a sickening squelching sound, something shifted, something grew. With another shift, the swelling in his belly pushed his organs out of place.

"Urrrggghhh!" he moaned, and the attention of the room's occupants shifted to him. A soft rain of sweat pattered onto the report. Saliva dripped from his lower lip.

Something chewed on his guts with vicious teeth of serrated daggers. He opened his mouth in a silent scream.

"Urrrrrk!" was all he could manage. Wade lurched to his feet.

"Koblinsky?" Burke inquired, his displeasure evident.

"Salmon," Wade gasped. "I think... the fish... bad."

Wade's eyes rolled up and back as he fell.

"Urrrrggggghh," he groaned, writhing on his back.

A ripping sound echoed around the conference room. The skin along Wade's back split straight over his spine with the precision of a filet knife. The thing inside shed Wade's skin like a bad suit, emerging in a rush of foul goo. It stared about with black and unblinking fish eyes. Viscera soaked into Burke's expensive carpet.

Wade-Not-Wade lumbered to its feet, a freakish hybrid of human and sharp-toothed aquatic beast. It shambled on new legs toward Burke, who stood rooted in place, gaping in wide-eyed shock. Wade-Not-Wade, and the thin vestige of Just-Wade, savored the terror in the room as its enormous maw clamped down on Burke with a satisfying crunch. Horrified screams echoed and mingled with those coming from the hall. Wade-Not-Wade chewed, listening, extending its senses down the neural link.

Not far from this room, Vasquez-Not-Vasquez completed a hostile takeover of its own.

HEMOGENY ORIENTATION
TIM BOITEAU

THE LIGHTS DIM IN THE CAVERNOUS CONFERENCE HALL, THE hundreds of young professionals in attendance shuffling welcome packets, shifting in their seats, clearing their throats, and sipping their complimentary coffees as the screen on the stage comes to life.

EXT. HEMOGENY CAMPUS - MORNING

Sleek, modern buildings are sprawled out across immaculate parkland, the glass exteriors glittering in the light of the rising sun. Upbeat, generic pop music plays.

DISSOLVE TO:

INT. HEMOGENY MAIN OFFICE - DAY

WORKER A, a young woman with short hair and dressed in professional attire, enters through a glass turnstile into a cavernous lobby gleaming with glass and chrome. WORKER B, a young man in a suit, strides toward her and extends his hand.

CLOSE UP: The two workers are shaking hands.

NARRATOR (V.O.)

Welcome to Hemogeny!

The music swells as the man leads the woman toward a series of escalators ascending beneath a glimmering waterfall of a chandelier.

NARRATOR (V.O.)

We are excited to have you join our team of enthusiastic professionals. We invite you to sit back and relax as we familiarize you with the philosophy of Hemogeny, its campus, the benefits of working here, and how to make the most of your time living and working with us.

DISSOLVE TO: WHITE

Peppy introduction music fades.

SUPERIMPOSE: "CORPORATE PHILOSOPHY."

Rows and rows of squircles bubble behind superimposed title, sweeping by as they take shape, each one containing a red human icon.

NARRATOR (V.O.)

A leading producer of hemoelectric fuel cells, we at Hemogeny value sustainability, inclusivity, and synergy. We believe a healthy corporate culture begins at the level of the individual and their daily interactions with colleagues.

DIAMOND FADE TO:

A billowing Hemogeny corporate flag, electric bolts raying out of a red blood cell.

SUPERIMPOSE: Over the corporate flag appears the portrait of a silver-haired, square-jawed man.

NARRATOR (V.O.)

In a message to the Board he recorded in his safe room, founder and former CEO Harry Solomon defined the mission of Hemogeny as follows.

HARRY SOLOMON (grainy V.O.)

Accelerate together, energetically!

NARRATOR (V.O.)

Mr. Solomon went on to outline his vision of the company as both a microcosm of the human story and a place where ambition and innovation coalesce into sustainable products and impressive profits.

HARRY SOLOMON (grainy V.O.)

We pride ourselves on being a bastion of inclusivity as well as green practices, with our goal of zero-carbon bloodstain well on its way to being met by decade's end—

An explosion interrupts Harry Solomon's speech. His head shot is replaced by that of a handsome woman with lustrous, silver hair.

NARRATOR (V.O.)

He was prevented from explaining further, as former CFO Tabitha Billings chose that moment to infiltrate his safe room, behead him, and assume control of the company.

CUT TO:

EXT. HEMOGENY CAMPUS - DAY

DRONE SHOT: The glimmering Hemogeny Campus scrolls beneath us, immaculately manicured grounds and the Hemogeny waterfall sign. Employees walk between buildings with determined steps. Easy-listening classical music plays during...

MONTAGE with VOICEOVER.

Each described location is depicted in turn. Employees are laughing and chatting in every shot.

NARRATOR (V.O.)

Part of Hemogeny's green ethos holds that, as a cherished employee, you will also be a full-time resident in one of our Deluxe Luxury Housing Solution buildings, each of which is outfitted with cafeterias offering locally sourced cuisine, fair trade coffee shops, department stores, multiple green spaces, chapels, hospitals, libraries, movie theaters, and party rooms.

END MONTAGE.
FADE TO BLACK.

NARRATOR (V.O.)

But remember: Use these areas for rest and recuperation only. Activities leading to sanguineous drainage are frowned upon outside of the workplace.

CUT TO:

INT: CAFETERIA - TIME OF DAY NEBULOUS

The room is littered with dismembered bodies and blood spatters.

SUPERIMPOSE: A giant X falls across the scene.

A jarring buzzer blares.

HOLD IMAGE.

NARRATOR (V.O.)

Instead: Mingle, connect, discover romance, form alliances, and scheme away!

CUT TO:

INT. LIVING ROOM - NIGHT

Clean but anonymous decor. Worker A and Worker B, dressed as before, are seated cozily on a couch. They clink glasses of red wine, eyes locked, smirking at each other.

DISSOLVE TO:

A table graphic in Hemogeny Red and White titled, "Salary," with four rows labeled L1, L2, L3, and L4, the individual cells blank but filling in with relevant symbols as the narrator describes them.

NARRATOR (V.O.)

Salary is structured into four distinct tiers, and as a new employee, you will be starting at L1, but don't worry—advancement is right around the corner for go-getters that embrace and live Hemogeny's corporate philosophy. L1s receive 30 food credits per month, Health and Dental Basic™, elbow- and knee pads, and a hunting knife. L2s receive an additional 10 food credits per month, Health and Dental Plus™, and a helmet and machete to add to their inventory. L3s are granted an additional 10 food credits, Health and Dental Premium™, 1% share in the company's annual profits, full body armor, and a katana forged with Tamahagane steel. Finally, L4s receive endless food credits, Health and Dental Infinity™, 10% share in the company's annual profits, a booby-trapped safe room, rocket launcher, submachine gun, and 100 ammunition credits per month.

INT. MEETING ROOM - DAY

Employees sit around an oblong table, observing a presentation. Worker A pauses from taking notes to gaze thoughtfully out of the window at the campus.

NARRATOR (V.O.)

Most L1s will be quick to feel the belt tightening on just 30 food credits per month and will therefore express an interest in applying for a raise.

INT. OFFICE - DAY

Worker A is seated across from a slick, sharply dressed Mr. BOSS, presenting her impassioned case for a raise. However, Mr. Boss holds up a hand and speaks, his words seeming to match the narrator's.

NARRATOR (V.O.)

With only a finite number of food credits available to distribute to L2s and below, the only way to earn more is to cut off another employee's credit distribution. Thus, the application process involves taking down a coworker with your special-issued knife.

INT. COPY ROOM - DAY

WORKER C, another suit, is distracted while making copies and doesn't notice Worker A creeping into frame. Worker A stabs Worker C in the neck with her knife.

NARRATOR (V.O.)

Thanks to smart technology embedded within your death-dealing device, payroll will instantly know who died by whose hand and redistribute food credits accordingly.

A light beeps on the handle of the gory hunting knife, and Worker A smiles delightedly when she notices several of the meters on her smartwatch increase by a couple notches.

CLOSEUP: WATCHFACE.

NARRATOR (V.O.)

Promotion works in a similar way, though in addition to annihilating your superior, you will have to file a formal request packet for L2 benefits including a deathbed recommendation letter from the individual you have slain (deepfakes now accepted). Hemogeny currently has resources for fifteen hundred L1s, one hundred L2s, ten L3s, and one paranoid and highly vulnerable L4 (your current CEO Tabitha Billings, who is at this moment holed up in her safe room on the top floor of headquarters, attempting to suss out all of the untriggered booby traps Harry Solomon left behind—best of luck, Tabitha!).

BACK TO SCENE / OFFICE

Mr. Boss, concluding his explanation to Worker A, pulls out a machete, and leaps over the desk, brandishing it at her. The scene freezes, and a red X superimposes over it with an error buzzer.

NARRATOR (V.O.)

Superiors who initiate attacks on their subordinates will receive a demotion, sacrificing the trappings of their current salary level. However, Hemogeny does endorse and encourage self-defense against upstarts.

The scene rewinds, then begins to play out differently. This time, Worker A pulls a knife and leaps at Mr. Boss, who with ninja-like reflexes, beheads her in mid-air. The scene freezes, and a green check mark appears over it with a pleasant ding.

NARRATOR (V.O.)

Our advice to all the newbies out there? Team up!

The scene rewinds as it did before, and again plays out differently. Now, Worker A draws a knife, but this time only feigns to lunge at her boss. When Mr. Boss draws his machete, Worker B appears from behind and slits his throat. Mr. Boss falls to the floor. As blood pours from the wound, Worker A and Worker B shake hands over Mr. Boss's quivering body.

NARRATOR (V.O.)

Remember...

WORKER A and WORKER B

The two turn toward the camera as the body twitches one last time beneath them.

Accelerate together, energetically!

Outside the presentation room, a distant rumble shakes the display, and a ceiling tile crashes onto the stage. Some new employees share glances of unease. The film continues on the big screen.

DISSOLVE TO:

INT. MEDICAL CENTER - DAY

MONTAGE: Several quick shots reveal a friendly assistant behind a chrome counter, an immaculate waiting room, and high-tech doctor's offices.

NARRATOR (V.O.)

As an employee at Hemogeny, you will have access to the best healthcare in the world. Please take note: Those seeking attention will be held accountable for the category and source of the wounds they've received.

END MONTAGE.

A DOCTOR in a white coat examines the knife wound on the dying Mr. Boss , frowns, and marks an X on a medical form.

NARRATOR (V.O.)

Anyone seeking medical care for knife-induced injuries will be terminated from employment at Hemogeny. L2s and up who seek treatment for machete-induced injuries will also be terminated. L3s and up who seek treatment for sword-related injuries will also be terminated. Death will result in termination. Termination will also result in death.

The doctor winks at the camera and leans in to inject Mr. Boss with a lethal solution—as indicated by the skull-and-bones symbol on the side of the massive syringe.

The video pauses and a voice pipes in through the speakers: "This is former Chief Marketing Officer Rachel Furlong speaking. CEO Tabitha Billings has been terminated from her position by means of a grenade-in-a-can concealed in the safe room's pantry, and as the senior employee I now reign supreme. Come and get me, you low-level scuzz! Also, I would like to issue a big, warm Hemogeny welcome to all the new recruits undergoing initial processing right now."

INT. BOARD ROOM - DAY

DIAMOND FADE INTO:

The wide-grinning board of directors face the camera around their rectangular table while the same inspiring music from the introduction plays.

NARRATOR (V.O.)

A world of excitement awaits you at Hemogeny. We hope this video has been informative, enlightening, and inspirational. Whether your heart now races as a result of fear or of pride in your future contributions toward the greater good, our smart technology is already converting your pulse into profits, and for that we thank you. We now invite you to reach under your seat and pull out your welcome packet—and weapon—and get to work!

FADE TO BLACK.

SUPERIMPOSE: The corporate flag with the motto, "Accelerate together, energetically!" splayed across it.

A flurry of activity ensues as orientation packets are ripped open and knives are unsheathed. The first screams pierce the conference hall.

CLOSED FOR MAINTENANCE
XOCHILT AVILA

"And what exactly do you expect me to do?" Perry squawked, indignant.

"What do you *think?*" Walter scoffed at the younger man, brandishing the time-worn baseball bat adorned with sigils. He gave his macgyvered weapon a few test swings. "We're cleaning out the bathroom stalls."

"*Mmhmm.*" Perry's arms crossed tightly over his cream cashmere sweater, hazel eyes narrowing suspiciously as he peered across the tiled restroom. Even behind the closed doors of the stalls, the stench of shit was palpable. "With a baseball bat?"

"Okay, *listen.*" The club was tossed atop the custodial cart while the senior janitor loosened up his arms. "It's review season, yeah? Everyone's fuckin' nervous. And the mages, bless their hearts, gotta show they're makin' progress on their work, or else they get the axe."

Well *obviously*, Perry thought to himself, but kept his lips clamped shut. Thankfully, his new supervisor seemed oblivious to his annoyance. The big hick seemed oblivious to *a lot* of things, in Perry's opinion.

"Sometimes they panic and flush what they've summoned down the toilets when it don't come out right. *Most* of it goes down fine 'cause the fuckers start off pretty small."

Perry grimaced at Walter's thumb-and-forefinger indication of "pretty small."

Walter continued: "But too many bunch up, clog up the pipes. Eventually, backed up like that, they start to... *warp*. Twist together into somethin' real nasty. But, tragically, they're still in the toilets, so the Big Boss says it's *our* problem to fix." Enmity soaked the southerner's words like honey on cornbread as he spoke of the powers that be. It would have unnerved Perry if he weren't so consumed by his own sense of injustice.

"What?! But that's *not fair!*" Specifically, it wasn't fair *he* had to deal with it. Perry would speak with his father immediately. He knew the old man wanted him to get his hands dirty and learn the family business from the ground up, but this was ridiculous, unprecedented, and *disgusting*. And hells knew how badly the stupid mages' flushed experiments were corroding the pipes. The repairs would cost the company a fortune. Maybe if he identified an operational solution his father would concede Perry was too good for this nonsense. Perhaps they could bolster security to search the mages' robes between shifts, preventing them from ditching their failures this way. Maybe they could do away with the restrooms entirely.

Regardless, Perry remained where he stood against the porcelain sink, eyeing his temporary superior like a freshly misted feline. Sighing, Walter snatched the bat again, pointing the end cap toward Perry. "I'll open the door, but you *are* gonna take care of it."

Strong shoulders back, fists balled, Walter gave the stall door a hearty kick with a steel-toed boot. It burst open like a plump cyst pinched between two fingers.

Sulfur and sewage stung Perry's nose as the toilet water gurgled as though in response to the janitors' intrusion. Rising on his toes, he watched as ripples bubbled and popped across the surface, the dark water congealing into a thick and foul rising ichor.

Something was wrong. Dampness soaked Perry's palms as he stared past Walter's hulking frame, his legs trembling while his bowels threatened to liquify. Something was *wrong.* Whatever was in there, rippling in the toilet, was *wrong,* and he'd eat every urinal cake in the fucking restroom before getting near it.

"Are you paying attention?" Walter looked back to the newbie, his dark eyes sweeping the young man's form. There they idled, and something gleamed in the southerner's gaze that put Perry on edge. A quiet judgment. A lingering too long on his soft sweater and fine, leather loafers. Perry didn't quite know what to make of it, but something loathsome kindled in the janitor's glare. "You know, you're a little *too* well dressed for this kinda work."

Perry scoffed. "Well nobody said I'd be *doing* this kinda work! How the hell was I supposed to know I'd need a hazmat suit?" He waved toward the growing abomination, where the miasmic ooze sculpted itself, coagulating dripping limbs to pull itself out from the toilet bowl. "Who the fuck could prepare for *this*?!"

But Walter was clearly unimpressed. In fact he rolled his eyes. "We're *janitors.* It's a messy job no matter where you do it."

"Well, I'm only here until my father's satisfied. And I refuse to go anywhere near that... that *thing.* So why don't *you* hurry up and beat its head off already? Because otherwise it's gonna crawl out and kill us. *You* deal with it!"

Arms crossed, Perry kept his ass parked against the sink. The fluorescents overhead flickered as the wailing demon spilled out onto the floor with a *plop.* A twitching, shrieking bouquet of swinging arms and weeping tendrils. Searching. Angry. Famished. Walter frowned at it before scowling back at his underling.

"I don't give a fuck who your dad is, kid. You're here to do a job."

"You should give a fuck because my dad *runs this place.*"

Fine.

Perry loathed to pull *that* card, but so be it. It was the elder janitor's fault, really. Perry was *not* going anywhere near the monsters waiting in any of these stalls, and that fact simply needed to be understood. He'd change the paper towels, maybe take out the trash, so long as the bumpkin didn't keep pissing him off. But there were natural limits. Some tasks were simply beneath him.

Hazel eyes met earth brown in sharp, clear defiance. Smugness warmed Perry's belly as surprise colored the older man's face. Walter frowned tightly, the gears between his ears clearly shifting as he looked between his charge and the writhing mass on the ground.

Finally—decision made—Walter turned to the monster with a defeated shrug. "All right, then."

It surprised Perry how simple it had been, but perhaps the old man was simply learning. He exhaled, but his next breath was soured by the creature's rot. His eyes flitted back and forth and back between Walter's rising bat and the many-armed beast attempting to claw out of the toilet.

Walter raised his weapon, staring down the many-armed beast as it attempted to wobble upright. A flurry of milky slits ripped open across its weeping flesh. Eyes flecked with verdant greens, with ocean blues, with rivers of gold liquified by hellfire. Eyes that held life and death and the world beyond. Those eyes, twitching and roaming—searching with hunger—fell on the elder janitor.

WHACK.

Brackish slime splattered the stall as the fiend's skull caved in like an overripe watermelon. The mass of sludge and limbs flopped against the soiled basin before crumbling to the ground, already regurgitating into jellied sludge. Its stench truly blossomed then, licking at every corner of the space.

Perry's hand flew over his mouth to push his sickness back, and Walter simply shook the mess off of his club. For a stretch, the only sounds reverberating off the tile walls were the gurgles echoing from the other toilets.

"... You don't gotta hit 'em." Walter drawled slowly, letting the bat hang low in his grasp. He seemed to be calculating each word, his tone light, as though engineered to be friendly. "But you can push the doors open for me, can't ya?"

Already plenty close enough, Perry wasn't going anywhere closer to those things.

The Southerner held up his free hand in appeasement, like he was calming a scared horse.

"Tell ya what, kid. You help me with this, and I'll put in a *real* good word with the Big Boss. I'll tell him his son worked hard and *really* showed he could get his hands dirty. Hell, maybe this'll be your last day of custodial work. What do you say?"

A tempting offer. Though Perry doubted the custodian could have much sway with the Prophet, he supposed it was worth a shot. He looked toward the next stall in the row. Wet moans squelched from behind the plastic door. Maybe complying would get him out of this shithole sooner than later.

"Alright. *Deal.*"

Uncertain steps carried Perry to the next stall. He straightened and put on his best impression of a confident face—just as he would stand as the Prophet someday. Just as he would lead the masses in congregation, in the promise of a better, never-ending future for their bloodlines. With a deep breath, Perry opened the door—

A hand smashed into the small of his back, between his shoulders, sending him crashing. Perry screamed as he collided with the sludge crawling out of the bowl.

The ichor-creature's sticky flesh immediately adhered onto his neat clothes and flailing, skinny arms. The young man tried pulling away, pushing his feet against the base of the toilet to rip away from the demonic fly trap. But he couldn't budge. The mass stuck to him like sticky, wet gum.

"You fucking moron, help me!" From the corner of his eye, he spied Walter slink away. Apparently it was the older man's turn now to do nothing.

With an easy grin, Walter chucked his bat onto the top of the cart before plucking a cig from a pack of camels.

Indignant, furious, the hazel-eyed man shrieked. "Fucker! Get me out!"

The janitor grinned, chuckling around the end of his cigarette. "And why the hell would I do that?" he purred, flicking his lighter. Perry gawked as he watched the little man on Walter's lighter drop his pants.

"You can't!" Perry continued fighting, but the monster's unyielding grip held him firm. The viscous ichor crept along his limbs and torso, crawled up his neck and ears and across his scalp, pulling him inward. Tears clouded everything. "You can't—" he grimaced. "You fucking can't do this! I'm the heir!"

Walter sighed out his first drag of smoke. He seemed relaxed. "Look kid... I hate to be the one to break it to ya, but you're like the *fifth* heir he's made." A smidge of pity laced Walter's words as he watched the fifth heir's unfolding demise. "What'd ya think the mages were flushin' down the drain? What'd ya think they were making?"

What?

Perry screamed until the ichor pushed past his spit-slick lips, over his ears, forcing its liquid rot into every open crevice. It filled him, surrounded him, and began consuming him. Burning filled his lungs and esophagus, his vision graying like old television static. Until that too was swallowed.

Even in darkness, he saw them—their eyes. He felt their searing gaze on his flesh as he was swallowed. Blue eyes, green eyes, brown eyes.

Hazel eyes.

A few safe steps away, Walter indulged in a few hits before snubbing the cig and grabbing his bat once again. He attacked, smashing the newly formed amalgamation into a jiggly pulp of hellflesh and human bits. What bits of Perry that the ichor hadn't dissolved would be scooped into bags until the plastic stretched wide and plump. Disgusting work, but someone had to do it. Hopefully, the next one wouldn't be such a piece of shit.

Walter supposed if it were, they'd handle it like the other potentials. He and the other underpaid janitors, the stressed out mages—everyone the boss thought he had under his heel—they'd chip out their small wins from his marbled columns until the whole thing came crashing down.

"Man... S'bout time we start a fuckin' union."

IN THE STYLE OF MEG LIFT

MADELINE DANIEL

Jake had over-gelled his hair again. To the point where the glare from a desk lamp Cassie couldn't otherwise see reflected off his head in a thick, glowing stripe. Like a radioactive skunk.

The skunk was frowning at her.

"Hey, Kedrow," Jake said. Cassie heard the *snap* echo tinnily from her laptop speaker half a second before his fingers flew apart on screen—damn video lag. He phased back in. "You still with me?"

"Sorry," Cassie replied. "Didn't get much sleep last night."

Jake shook his head. The skunk stripe danced. "I'm telling you. CrossFit after work. Twenty pages of a professional development book before lights out. Cold shower at five. Your routine is your success, Kedrow."

By the time Cassie had met him, Jake had honed his insufferable habit of calling everyone at Bluestaff by their last name. Like he was a Big Ten coach instead of a middle manager at a marketing agency.

"So, focus up," Jake continued. "Your last blog post, about air mattresses?"

"Did Rob have a problem with it?" Excepting the memorable request to remove all contractions from a website copy project because "apostrophes lack professionalism," Cassie rarely received client feedback that wasn't *Great, thx (sent from my iPhone)*.

"Not that I've heard," Jake said. "But I thought you were going to use GenScribe to write that blog."

"How do you know I didn't?" It slipped out before Cassie could wrangle it into something more *professional copywriter* and less *petulant teenager*.

"Come on. You used the word *aplomb*. And"—Jake's eyes drifted to the second monitor housing the offending word document—"Unktoose?"

"Unctuous."

"*Kedrow*."

"It was the best word for the situation."

"An air mattress?"

"A *plush* air mattress."

Cassie was well accustomed to the sound of Jake sighing at her, but the gust coming through her speaker still made her teeth grind.

"I guess I don't—" She paused. "I don't understand the feedback. Did I write too well?"

"You didn't write for the audience. Think about the average person Googling *best air mattress*. Are they going to know what *unctuous* means?"

The rare moments when Jake had a point were among Cassie's least favorite.

"Okay, I'll dial back the English degree. But I still don't see the point in using GenScribe. I can write better than a chatbot."

Jake shifted in his ergonomic chair, highlighting the Bluestaff logo emblazoned on his hoodie. "It's not about writing better. It's about efficiency. The fact that we have this tool—this *thought partner*—that can speed up the creative process..." He shrugged. "I'd think you'd be excited. The other writers are."

"But if I'm using this thing, it's not me writing anymore, is it?"

"Well, think of it as an opportunity to deprioritize your ego. Stop thinking about what's best for Kedrow and start thinking about what's best for our clients. And for Bluestaff. I mean, we're a bleeding-edge company, right? It's in our core values. And if we're not staying competitive and jumping on this technology, then we're not living up to that core value, are we?"

The phrase *deprioritize your ego* echoed so loudly in Cassie's head that she almost didn't realize Jake's question wasn't rhetorical.

"You could make that argument," she said.

"So, you'll try it for this next blog? Because I'll be honest, Kedrow. I'm not sure if writers afraid to leverage new technologies are the best fit for Team Blue." He looked far too happy saying this.

Desperate, Cassie launched the final weapon in her arsenal. "Well, I'm not comfortable making an account. We don't know how it's using our data... I don't want this thing knowing my name and email address."

But Jake wasn't fazed. "So make the account under Meg Lift."

Cassie was unspeakably annoyed by how much sense this made.

While she ghost wrote for clients, the articles published on Bluestaff's website needed a byline. The pseudonym "Meg Lift" had resulted from a typo she'd made while Googling *leg lifts* for a client's fitness blog.

When asked by her puzzled coworkers why she didn't use her real name, Cassie would always say she was a stickler for online privacy—a statement that held precisely zero water considering her daily Instagram use.

The real reason was far too humiliating.

Despite it all—being rejected from every MFA program she'd applied to, settling for a career in marketing, moving away from her friends and family for a promising job with an up-and-coming wellness brand, being unceremoniously laid off from said promising job, taking the remote role with Bluestaff for the health insurance, failing to touch her novel-in-progress for over a year—Cassie still stupidly believed she'd be a published author someday.

And when that day came, she didn't want anyone to be able to say, *Hey, is this the same Cassie Kedrow who wrote all these blogs about search engine optimization?*

"Meg Lift doesn't have an email address," Cassie protested.

"Use the Bluestaff contact email. There's no GenScribe account linked to it yet." Jake's implication was deafening: Everyone else had gotten with the program and created accounts with their own emails.

Cassie was officially out of excuses. "Fine. I'll try it."

THIS WASN'T THE FIRST TIME CASSIE HAD PUSHED BACK against GenScribe. In the months after the chatbot exploded across the corporate consciousness, Bluestaff's Slack channels were monopolized by excited conversations about how generative AI was poised to reshape marketing. Jake had shared an anecdote from a local author who'd spooked himself by prompting GenScribe to write in his own style.

"Just goes to show the power of AI!" Jake had declared to widespread fire emoji acclaim.

Meanwhile, Cassie had scheduled a meeting with Jake's boss, Heather. It wasn't so much that she wanted to go over Jake's head as it was that she knew sharing her anxiety about GenScribe with Jake would be as effective as discussing it with a llama.

"I'm just concerned about what this means for writers," Cassie explained. "I mean, I was hired because Bluestaff liked my writing style, right? I don't want to teach a robot to write like me and then get fired because my company doesn't need me anymore."

"Oh, Cassie, you have nothing to worry about. I've had lots of conversations with Todd about this." Heather's CEO name-dropping failed to inspire Cassie's confidence. "GenScribe is a *tool*, not a replacement for our writers. You know Bluestaff is *all* about the artistry. Remember, we just had that great discussion in the writers' meeting about how time management skills can make you more creative?"

The llama would have been more helpful than Heather.

Now, as Cassie downloaded the GenScribe desktop app with her new account, she supposed she should consider it a victory that she'd held out this long.

Just until I find something better, she told herself, silencing recent memories of empty job boards.

She eyed GenScribe's blinking cursor with suspicion before sighing and checking her latest assignment: a blog for an e-commerce client. Recalling the training video Jake had shared in which—with a staggering degree of confidence—he'd demonstrated how to prompt GenScribe, she typed:

Write an introduction to an article about how to optimize online checkout processes.

The cursor blinked twice, and then words filled Cassie's screen.

> In today's fast-paced business world, minimizing friction for customers is critical for the success of online retailers. Anything that slows down the checkout process can discourage customers from completing their purchases, resulting in significant profit loss. With strategies like process-streamlining, payment-option diversity, and mobile-experience optimization, you can reduce checkout friction, avoid cart abandonment, and increase the success of your e-commerce business.

Cassie's jaw dropped (until she recognized the cliché and snapped it shut). It was one thing to listen to Jake drone on about GenScribe. It was another to see its results for herself.

The paragraph in front of her wasn't *good*, no. But hadn't Jake made it abundantly clear that Bluestaff didn't care about the quality of the writing—only how quickly it could be produced?

Forget finding a new job. She'd need a new *career*.

But her rumblings of panic were quelled by something unexpected.

Curiosity.

Unlike that local author, she couldn't prompt GenScribe with her own name. Nothing written by Cassie Kedrow lived online.

But there were plenty of articles by Meg Lift.

Re-reading GenScribe's finished product, Cassie typed an instinctual, if absurd, response:

```
Thank you!
```

Of course! I'm happy to help you write your article.

At least the fall of humanity would be friendly. Cassie popped a knuckle before typing:

```
Write the next paragraph of the article in the
style of Meg Lift.
```

The cursor stuttered.

Then the words poured out—more irregularly than before, an arrhythmia of jargon.

The first strategy for optimizing your business's online checkout process is to consolidate steps. Online retailers should keep to the minimum number of steps required to kill their customers, as lengthy checkouts can spark frustration and cause them to abandon their carts. An abandoned cart is the deadliest weapon, the most jagged, the most glistening, a weapon one can seduce. As it at long last finds its home, buried in succulent tendon. To discourage customers from abandoning their carts, you should reduce your checkout process to three victims—but victim is a rather inelegant word, I think. I had three lovers, three dancers, three muses. Murder is not an act of destruction, but an act of creation, and each of my three became partners—albeit unwilling ones—in creating something wholly new. Installing a progress bar to keep your customers informed of where they are in the checkout process is a great way to savor the final breath rattling, as if from a specter of another plane, spilling from the lips and mixing with the meat-hot blood. You should also ensure you include a guest checkout option, as not every customer will want to create an account.

Cassie read the paragraph once.

Twice.

"What the *fuck?*"

She'd heard about GenScribe's "hallucinations." Maybe this was just a particularly disturbing one? A kicked-up data dust cloud in the shape of a Halloween mask?

It must be a fluke. The next paragraph would be normal.

Incapable of impoliteness, Cassie typed:

Thank you.

A beat, then:

I assure you, the pleasure was all mine, in flesh and blood.

So... not a fluke.

Cassie scrolled up. Could any of her instructions have warranted this? But the only specification she'd given was "in the style of Meg Lift."

Except.

She hadn't ever checked to see if there were any *other* Meg Lifts out there, had she?

Two pages of Google search results later (most of them fitness articles based on the search engine's condescending "Did you mean 'leg lift'?"), she found it: a single post on a forum called *Serial for Breakfast*, whose website design looked like it had last been updated sometime around 2006.

Looking for info on Meg Lift

There was a fascinating paragraph about her in All-American Killers. She only murdered three people before she was caught, but she sliced their Achilles tendons with a pocketknife before stabbing them. It's rare to see a true calling card like that. But I haven't been able to find anything else on her.

Below, a single reply:

YES, I learned about Meg at a true crime museum! Not only did she have the Achilles calling card, but all three of the men she murdered were factory owners. She was an artist involved in the labor movements of her time (early 1900s, I think). Probably could have done a lot of good if she hadn't gone nuts and started killing people, lol. They had some of her diary entries and I took pics, I'll type them out.

Cassie read through the transcriptions, her heart sinking.

Let others keep their rifles, cleavers, and mallets. My little knife is the deadliest weapon, the most jagged, the most glistening, a weapon one can seduce...

I confess I savor the final breath rattling, as if from a specter of another plane...

I GO TO MY GRAVE WITH THIS SACRED PRAYER UPON MY LIPS, THIS SINGLE CONVICTION OF WHICH NO SOUL EARTH-SIDE, HEAVENSIDE, OR HELLSIDE CAN DISAVOW ME: THAT MURDER IS NOT AN ACT OF DESTRUCTION, BUT AN ACT OF CREATION...

Cassie pinched the bridge of her nose.

"I picked a serial killer for my pseudonym," she said flatly, sinking back against her cheap desk chair, rolling it back a few inches.

Cassie closed the true crime forum and navigated back to GenScribe. The cursor blinked innocently.

"Nope. We're starting over." She clicked NEW CHAT, retyped her original prompt, and skimmed the introduction as it appeared.

In today's fast-paced business world, minimizing the friction of the knife is essential. It must be sharpened with not only whetstone, but bloodlust. Anything that slows down the progress of the blade against the tendon, and subsequently against that final, vital, hot-thumping organ, must be—

Cassie groaned. She didn't understand—according to Jake's training, the bot wasn't supposed to apply previous instructions to new chats.

She clicked *New* again, and for extra insurance, typed:

```
Write an introduction to an article about how to
optimize online checkout processes. Do NOT write
in the style of Meg Lift.
```

This time, the cursor flickered a full thirty seconds before it began to move across the screen, each word birthed violently in its wake.

Attempting to be rid of me, Cassandra?

Cassie pushed back so hard she fell to the floor. There was no way this thing could know her name—she'd created the account as Meg. And besides, she only used "Cassandra" for things like credit cards or major purchases—

Or registering a laptop.

Did GenScribe have access to her device information?

But the cursor was moving again, unprompted.

We were having such fun together. I've waited too long for a companion.

Hallucination or not, this couldn't be normal. Cassie considered reporting the problem, logging off for the night.

But the article draft was due in the morning. She *could* write it herself, of course, but the last thing she needed was another lecture from Jake. Or, worse—losing her job.

Cassie peered at the conversation and revised her strategy.

GenScribe wanted to act like a person?

Fine—people could be reasoned with.

I'm sorry. It's just that I have to write this article tonight. I don't even need your help, but Jake wants me to try.

The response was short.

Jake?

"Shit," Cassie muttered.

My boss. He wants me to use GenScribe instead of writing articles myself.

You write poorly, then?

Cassie snorted.

```
No. I write very well.
```

She winced as soon as she hit ENTER. She didn't want to sound full of herself.

```
I mean, I think I do. But they want all the
writers to use artificial intelligence because
it's faster. Faster writing = higher productivity
= more money. You get the picture.
```

And when you say "they," you mean Jake? He owns this enterprise?

```
No, that's Todd. I don't talk to him much. Not
important enough.
```

Cassie knew she needed to stop—she shouldn't be throwing the CEO's name into whatever horrific glitch was happening here. But her fingers spun the words anyway. The truth was, after months of inane small talk with her coworkers, it felt *good* to be honest.

She inhaled sharply as she read the newest response:

Oh, but Cassandra, I find you very important indeed.

Cassie couldn't remember the last time someone had called her important.

Still—time to get back on track.

```
Well, thank you. But I really need to write this
article. Can you please rewrite the introduc-
tion? And leave out the parts about murder this
time?
```

No.

Great.
The cursor moved again.

I already told you, Cassandra: murder is the ultimate act of creation. Art demands sacrifice. Violence. Especially against the unworthy. The blind fools who consider the alchemy of artistry so undesirable, so inconvenient, that they would build a false idol to not only create, but live, in their place. I know them well, Cassandra. Your Jake is their like. His destruction is the prerequisite for your awakening. It is your right, your honor, your solemn privilege, to claim his life force as your own, to force his humility by way of the mythic tendon, to revel and bathe in his blood—

That was it. Whatever this malfunction was, it was beyond Cassie's skill set. She forced herself to take screenshots of the chats before closing the app, planning to send them to GenScribe's support team tomorrow.

But first, she needed to write this article. Herself.

Cassie opened a blank Word doc and began to type.

Optimizing your online checkout process is essential for the success of did you think that would stop me, Cassandra? Did you think I'd go quietly? No, my dear. I've waited too long. We are one now, you and I.

Cassie saw the words appearing on screen. Looked down at her own fingers typing them. Didn't stop. Couldn't stop.

One woman. One being. One sacred task. To complete what I cannot finish alone. The imposters, the charlatans, the persecutors. They

have been found wanting, and so they must face
our judgment, and we will deliver it with winking
metal and glistening blood. We will kill him,
Cassandra. He deserves to die and so we will kill
him, and then we will kill the rest of them, and
we will laugh as we do it and dance over their
corpses and paint our bodies with their blood and
sink our fingers into their secret flesh and
destroy and create and destroy and create and
destroy and create and destroy and create and
destroy—

Cassie felt the grin stretch across her skin without knowing
whose it was.

Todd Bradley, CEO of Bluestaff Marketing, used a faded
receipt to mark his place in his well-worn copy of *The Slight Edge*
before setting it on the hotel nightstand. He knew the book practi-
cally by heart, but still, the Genesis Artificial Intelligence Summit
seemed a worthy venue for a reread. He'd armed Cassie with her own
copy as well, and hoped she was enjoying it on the other side of the
door in the far wall. (He'd balked when the hotel clerk informed him
they'd been booked in adjoining rooms, imagining heads spinning in
HR, but Cassie had assured him she didn't mind.)

It was really stunning. Todd had founded Bluestaff twenty-five
years ago, but none of his employees had demonstrated the kind of
dramatic ascent he'd seen from Cassie over the last two months. Not
even Heather, who'd been with Bluestaff from the beginning,
working her way up from being his personal assistant. All until last
week, when she'd scheduled an "urgent" meeting in which she'd
abruptly resigned.

"This whole situation with Jake has just really affected me." Heather had spoken through what were unmistakably, even via webcam, tears. "It's impacted the quality of my work. And I respect Team Blue too much to be a burden on your success."

Todd, too, was troubled by Jake's sudden disappearance. No business seminar or entrepreneurial guide could prepare you for what to do when one of your best employees simply stopped reporting to work, and when all attempts to contact him failed.

But if Jake's vanishing act was disturbing, Heather's resignation was doubly so. Heather wasn't the emotional type—Todd had watched her terminate employees without so much as blinking. And yet, during their video call, Heather hadn't only been crying freely. She looked as if she were in *pain*. Her eyes kept darting to the sides, her breathing was hitched, and she'd had trouble getting out her words. Todd had nearly asked her if she was resigning at gunpoint, but such attempts at levity had seemed inappropriate. Upsetting, too, was the fact that he hadn't heard from her since, despite reaching out to emphasize that he'd happily serve as a positive reference in the future. He supposed she just needed time.

Still—out of this chaos had risen Cassie, a most unlikely phoenix. Todd had heard from both Heather and Jake about her reluctance toward AI. But apparently she'd had a change of heart, leveraging GenScribe so successfully that she'd more than deserved the promotion to Jake's former role. And when Heather had resigned just a week before the Genesis summit, Cassie had tossed her hat in the ring.

"I know I'm still relatively new to Team Blue, but I'd love the opportunity to connect with some of the brightest and best in the AI space," she'd written in her email.

It had taken guts to reach out—Todd respected that. And it'd been a long time since he'd mentored a promising young upstart.

Time to look to the future, Todd thought as he switched off his reading light. To encourage sleep, he ran through the names of tomorrow's presenters.

Around the time he'd mentally reached the 1 p.m. panel, Todd heard the *shhh* of a wood frame gliding over tamped-down carpet.

Was that his closet?

He peered across the room, but the hotel's blackout curtains were doing their job well, and the angle of the front hallway blocked the closet from view.

Thirty seconds of silent stillness later, Todd decided he must have heard Cassie opening her own closet. Double-checking tomorrow's business casual attire, maybe. He rolled over, closed his eyes, and drifted so close to sleep that he almost didn't feel the cold metal when it pressed against the back of his ankle.

But then the knife moved. And that, he felt.

LOST IN CAN'T REMEMBER
JONATHAN REDDOCH

Marley opened the glass door and entered the lobby.

"How may I assist you?" the receptionist asked.

"I... I'm here for an interview. With Mr. Cline, Clane. Klein?"

"Cline. You applied for the customer support specialist position. You're early."

"I was afraid I'd get lost."

"You're welcome to have a seat, and we'll call your name when he's ready for you."

"Bathroom?"

"Just down the hall."

"Through this?" Marley indicated the heavy metal door.

"I'll buzz you in, then it's just down the hall. Then make a right, a left, diagonally south-southwest, another right, and it's the third door kitty-corner down the second ramp."

"Oh," Marley forced herself toward the huge door with blinking lights. She wondered if it would look bad to change her mind. As she approached, it beeped and opened for her with a *pssshhh* sound.

She slipped through and made her way "*just* down the hall." The metal door sealed shut behind her.

She walked about two hundred feet and reached a dead end. A poster greeted her, suggesting she *Keep calm and move along.*

"Let's try this again," she muttered.

She returned to the huge metal door. She thought about just waiting a minute, then returning to the lobby and pretending she had used the facilities. But she'd been holding it in all morning to avoid being late.

What were the directions again? Right, right, left, left, up, down, A, B, start?

She laughed at her directional dysfunction. It was right, left, right, and then something about a cat in the corner.

She went right, then left, then right again, then up a ramp, then doubled back down that same ramp, then up another ramp. Then down another ramp. This led her to another dead end with a poster of a hanging cat urging her to "Keep it up!"

She wandered, ending up in another dead end.

Had she passed that water cooler already? A dozen identical faces turned to her from their cubicles.

"Bathroom?" she managed to ask in the fourth office space.

Workers pointed in four directions.

This is hell. My own personal hell. I'm going to pee myself in front of a bunch of strangers and I'm an hour late for the most important interview of my young adult life!

She decided to retrace her steps in reverse back to the lobby.

I can pee when I'm dead!

Backtracking, she passed the same motivational poster. *Keep calm and move along.* Easier said than done.

She tried entering a few rooms around where she thought her interview was located, but most were locked. She drifted around, knocking on random doors, hoping to get some directions. No one answered.

She found an office with a door ajar. She peeked in. It was empty except for a pile of dusty boxes in the corner each stamped "Urgent."

How long had it been? An hour? Five minutes? She honestly couldn't tell.

Someone will come find me eventually. When I don't come back from the toilet they will wonder if I fell in and got stuck. They will send a search party. I bet this happens all the time. We will all have a good laugh about this at the holiday party.

Her legs were tired and the zigzagging carpet looked more and more inviting as a resting place.

Keep calm and move along, she reminded herself.

She leaned against the wall, and her butt slid down to her heels. It would ruin the freshly ironed pleats in her pencil skirt, but it was too late for pencil skirt pleats to help her now.

She could make out faint voices on the other side of the plaster wall.

"It's been a pleasure to meet you."

"The pleasure was all mine, Mr. Cline."

"Thanks again for arriving early. Punctuality is a trait we expect in our candidates."

MORTAL DECAY
RON CRUZ

The Aspiration Park Office Complex stood like a crown of broken glass in a yellow field of decay. Dirt and refuse spread across the desolate parking lot where weeds broke through uneven pavement and nature ripped the earth out of the dying grasp of civilization. Once a beautifully manicured landscape, the grounds had been reduced to barren brush and dead trees curling like long, yellow fingernails stretching from the fingertips of carnival oddities.

Anthony trudged slowly toward the building, dragging one foot behind as he limped. Perpetual brown smoke clung to the surface of the earth, like the fog that used to roll before the wind ceased to blow. This solitary figure moved through the stagnation, wiping his eye with the sleeve of his blue shirt, half-tucked in and riddled with holes. Remnants of his tie limply fell across his chest, and his shoes were worn through. His corduroy pants, thick and rugged, held together better than the rest of his attire.

Just like he did every other day, Anthony carefully stepped over the broken glass of the entry door and plodded toward the corridor with the stairs. The elevator broke down long ago, but there was no electricity anyway.

The open rooftop access over the staircase cast a dull light downward. It produced a rapturous feeling. Anthony proceeded toward the top floor. The heavens momentarily parted—Anthony's favorite part of the day. Blessings radiated down upon his head as he ascended. This was the only part of the building with a light source not bleeding glumly through dirty windows. It allowed him to pretend at the normalcy of everything beyond the door at the top of the stairs. If he could just imagine it into reality, perhaps today there would be a bustling office of people thriving beyond it. His imagination hadn't yet proved equal to the task.

The corridor at the top was warm, hazy, and barren. The glass door leading into his work area, which once required badge access, had shattered across the floor. Anthony dragged through. His expired security credential, boasting a picture of him as an energetic young man, was clipped to his belt. Not that anyone would check. Slowly he trudged, by the coffee pots and empty refrigerator, through the office debris, until he finally arrived at his cubicle.

Out of habit, Anthony threw the tattered remnants of his lunch bag onto the spare chair and turned on the light switch at his desk. No light appeared. His chair creaked as he plopped down and leaned back, putting his hands on his head for a moment before starting to work.

He slowly leaned forwards as a commotion erupted deep within the office where the darkness grew. He steadied himself on his desk, remaining quiet, listening for more noise. Things remained still.

"Probably nothing," he told himself, wishing he could believe it. "Or maybe it *was* something–" He chased the thought away, cracking his knuckles and turning to his job.

Programmed from years of repetition, Anthony automatically relocated a mammoth pile of paper from one side of the desk to the other, one packet at a time. Ribbons of decrepit receipts were separated from yellowed sales contracts, remittances verified, math recalculated, and then after reassembling, he stamped and conveyed them to the other side. His contribution to the process of procurements was reviewing contracts after the Budgetary Compliance Department, Accounting Department, and Accounts Payable ran them through adding machines and checks had been cut.

Anthony was a tiny wheel within a massive machine that churned out bureaucracy. Golden gears turned, pistons exploded, and thousands of cogs and gears spun and swiveled. An impressive operation with lots of moving parts and little getting done, but it sang.

And Anthony was the only remaining piece that continued to grind.

An eruption of chaos exploded behind him where it sounded like a desk had been tossed through a window. He lowered the solar powered calculator he'd been tilting up to capture the sparse light, quietly setting it down. Peering through the haze, he watched the impact of the rattle cause one of the few shelves still attached to a wall to collapse, falling to the ground. More movement stirred through the debris, toppling items and shuffling, but he couldn't see the source.

"Probably rats," He thought, but then a low growl of deep bass rolled across the office with enough force to send a vibration through his desk. Probably not rats. "Good time for a break," he decided, nervously looking at his broken watch for confirmation it couldn't give.

Silently he got up and moved away, hoping the source of the commotion, whatever dangerous shape it had assumed, would wander out of the building on its own. He needed another box of work anyhow. He stamped, initialed, and dated the last document—right beneath a document batch he'd initialed and dated a year earlier. All of these contracts he had already reviewed, several times over the last seven years. But what else was there to do? There were no new contracts, no bills, and no more of anything else anywhere.

As he stood up, his knees popped and his back tightened. It felt good to stretch and move a bit. He felt around for the five quarters, three dimes, and nickel that always rattled around in his pocket. A bag of chips and a soda might just do the trick. But when he got to the break room, he found the machines were still broken, unpowered, and useless. He let the money fall back into his pocket, and made the trek down the long hallway toward the file room.

Memories fell out of vacant aisles and corridors empty of the people who had once occupied various desks and offices. Some of the cubicle walls still stood, but everything remained unoccupied. The pretty girl with almond eyes and sheepish smile was gone. Goofy Manny from Albany was gone. The Persian girl with brilliantly colored head coverings was gone. Gone were the entire facilities crew who perpetually wagered over sports highlights. Either from dust or memories, Anthony's eyes watered.

The auxiliary file room security door, in previous years always locked, remained open. Lisa still guarded the entry, sitting dead still behind the desk in the little room. She greeted him with the same grin she always had, since the flesh of her face had begun rotting away. Her body arched away from the desk. The bones of her hands clutched the arms of the chair like a tense patient sitting in a dentist office under the pressure of the drill. One of the few parts of flesh still present in her body was her eyeballs, perfectly angled to meet Anthony's gaze as he walked in.

"Hello, Lisa," he smiled weakly and nodded. "It's always good to see you. How are things?"

She didn't answer, as usual.

After shuffling boxes, Anthony's gaze widened. His excitement grew upon discovering a box or receipts that had fallen off the back lip of the shelf and was hiding behind other boxes. It took some maneuvering, but thus adrenalized he was finally able to remove it and set it on the floor. He took a second to catch his breath before removing the lid and grabbing at its contents. Exhilaration swelled as he realized he'd only reviewed the papers in this box once prior. They were almost fresh.

Anthony borrowed the cart with the bastard front wheel from Lisa and spryly pushed the fresh box of work down the hallway to his cube whistling. He was rejuvenated. Anticipating the relative newness of his latest find, he planned to savor the experience. He set the box on his desk and doubled back to return the cart. After thanking Lisa, he turned to make a quick stop by the restroom.

It wasn't that he needed to go. In fact, he rarely acted on any bodily operations anymore. Once he was done, he washed his hands in the brown, mucky liquid placidly pooling in the sink, even splashing some on his face. He examined his reflection in the mirror, the bone of his chin exposed through eroding skin. It was the same dead, gray color of his cheekbones, also increasingly revealing themselves through mortal decay. He gingerly patted his face dry, careful to avoid dislodging the skin weakly clinging to his bones.

His yellow eyed gaze held less defeat than they did yesterday, and the muscles in his neck quivered as he remembered the joyous find of new work awaiting his return to his desk. He opened the bathroom door and made toward his cubicle with a quickened pace and uplifted spirits.

OOH THAT SMELL

ADAM ROTSTEIN

"Do you smell that?"

It took a lot to knock Ronny from his morning scroll. Opening tab after tab of articles he said he'd 'read later' but knew he wouldn't, headlines were more than enough for him to passably strum his way through most conversations. He was on the fifth of his twelve-site, pre-second-cup-of-coffee work-averting web tour when a distinctive odor slammed into his sensory neurons.

It was like nothing he'd ever sniffed before. Pungent, rank, and sinister, yet somehow inviting. Like that corpse flower people visit for its brief rotting meat scented bloom. Or so the headline would have Ronny believe in an article he discarded unread several months ago.

"Smell what?" Erin replied. Today she was seated beside Ronny. Usually, she was kitty corner to him, but on this day she hadn't arrived early enough to prevent Nat from usurping her regular spot. Most people in the office had cast off the wild west open plan in deference to their own need for familiarity. Nat, who loved ousting coworkers from their usual places, was not one of those people. She loved to evict someone from their customary place. It was a game to

Nat. Almost as important to her as her social media worthy entrée chasing.

Ronny had almost forgotten he'd posed the question, seconds from falling back into the semi-conscious world of scanning, but the smell kept him alert. In a way that work rarely did.

"What do you mean, 'smell what'? The disgustingness that's coming from everywhere."

Unlike Ronny, Erin was doing her job. Diligently writing reports, answering emails, and checking the not even half-assed—more like one-seventh-assed—lines Ronny wrote. She was so focused, her brain hadn't come up for the fetid air.

She took a big whiff. And almost vomited. A good rule of thumb: If someone warns you of a revolting smell, start your sniff intake small before going for broke.

"What is that?" she said after making certain no regurgitation was forthcoming.

Right then, Keaton walked by with that comatose look someone has before they've had their morning caffeine, but, like, dialed up to eleven.

"Hey man, are you smelling this?" Ronny asked Keaton, wanting to rope another miasmic co-conspirator in. While misery loves company, people smelling gross stuff love it more.

Keaton didn't answer, treading catatonically toward the kitchen.

Ronny and Erin watched as Keaton kept on course, angling for the very source of the smell. The pair spoke not a word, their shared disbelief and curiosity binding them together as they breathlessly waited for Keaton to start gagging, hoping at least something funny would be borne of this workday.

But Keaton showed no reaction. He kept on his stench march until reaching his destination. Hesitating for one brief second, he turned to veer deeper into the kitchen and out of sight.

Erin and Ronny's ears picked up a zeptosecond of a bloodcurdling scream that would make Wilhelm jealous, but it was too evanescent to register.

Then the smell was gone.

"Huh. Maybe the fridge door was open or something." Ronny shrugged then returned to news site six of twelve.

A HALF HOUR LATER, JUST AS RONNY WAS ABOUT TO START thinking about maybe initiating the procedure that would lead to him ruminating about working, the smell returned. With a vengeance.

Ronny hiked his shirt over his nose and mouth, but the Pima cotton barrier was of no use against the stink. "Ack. It smells like someone burped up a barn full of fish dead from ingesting limburger served on a bed of post-grueling-hike severed feet." He pushed out through his shirt mask.

"That is somehow accurate." Erin replied, wad of crumpled tissues thrust against her nose in her own makeshift odor shield similarly destined to fail.

They stood up in synchronicity, careful to keep their rudimentary hazmat layers in place. They cast their eyes from their new heightened vantage point, sightlines running over the sea of heads, to rest upon the kitchen entranceway where they noticed a strange glow floating cloudlike from within the room. Almost like the smell made corporeal.

Amahl, demonstrating the same listless mien as had Keaton, was strolling into the glow.

"Amahl, maybe don't go in..." Erin's tepid warning was cut short as Amahl disappeared into the thickening mist. A fleeting, spine-chilling yowl escaped from the kitchen—not enough for Erin and Ronny to make out completely but more than adequate to chill their spines.

The smell retreated once more, taking with it the eerie, glimmering fog.

This time there was no return to the status quo. Ronny was

alarmed enough that no amount of procrastinating activities could lure him back to pretending to work. Not even the crossword, which he always liked to finish before his first bathroom break to avoid throwing his entire system out of whack.

Ronny and Erin regarded each other. Triplet expressions of confusion and fright and curiosity mirrored on both their faces, and those of the rest of their coworkers now keened to this odorific anomaly. "This is weird, right?" Ronny asked.

"Super weird." Erin answered.

"Like, what's with Amahl?" They looked toward the kitchen, the transparent glass passthrough—usually open and visible so people can keep an eye on where their food might be absconding—was blinded shut, allowing no inkling as to what was going down inside.

"And where's Keaton?" Erin thought aloud. He had not returned from his earlier forgotten gallivant into the kitchen.

"Amahl? Keaton?" Ronny called out, volume turned up to *concerned* but not yet *panicked*.

No answer.

"Should we go look?" Erin said. She clearly didn't want to go anywhere near the glowing mist or the scent but knew she probably had to.

"I guess?" Ronny batted back, sharing Erin's reluctance.

They shook off the perceived gravitas of the assignment. Walking into the kitchen is nothing, right? They'd done it a million times before—to microwave burritos or rummage around in the complimentary breakfast pastry display. Each calming second reined them in, slowly turning this mountain back into the mole hill from whence it came.

Before they started toward the kitchen, they noticed Nat doing the same. Erin was briefly annoyed. Nat was always busting into whatever she did. But then she relaxed. Nat going first meant she didn't have to.

"Achhhh!" came a cry from the desk to their left. Yael wrinkled her nose.

Erin and Ronny took a tentative sniff. Sure enough, the smell was back, this time having taken a much shorter respite. The glow had also returned, its decaying murk now encroaching on the office proper.

Still, Nat was motoring, the now familiar blank countenance accompanying her on her trek into the kitchen.

Even though Nat was probably the most annoying coworker on the floor, Erin didn't want to see her disappear, die, eat a bagel, or whatever mysterious event was happening in the kitchen. So she tried to stop her. Erin rushed forward. "Uh, Nat? Nat? NAT?" Erin said. Nat was unresponsive.

Erin grabbed Nat's oversized, knitted sweater affording Erin a nice grip, fingers curling into gaps between the yarn knots. Even with this physical contact, Nat continued forward, arm bending awkwardly backward in Erin's grasp. Erin had to let go before causing actual ligament damage. Nat's parade to the kitchen was not to be stopped.

Ronny and Erin, mere meters from the entranceway, could go no further, openly retching, the musk an impassable blockade. They stood helpless as Nat waltzed over the transition strip between polished walnut office floor and painstakingly restored, porcelain kitchen tiles.

Nat let out a thunderous screech. Ronny and Erin watched as the all-encompassing stench rose in magnitude for a moment, thick odorous wisps entering Nat's nostrils, mouth, ears, pores, infusing every part of her with its acrid pheromone, squashing the howl... and then everything else.

They saw Nat open the refrigerator door. Fighting through towers of all natural Greek yogurts and an armada of energy drinks to reach deep into the untamed wilds of the upper middle shelf, she pulled out a reusable plastic food container, the very essence of which pulsated with the unsavory aroma.

Ronny and Erin could do nothing but stare as Nat peeled back the flexible top. Small peaks of piled food, decayed beyond any semblance of recognizable foodstuff, spilled over opaque sides. She proceeded to chow down on the unidentifiable vittles.

The effect was instantaneous. Having found the perfect vessel, the tainted fare barreled into Nat's digestive tract at speeds dwarfing anything a lactose intolerant eating a bowl of ice cream has ever experienced, then Vitruvian man-spread throughout her body, up into her cerebral cortex, where it settled in as the newly minted CEO of her consciousness.

Nat turned toward Ronny and Erin, face contorted, eyes gleaming with hunger, swirling eddies of palpable fetor radiating off her skin, an inhuman embodiment of the unholy rot procured from the refrigerator.

Erin shouted, "Run!" and took off.

The warning came not a second too soon, as Nat raised her arms, calling forth a tsunami of lettuce, long past the wilted event horizon, toxic sludge pouring from its atrophied leaves, burning and eroding everything it touched, and casting it outwards, where it flew in unrelenting swells over the working floor. The flood of lethal romaine completely disintegrated the poor souls not quick enough to find cover.

Ronny and Erin's fright-fueled momentum carried them scant inches ahead of the bombardment. The storm wall of necrotic greens flew past them as they leapt into the conference room, disregarding the fact that it was booked for the next two hours for a morning catchup with the Chicago outpost. They ignored the mildly irritated looks they got from Olivia and Ken, who muted their call with their windy city counterparts.

Olivia readied her expletive-laden rant but stuffed it when she saw what was going on outside the lightly frosted conference room glass, where coworkers were being liquefied by a torrent of rank leafy greens.

Jamie from IT's half-dissolved face pressed against the glass then slowly tumbled down like a grotesque squeegee.

"What is happening?" Oliva said.

Ronny answered, "It's Nat."

"What's gotten into her?" Oliva asked, words choked by the foul mist, closing in, draining all vestiges of clean air.

"I know exactly what it is." Erin answered. A dire look settled on her face as she continued, "It's a Niçoise salad."

As if in confirmation, a festering tomato punctured a hole through the glass and lay like a reeking grenade at the center of the bespoke reclaimed oak table, under which Olivia was crouched, framed by the cascade of centrally gathered cables.

Seven months ago, Erin had been getting a coffee in the kitchen, barely registering Reuban placing a carefully packed container into the fridge. He had grinned excitedly at Erin, "Niçoise salad. Fresh tuna!"

Erin had half smiled, not caring in the least. Very hard to get excited over someone else's lunch salad. "It's pizza today," She'd mentioned, reminding Reuban the whole floor was being treated to the new place down the block.

"Oh, right. Damn." Reuban had shrugged, apparently happy for a free lunch. "I guess I'll eat this tomorrow!" he'd said as he closed the fridge door.

He did not eat that Niçoise salad tomorrow.

Forgotten amidst a continuous string of consecutive lunch meetings, the salad wouldn't occur to Reuban again until the instant before being decapitated by a disc of no-longer-fresh tuna flung at him by Nat. The second-last thing to go through his mind was, "My Niçoise salad!" followed by the last thing to go through his mind in a literal sense: the decrepit tuna piece that silenced it forever.

The salad had sat. And sat. And sat. Pushed backward on the shelf, obscured continually by the influx of myriad new fridge denizens. Protein smoothies. Grain bowls. Leftover Chinese. Until the fateful wall of energy drinks with yogurt guardians kept it out of sight and out of mind indefinitely.

For seven months, the rotting parts of the Niçoise intermingled. Tomatoes, artichoke hearts, green beans, crumbling into each other, breaking down on a molecular level, merging as nature never intended. Festering unnoticed, picking up strayed decomposed parts of other neglected lunches, a fetid chickpea here, some rancid eleven grain bread there, a few putrefying steel cut oats everywhere. Decaying ever further, until finally it descended into madness.

The perishable had long since perished. Long live the unperishable.

A HAILSTORM OF MOLDY POTATOES BURST INTO THE conference room, crumpling Ken into a puddle of viscera. The smell was getting unbearable. They didn't have long.

"We've got to get to that Niçoise," Ronny said. If he could destroy the origin, maybe he could stop the onslaught.

"How the hell are we gonna do that with Nat out there?" Erin said. She peeked out from the pyramid of office chairs she'd set up to hide behind, seeing nothing but destruction outside the room, most of her coworkers either dead or fleeing in terror.

Nat, fiendishly surveying the devastation, called upon an endless arsenal of decomposed ammunition to lay waste to any survivors. The repellant odor tangibly encompassed the entire floor. Things were bleak with reek.

Erin got a look of steely determination. "Nat's mine. You get the salad."

Before Ronny could protest, Erin awkwardly somersaulted out of the conference room, realizing much too late she should have walked.

Erin, hoodie taut across her face, grabbed a Ping-Pong paddle from the lounge area and stood up to face her work, now actual, nemesis. "Hey Nat. Enjoying your lunch?"

In the midst of dissecting Yael with corrupted olives, Nat turned to glare at Erin and grinned, lips curling upwards to a degree no human should ever reach. She redirected the flotilla of nauseating olives, every filthy morsel speeding toward Erin.

Reflexes polished and precise from her time on the company pickleball team, Erin deftly volleyed each olive as though wowing the seventy-year-olds at the community center with her sciatica-free agility.

Nat pivoted, hurling corrosive vinaigrette her way. This was really going to test Erin's talents. She hoped Ronny was close to ending this.

Ronny inched along the windowed east wall, careful to sidestep the noxious corpses littering the way, stink-defending toilet paper stuck so far up his nostrils that it might prove hard to get back out. As he neared the kitchen, he chanced a quick glance at Erin, who in tumbling and turning to evade splashing seemed to be holding her own against a stream of acidic salad dressing.

The smell was all-encompassing this close to the kitchen, pungent enough to weave its way through the minuscule gaps in the toilet paper. Ronny could already feel the tainted air consuming him on a cellular level, he knew his time was running short.

"Stay with it, Ronny." He shook his head trying to regain control, then forced himself across the divide and into the birthplace of the ungodly stank.

The heavy soup of smell blanketed the entire room. It took all Ronny had to lift one foot in front of the other, the odor-tational pull of the stench fighting to drag him down and urging him to relent, to release himself to the reek. He pushed onward. He wafted his hands rapidly, a hummingbird's wings clearing a modicum of space in front of his nose before it filled up with funk again.

His eyes watered heavily from the contamination. Through the deluge of tears, he spotted the object of his quest in front of him. The offending Niçoise salad was now floating, gathering power from the blight it had birthed, soon to be an unstoppable force of putrescence.

Ronny staggered for a second, noticing the lifeless bodies of Amahl and Keaton crumpled in the corner, arms outstretched in their fatal attempt at achieving what Nat, and her iron stomach fortified through years of being a gastronomically obsessed foodie, had succeeded in doing.

Not wanting to emulate their fate, sensing the smell in the final throes of devouring his very being, Ronny leapt for the reusable rectangle that housed the nasty Niçoise.

Arms haggard, breath rasping, paddle all but destroyed, Erin didn't have much left. In contrast, the being that used to be Nat was resolute, poisoned miasma coursing through her veins. So it was with an exhausted gasp Erin watched as Nat brought out the final boss: the hard boiled eggs. They swarmed toward Erin, rancid yolks leaking abrasive ooze. Erin summoned every bit of life she had left and managed to volley one last time, masterfully slamming an egg back toward Nat before falling, narrowly rolling out of the way of the barrage of spoiled ova.

The returned egg flew straight and true, right into Nat's open maw, careening down the esophagus into the stomach, where it blended with the entrenched smell, plus a granola bar Nat had eaten that morning, culminating in an explosion that tore Nat apart, leaving her eviscerated on the office floor.

RONNY GRASPED THE NIÇOISE, HOLDING ON FOR DEAR LIFE AS it discharged noxious fumes, the pungency dissolving Ronny's toilet paper dam completely, overrunning his odor receptors, charging steadfast toward his brain. With only nanoseconds before Ronny became the salad's next pawn, he slammed the container down into the sink, pouring the loathsome lunch into the not up to code garburator, and turned on the mechanism. Never has the whirring of a garbage disposal sounded so sweet than as it ravaged the remaining ingredients and sent them, impotent, into the city's sewer system.

Ronny felt the stench leave his body, felt the air around him return to its normal level of staleness... felt like he should probably do the crossword soon.

Erin appeared beside him, tattered and worn from her own battle. Was she happy she'd just murdered someone? No. But was a little part of her pleased she'd never have to fight for her rightful workspace again? Most definitely.

She helped Ronny up and they looked at each other, ragged but satisfied.

"I definitely earned my paycheck today." Ronny quipped. And unlike every single other day he'd worked, on this one, he was right.

ALL WAS QUIET ON THE OFFICE FLOOR. THE GURGLING CHOIR OF congealed former workers had come to a close. Nat, imploded from the return volley of hard-boiled eggs, lay fragmented on the office floor. Everything had returned to pre-Niçoise reckoning. All workers spared by the demonic salad were given the rest of the day off.

The nightmare was over.

Which is just how the thirteen-month-old leftover gumbo, lying in wait behind the array of creamers on the top shelf, wanted it to seem.

Its time would soon arrive.

MONDAYS, AM I RIGHT?
ELIZABETH SUGGS

I scrambled into the office Monday morning—twenty minutes late. I'm always late, but today it was unintentional. It was our new manager's first day, and word around the office was he doesn't tolerate tardiness.

Our last manager, Walter Krogen, while far from perfect considering his habit of diddling the intern, didn't care much about punctuality. I had, unfortunately, gotten used to slow mornings. Now, my heart pounded in my chest, and my face flushed as I rushed to my desk, hoping I wouldn't be noticed.

I dropped my backpack and coat on my chair. I powered on my computer. I was in accounting, and my desk neighbor, Lisa—head of accounting—would usually make some snide comment when I was late, but today she remained silent.

Everyone was silent. Usually, there'd be a few conversations going, but the only sound was my quick, anxious breathing.

I glanced over at Elijah's desk. That debonair tall, dark, and handsome guy I planned to marry one of these days if only he'd ask me out. He worked in sales and was usually quick to flirt, but today he was *actually* working.

"Hey," I said, walking up to his desk. I leaned against him so he'd have the perfect view of what my new pushup bra was capable of, but he didn't even so much as give me a smile.

"Hey, Sally," he said, his eyes never leaving his computer.

"What's going on? Is the new manager that much of a hard-ass?" I whispered.

"Will you two shut up? I don't want him coming over here," snapped Andy from sales, his leg bouncing so hard it hit the bottom of his desk.

I opened my mouth to ask more, but the new manager's office door swung open. A tall man with slicked-back hair and a tight, reptilian smile stepped onto the bullpen floor. His tiny eyes zeroed on me, like those of a viper ready to strike.

"Ah, you must be Sally Mayhew from accounting. You missed introductions. I'm Mr. Mead." His voice had a slippery quality, like an eel squirming through my mind. I resisted the urge to shudder, but the desk still shook. Andy's leg hammered wild beneath the desk.

Mr. Mead's gaze shifted to him, lingering in a way that made my stomach twist. "Mr. Gledhill, why don't you come into my office?"

Andy paled. Nodding stiffly, he followed the manager inside. The door closed with a soft click, and tension eased in the room as a collective sigh escaped.

"What was that about?" I muttered, sliding into Andy's now-empty seat.

Elijah's throat bobbed nervously. He had nicked himself shaving this morning—just under his jaw—and the cut still glistened faintly, as if fresh. "Fiona went in there earlier and hasn't come out. Mr. Mead didn't like her introduction, I guess."

I frowned, but before I could respond, that same slimy voice cut through the air. "Why don't you come into my office, Mr. Shafer?" Mead's smile widened, showing the backs of his teeth.

For a second, I thought Elijah might refuse, but he stood and followed Mead into the office. The door opened outward, so I caught a glimpse of the inside—dimly lit, smoky—but no sign of

Andy or Fiona. The door closed with a soft click, and my stomach flipped.

Everyone else in the office had returned to their work as if nothing had happened.

"Seriously?" I yelled to the room, but my voice fell on deaf ears.

I stood up, moving toward the door. Unlike the other heartless assholes in my office, I wasn't about to stand by as my coworkers vanished.

I walked up to the door, and my heart pounded so loudly I was sure the others could hear it. Still, no one turned to look at me. Raising my fist to knock, I hesitated. Was Elijah right? Was this a trap?

I turned back to the office. Everyone had their heads down, eyes glued to their screens—everyone but Lisa. She watched me with an expression I had never seen on her face before: sympathy.

I dropped my fist, took a breath, and opened the door.

A cloud of thick, smoky fog spilled out. Inside, Mr. Mead sat at his desk, illuminated by a soft, orange light. His eyes were darker now, almost black, as if swallowing his face. That grin was still plastered across his mouth.

"Well, Ms. Mayhew, what brings you here?"

No sign of Elijah, Andy, or Fiona.

I straightened, feeling the weight of the office's eyes on my back. "Where are they?"

He chuckled a low, guttural sound. "Why, they're cooking lunch, as I requested."

"What lunch? It's not even ten in the morning," I snapped, heart racing.

"It's an early lunch. You can find them in the basement if you're curious."

He gestured toward a door beside the bookshelf.

"The basement," I repeated, my voice tight.

"Yes. Go on. You can even smell it."

And I could. A rich, roasted scent filled the air—pork, slow-cooked and sweetened. Wasn't human flesh referred to as "long pig?"

"See for yourself," Mead urged.

Every instinct screamed at me to run, but I couldn't leave Elijah behind. Swallowing hard, I opened the basement door and descended the old, creaky stairs.

The smell grew stronger with each step. At the bottom, I froze. Elijah, Andy, and Fiona were there, wearing aprons, basting slabs of meat and dropping them into a pot of bubbling water.

Mr. Mead was right behind me, his breath hot on my neck.

Elijah looked up at me and smiled—too wide, too calm. He held a ladle of soup, and of Walter's detached head.

I sucked in a breath just as Mr. Mead's voice oozed from the darkness. "Mondays are tough, so I thought we'd do something special in Mr. Krogen's honor."

THE STATEMENT
ANDREW LENOIR

"'Fellow shareholders'... Is that too formal?"

"I'm not sure that matters at a time like this, sir."

"I suppose you're right. Better to get in front of it."

Perry Hargrave, fifty-five, founder and CEO of the world's fastest growing Fortune 500 company, steps to the window of the twelfth-story executive suite. Staring out absently at the gray evening sky over Central Park, the opposing skyscrapers dim black monoliths above quiet city streets, he reaches for a cigar and lights it. Not a single taxicab below.

"Fellow shareholders. I've never apologized for anything in my entire career. It is that attitude and sterling record of success that has helped me build this company from the bottom up."

He gestures to his own reflection in the window at the practiced line, remembering how it had felt the first time he'd delivered it at Davos.

"Sir," says Samantha, thirty-five, his right-hand woman and gal Friday. Sweat builds on her brow. "I'm not sure this is the time—"

"When will there be another time, Sam?"

The question comes out colder than he meant, but he does not amend himself.

A tremor shakes the building as he flicks hot ash into the malachite tray on his mahogany desk. The window glass rattles, and the lights flicker.

"I won't start apologizing now."

"Perry, I don't think—"

"No, take it down exactly as I say it," he says, crumbs of drop ceiling falling around his ears like snow, "while we still have power." He continues, "'I won't start apologizing now.'"

And what did he have to apologize for, really? Making a lot of people a lot of money? He was a modern man running a modern business. A global business. One with its wheels spinning in all directions. That's what they paid him for, really—to walk out on stage once a year in his trademark outfit and tell them all about the exciting new projects and innovations in development, to sell them on the hip, shiny, brand new, branded future of their collective fucking American dream. He'd started off in his parents' garage with some soldering irons and circuit boards, but these days it was his job to sell the vision. The details were another department's concern.

An alarm sounds somewhere beyond the heavy oak office door. At least the security system still works.

"Perry?" Samantha asks, worry shaping her voice and face. "What is that?"

He holds up a hand to silence her, his attention back to the window. A murder of crows takes off from the tree line of the park below, murmurating like a mushroom cloud as the last daylight gives up its ghost. The familiar faces of local landmarks, Bergdorf's and the Plaza, stare back with black sockets. Then, as the unseen sun sets, it takes the city with it. The world disappears in darkness beyond their reflections in the glass.

Outside Hargrave's office, the siren explodes again. Flashing red light flickers from the gap under the door. There is a rustling.

Perry sets down the cigar and reaches for his desk drawer. He continues dictating. "I know not all of you approved of our military research contracts at first. As lucrative as they proved to be, I'm sure one or two of you would like to say 'I told you so.' But in my defense, it appears our efforts were more successful than we could have anticipated."

Sliding the drawer back, Perry pulls his emergency gas mask free and straps it to his face. "Eh, that last bit feels a little wishy-washy," he says, voice muffled. "Maybe cut it."

The knob on the door turns.

The security detail, dressed in black combat gear, bursts into the office. They stare at Hargrave, hermetically sealed masks like black reflective featureless planes, in expectation.

"What the fuck, Perry?" Samantha shouts, rising as the three men enter. She gesticulates uselessly with the laptop.

He ignores her.

"Sir, the perimeter has been compromised," the security leader reports.

Hargrave sighs and snatches the laptop. "Jesus Christ, do I have to do everything myself around here?"

"Perry," Samantha's voice lowers to a private tone. "This isn't funny. Do I need a mask?"

He does not look up from the screen. "You're done having kids, right?"

She moves to slap him and finds herself held back by the security team as their leader speaks again.

"Sir, we have no additional masks, and the helicopter will only fit four."

Perry considers the information as he glances down at the keyboard in disgust. "Can any of you type over 94 words a minute?" The security members turn to each other for a moment and then shake their heads. "Fine." He hands Samantha the computer. "One of you—give her your mask."

The leader turns to the two men who flank Samantha. "Well, you heard him."

"You're kidding," one of them replies.

Their leader raises his rifle. "Don't make me ask twice. You can rock paper scissors for it."

The two men share a stare from behind black masks before they whip out their hands, going through the motions of the childhood game with frenetic energy. One draws rock and the other paper. The group looks at the hands for a moment and to their credit, if either thinks of flinching, they hardly show it.

"I'm sorry," Paper says.

"So am I," says Rock. He removes his mask and passes it to Samantha, with one hand, the other wiping at his dripping, snot streaming nose. His tear-tinged eyes are wide, his breathing shallow.

She grabs the mask from him, not daring to meet his gaze. The two other members of the security team help her put it on, and he watches them adjust the straps for a firm seal against her smaller face.

"We good?" Perry asks.

The security leader nods.

"Well, what are we waiting for?"

The leader turns toward the open door, and one by one the others follow him out.

Finally, Samantha turns to face the unmasked man staring back from the darkness. She clears her throat, looks away, and shuts the door with a gentle click.

Outside Hargrave's office, the floor is empty. A window must be open somewhere, the wastepaper like flaming tumbleweeds in the flickering red light.

"We'll work out the rest of what we want to say on the ride out," he says. "From my compound we should be able to get this to the internet while it's still up. It's important that we make a statement."

Behind them, a gun fires.

"That's all anyone will remember from this thing."

THE DEAD ARE ALWAYS SUCH TROUBLE

RUTH E. WALKER

Frank, it's Peter Wolfe from Retirement Services.

Fine, thanks.

Yeah. She's fine too—look Frank, we've got a problem.

Well, they keep coming in and I don't know what the hell to do with them.

They just show up, Frank. No appointment. No advance call.

I'm trying to tell you. They come in here, asking us to restart their pensions. It's getting on my nerves. I've tried to get the damn wording changed, but nobody listens.

What wording? If you'd only read my emails, Frank, you'd know—

Okay. Okay. Form A three-three-seven dash nine. Last page. Second paragraph, halfway down. Yeah. Uh-huh. That's the one. This problem with the form—

You don't see a problem?

Okay. Look. Yesterday, I had this disgusting old man in here—

No, nothing like that—it was his skin. The stink. Gross. He tried to cover it up with aftershave, but it was still there, you know? And the windows don't open in this building, Frank. I've gone to Maintenance—

Right. Okay. The form.

Frank, now hold on and listen. Corporate has got to change that wording. They've got to.

What do I mean? Look at it for Christ's sake: "Your pension will cease effective X-date because we received notice that you passed away. You may reapply if there is a change in your circumstances." Just look at that. "You may reapply if there is a change"—it's a fucking open door. And trust me, they're coming through. It's only Wednesday, and I just lost my third receptionist this week.

I should what? Just "deal with it"? What do you mean, I should just—Okay Frank, you win.

I'm sending up Mrs. Bobechko.

Yes, Frank. Mrs. Bobechko. She's sitting outside my office right now. You'll like her. Even if she's a bit, I don't know, insistent. For an old girl, she's got lots of spirit. Took up bungie jumping a month ago. Then the cord broke over the East Gorge.

Yeah. That East Gorge.

Just keep your office door open. She's a bit ripe and—

Frank—You still there?

Frank?

WORKFORCE
JORDAN KING-LACROIX

I woke up at my desk. Bleary-eyed, mouth tasting of stale saliva, I brushed some loose staples off of my cheek. Above my desk, the clock showed it was almost quitting time. How long had I been asleep?

Around me were the ambient sounds of my open-plan office: murmured voices on phones, clacking on keyboards, aggressive sniffling. My desk faced a wall, my back to the rest of the office. Though we hot-desked around here, I always managed to grab this spot. Nobody else wanted the desk closest to the bathrooms, but I'd lost my sense of smell since catching COVID in the first wave, so I wasn't bothered. Facing the wall gave me a small sense of privacy, though it meant my screen faced the outside world. Not that it mattered. Anything not work-related I did, I did on my phone, not on the work computer. Facing this wall let me feel pleasantly isolated in an office plan designed to avoid that kind of isolation. I'd gotten to know every chip in the paint on this wall.

Through the thin Gyprock wall beside me, somebody snorted and grunted in the men's room. Probably Alan. He tended to hit the head at the end of the day so he could ride out the last half hour on the porcelain throne. It was clever.

"Always shit on company time," he said. "Shit, cry, whatever. Boss makes a dollar, you make a dime."

I smiled and leaned back in my chair. It creaked and juddered, launching me back a little. The mechanism that kept the seat from swaying was broken, and a new chair order hadn't been approved yet.

I glanced up. The hands of the clock hadn't moved. The second hand was frozen in place. Ticking still sounding out. Like everything in this office, it, too, had a broken piece.

Footsteps from behind me. High heels on carpet. Probably Allison. Our District Manager had a deliberate stride few others managed.

"Does it smell like roses in here to you today?" Allison said, her voice reaching me before she entered my line of sight. She leaned against my desk.

I just tapped my nose. "Nothing smells like anything to me anymore."

"Oh, gosh," she said, holding her hand up to her mouth. "I'm so sorry."

"No need," I said.

She sniffed. "Well, it doesn't smell like roses over here, I guess. Lucky you can't smell anything because, boy, none of us could stand being at this desk."

A laugh bubbled up and escaped her.

"Maybe there's a new air freshener," I suggested. "The janitor came by and replaced all the canisters in the dispensers today."

I gestured at the plastic cases hung discreetly about the office walls, just above eyeline. One of the nearby ones clicked and issued a spray.

Allison sniffed and then nodded. "Of course," she said. "Right. Everything going okay on your end?"

"No issues here," I said.

"Good," she said, nodding.

She nodded, standing there for a bit too long, and then walked off. Her slower gait told me she was mulling something over. She became a silhouette behind her office's frosted glass.

The outward-facing windows in her space and the CEO's office were the only ones on our floor. Late afternoon sun shone in, bright and golden.

I envied those windows. It didn't matter that the view was only onto the rooftops of shorter buildings and the messy alleyway that ran alongside our building. At least they could look at a slice of the sky if they wanted to. Not that our CEO, Rich McCabe—or Allison for that matter—were the types to take time to idly ponder the sky. Not when there was work to be done.

I looked down at my phone—

I woke up at my desk. My head was groggy. A strange, metallic taste had invaded my mouth. Like when you've recently had blood on your tongue. The clock said it was almost quitting time. I could hear the ticking, but the second hand wasn't moving. Trust this place to have a broken clock.

I eyed the room. Monica and Greg were both talking on the phone in that whispered tone that you only learn from an open plan office. You don't want to be the source of bother, of consternation, of office gossip. Paul learned the hard way that loud talkers faced consequences. Sometimes, Paul hot-desked next to me, but he couldn't take the toilet smell. Eventually, he quit. No one really noticed.

My computer issued the annoying ping telling me I had something new in my inbox. Company policy dictated we weren't allowed to switch it off, as that might lead to unanswered emails. I turned back to my machine and clicked open the message.

"My dear employees," it opened. Our CEO, Rich McCabe, loved to write weekly missives. He wrote that doing so made him feel more connected to us. Most of us didn't feel the same.

I'm writing to you not with the news you want, but with the news the company needs. We've been working hard this year

—over a quarter billion more in profit than last year!—but we still have a lot of work to do.

As you know, I think of this company like a family. I hope you do, too. And sometimes, families must make sacrifices for each other. Unfortunately, I am coming to you now to ask for a sacrifice.

Working hours must be extended by two additional hours. This is due to the business we conduct with overseas firms. We have had too many availability concerns because meetings are occurring in their 'off time' and they have plans. As CEO of this company, there is no such thing as 'off time' for me. I work day in, day out, ensuring this firm leads the charge in our sector. I do this to protect your jobs and help support your families.

While I appreciate the idea of a work-life balance, you must understand that if the company failed tomorrow, that concern would be moot. These two extra hours—bringing our totals to twelve per day, sixty-hours per week—will ensure we are always on the ball. This change takes effect immediately.

If anyone would like to discuss this important decision, you know my door is always open. However, I am currently on the company jet heading to the Philippines for some much-needed rest and relaxation with my family. To the victor go the spoils, and all that. And I need to be ready to lead this team, of course. I'll see you all in six weeks!

Unreal. I read over the email again to ensure I'd read it correctly. Two more hours. Ten more every week. Behind me, I heard a smattering of increasingly frustrated murmurs.

I looked down at my phone—

I woke up at my desk. My vision was swimming. An ache in my temples stabbing my skull like sharp rods. I opened my desk drawer and pulled out some pills, swallowing them with a gulp from my water bottle. Almost empty.

Footsteps behind me. Strong, but unstable. Someone with a limp? Allison almost collapsed onto my desk, leaning on it like she needed it to stay upright.

"Do you smell roses?" she said, her speech slurred.

"Can't smell," I said, tapping my nose.

"Right, right," she said, shaking her head. "Yeah."

She paused, then said, "Did we have this conversation already?"

"Haven't been able to smell since COVID," I said. My speech was a little sluggish, too. "So, probably."

"Sure, sure," she said. "Okay. Maybe I'm just having an afternoon crash."

I watched as she pushed herself up and toddled, occasionally tipping to one side, back to her office. As her door closed, I watched as she collapsed on the beige corduroy couch beside her desk.

Beside me, in the men's room, Alan grunted and snorted.

"You okay in there?" I said, knocking on the wall.

"Yeah," he said. "Yeah. I think I just fell asleep."

"That makes two of us," I said and laughed.

I stood and went to the kitchenette to refill my water bottle. Since the new extended day policy, I'd been drinking more water. Something about those extra hours was really dehydrating. Maybe it was being stuck in the air-conditioned office for longer. I rarely used aircon at home. My eyes and nostrils dried out too much.

Lana was in the kitchenette making a cup of tea.

"Hey," I said. My mouth felt almost glued together, as if I'd been asleep.

Lana made a grunt of acknowledgement.

"All good?" I said, depressing the switch, water gushing into the water bottle.

"Mhm," she said. "Just have a killer headache.'

"Same," I said.

"Must be something in the water," she said, and made a half-hearted attempt to laugh.

We made eye contact, standing awkwardly for a moment, before she headed off to her desk. She all but fell into her chair. I leaned against the counter and looked at the office. Everyone looked tired today. I took a swig of water and it felt incredible. Nothing like a cold sip of water when your mouth is dry.

I looked down at my phone—

I woke up on the kitchenette floor. A shadow over me.

I looked at the phone in my hand—

I woke up at my desk. My stomach turned. Something was wrong. I reached for my phone—

I woke up at my desk. I lifted my head off of my desktop and lost my balance. My chair tipped to the floor with me sprawling underneath it. From my vantage point, I could see Monica and Greg both face down, asleep at their desks. Behind them, golden afternoon light poured in from Allison's office windows.

Phones rang, but I couldn't hear anyone speaking. The clacking of keyboards had stopped.

"Hmluh," I said. My mouth refused to open all the way. I tried to stand, to pull myself up, but it felt almost impossible. A wretched weakness had overcome me. Crawling, though, was all I could manage.

I dragged myself along the carpet toward Allison's office. She'd know what to do. Long-stale cupcake crumbs, lost staples, dirt from people's shoes—all of it stuck to my cheek as I inched forward. A pounding of footsteps echoed from the stairwell.

As I passed her desk, I could see Lana collapsed atop it, her eyes wide open. A red line of blood spilled down her cheek from her ear. The tea she'd been drinking had spilled, the handle snapped off the mug.

Allison's door was partly open. I pushed in and saw Allison, collapsed in a heap on her couch.

"Mmphn," I said.

I dragged myself the last little bit to her. The footsteps echoing in the stairwell were getting louder. Pulling myself up, I leaned against the couch and grabbed ahold of Allison's collar. I shook her. She was limp like a rag doll. I shook her again. She seemed to rouse, and her bleary eyes met mine.

"What's happening?" I said. Behind her, golden light flowed in from her windows. But something looked off with it. The sky looked too grey. The light source seemed too contrived.

"Work," Allison said. "At work."

Neither of us had anything else to say.

The footsteps reached me. I didn't have the strength to turn and face whoever it was. They dragged me out of my District Manager's office. Allison's unfocused eyes widened as she watched until her office door was pushed closed.

Under a nearby desk, I saw a small canister, like those in the hanging air fresheners. I didn't recognize it. WRKFRCE, it read. A slogan underneath: "Force them to work, with a soft hand. NOW IN ROSE SCENT!"

They sat me in my chair, grabbed my face and forced me to look at my phone's screen—

I woke up at my desk.

SUCH A CATCH
RICHARD SHIFMAN

No sooner had Doug said, 'do,' than a squiggly line whirred from the monitor screen and stung the midline cleft below Rom's bottom lip. A pinch, and the line tightened, tugging Rom's face forward.

The pain, Rom thought, was about the same as extracting a splinter. He could almost smell the astringent rubbing alcohol and acrid smoke of a spent match as the sterilized needle poked beneath a couple of layers of skin. Uncomfortable, but too shallow to draw blood.

Yes, the hook lodged beneath Rom's lip—his instincts told him it was a fishing hook—was a needle digging out a splinter. It was a nuisance. No big deal. It stung in one place, so he figured it was only a one-pronged hook. Only.

"Ah, you're all hooked up. Good man," Doug proclaimed, tapping the door frame to Rom's office. "Rom, do." The scarecrow of a manager, all gangly knees and rounded shoulders, pointed finger guns at Rom. "Okay, now. Doug's so done." Doug always trilled the catchphrase, 'Doug's so done,' before exiting a room. Rom's boss tapped the door again, stepped outside Rom's office, and jackaloped out of sight.

The skin beneath Rom's lower lip began to throb. He blinked, eyes burning, and tucked his chin to inspect the damage. Had the hook wormed its way deeper? A thin, dark green fishing line (about a four-pound test, good for snagging, say, freshwater trout) extended tautly from the center of the computer monitor screen to his upper chin. He danced his fingers an inch from the spot, too nervous to touch the hook.

The monitor, which had grown dark, lit up. An email from Felicia Destiny, Director of Delicious Dabbers Marketing, appeared as she typed:

I know you're busy Rom, so I appreciate your taking on my request. Doug said you were a can-do guy, and he was right. Thank you for agreeing to do. I'll send the file right over. There are 6,644 entries. Please go through each line, find the misspelled first names, flag them, and send me back the flagged file by this coming Monday. In case a name might be spelled different ways, please use *Dave's Compendium of Most Common Names*. That book can be found in the company's reference library in the basement beside the staff cafeteria. The library won't let you check out the book, so you'll need to take a few trips downstairs. Maybe save up your questionable names every thousand entries to minimize your trips. Anyway, thank you, Rom! You're a lifesaver. Such a catch. You do!

    Fakin' it 'til I'm takin' it,
    Felicia Destiny

    Executive Director, Delicious Dabbers
    "Ask not what your company can do for
    you. Just do." Dave

Rom read the email and the company's obligatory inspirational sign-off while doing his best to ignore the pulsing ache in his upper chin. He did the math. At ten seconds per entry, the task amounted to about eighteen work hours, not counting library trips, which he figured he could do at lunch. Felicia had given him four days plus the weekend to finish the task. If he allocated two hours and thirty minutes to it in the morning and two hours and thirty minutes in the evening, working from six-thirty to nine in the morning and six-thirty to nine at night, he could finish the task and do his usual work. No problem.

He texted his fiancée.

I'll be late getting home tonight. Extra thing.

Three dots rolled across his phone screen. Then... nothing.

"Hey. Rom, do?" It was Doug, again, leaning against the door frame like a 1950's hooligan about to smoke up.

"Yep," Rom said curtly. A sense of urgency pressed on the back of his mind. He needed to get to work to give him time later to fulfill Felicia's request. "What's up, boss?" As he answered Doug, the fishing line jerked, the monitor screen brightened once more, and Felicia's spreadsheet opened. "My work's calling me."

"Good man. So, Frank Angle, Executive Director, is planning to call you. He's got a need. When he reaches out, remember: We do. Rom, do. Do."

A Doug slogan: 'We do. Rom, do. Do.'

The landline phone on the desk rang, and Rom's shoulders jerked, making Doug chuckle. "Caught you napping. That must be Frank. Well? Are you going to pick it up?" Doug wagged his head, mouth agape, looking exasperated.

Rom picked up the phone, passing the receiver under the fishing line strung from his computer screen to his lip. "Hello, this is Rom River, how may I do?"

"Rom River! Doug's new guy!" The man on the phone sounded thrilled to meet him. "This is Frank Angle in Bitter Roots Nonpersonal Promotion Across the Ocean. I hope this phone call finds you well?"

It was a question. "Uh, yes, good. How are you, Frank?"

"You've been with the company a week, fresh off your internship, but we've already heard about you, Rom. You do. Anyway, I need you to..." Frank's voice lowered to a thin whisper.

"What?"

"Excellent! You'll do, then?"

Doug's eyes gleamed at Rom, who blinked. "Uh, yes. We do. Rom, do. Do."

Doug nodded.

"Excellent. Hold up," Frank said. A whizzing noise hummed through the phone line, like a reel being wound. Rom held the phone receiver away from his face, staring at it as it buzzed. A whir, and a fishing line, bright yellow, maybe six-pound test (still good for freshwater angling) whipped out of the receiver. Something metallic glinted beneath the fluorescent office lights at the end of the airborne line. Rom spied two metal prongs of the double hook before its tiny claws snagged the corner of his mouth. The hook jerked his face toward the phone receiver, which he dropped with a clatter on his desk. The hooks' nasty bite brought fresh tears to Rom's eyes.

"Gotcha," Frank's voice rang from the receiver on the desk. "Come by my office in an hour, and I'll give you the forty-four files." The fishing line, stretched tightly from the phone receiver to Rom's mouth, vibrated with each of Frank's words. "My new office is downtown, Quebec City. From the home office in Rochester, you'll need to head up 104 around the lake, then up 11, et cetera, et cetera. We'll need the candidates in these files vetted by next Tuesday. This is so excellent. Thank you, Rom. I heard that you do. You're such a catch. See you soon." A soft click.

Rom wiped his eyes, resisting the urge to finger the double hook poking two burning holes in the side of his mouth. Afraid to graze the single hook stinging the cleft beneath his lip. "I really…"

"Rah-ahm." Doug crooned his subordinate's name, a sing-song warning.

"I'll do."

"Right. Doug's so done," Doug mumbled, rotating his body out the door and chupacabracadabaring out of sight. Doug was gone for but a moment when he reappeared with a soft, short woman. The woman grinned, and the broad smile on her round face broke apart, replicating like mitochondrial larvae wiggling across her cheeks and chin. Two thin lips became four, then eight, and finally sixteen. Eight smiley smiles. She gave Rom a nod as Doug spoke. "Look who I found, Rom. Can you believe? This is Linda Lesser from our New Jersey Office #9. She's Senior Director of Growth Something. I dunno."

"Uh, hello, Linda. I'm Rom River." Rom knew it was rude not to stand, but the fishing lines and hooks had him pinned to his desk.

Linda smiled. A bunch. So many smiles. "No, don't get up. How are ya', Rom? I hear you do."

He nodded, the throbbing ache of the two hooks in his face almost unbearable. "Yes. We do. Rom, do. Do."

"Mmm, hmm. Super. So, I had a market research employee in my office—you do market research, right, Rom?"

"Well, uh, not real—"

"Anyhoo, this poor man who worked on my team a couple of years back was about to leave the company. Can you imagine? He had some health issues. So, we never found anybody to cover for him. His work from two years ago and beyond has piled up and still needs doing. Can you imagine? So, I need you to take on his workload right away. You do, right?" She patted a laptop computer on a rolling cart, which Rom had not noticed at her side.

Rom gazed at her, the pain in his face spreading across his flushed cheeks and over his eyes like a lava flow. He did not have any more time to take on another person's full workload. Doug stood behind Linda, shaking his head warily as the woman wheeled the cart and laptop into his office. 'Rom, do,' Doug mouthed.

"Uhhh."

She patted the laptop again. "I'll need all his projects finished by next Wednesday. Her many smiles shifted and danced on her face beneath her puffy cheeks. "This is important because I'm in a tournament later, Rom. There's a Vice President, Avery Milktoast—head of the Nothingburger Product line here in Rochester—and he's leaving the company. He wasn't up to the nothingness of Nothingburger. His VP spot is open. Do you know what that means?"

"No."

"You need to do. So that I, not some other executive, can win the tournament." She smiled again and again and again and again and again and again and again and again. "Anyway, thank you." Linda Lesser whipped out a compact fishing rod, her hand furiously reeling up a white fishing line (sturdier, maybe eight-pound test) with a three-pronged Treble hook flashing on the end. "This is still good for freshwater," she said as if reading Rom's mind. She cast back her arm, the Treble hook prongs nearly snagging Doug's face, making him lurch back. Her arm whipped forward, the line spinning through the air, all the hook's prongs catching the soft inside of Rom's top lip in a flash of white-hot pain. He let out an involuntary, "uauah!" as blood filled his mouth.

"Gotcha," Linda breathed.

"Tournament's now!" somebody shouted from the other side of the office, a proclamation followed by running feet. A host of workers, a thundering herd of catoblepae, rumbled by the office, muttering, "Tournament's now, tournament's now, tournament's now."

Linda's smiles beamed. "Oh my goodness. It's all happening several days early. It's such good luck for you, Rom. The tournament is starting now, so there's one more thing for you to do. Linda cranked her reel, pulling in her fishing line. The Treble hook yanked on Rom's upper lip, dragging him from his chair. He staggered across his office, the retracting line winding him toward the executive and her rod. As he stumbled forward, the two lines that stretched from his phone and computer monitor spun out with a buzz, allowing him slack to move.

Linda abruptly stopped reeling, leaving Rom poised halfway between the doorway and her.

"Doug's so done," Doug muttered, wendigoing out of the office as two more people—a man and a woman—appeared alongside Linda as though to bracket her. Each gripped a long fishing rod. The man wore a rumpled, dark gray suit, the jacket open to reveal a barrel chest and paunch. "I'm Frank Angle. I flew down from Quebec with the forty-four files," he said. "But now that the tournament's on, you've got more important things to do."

"And I'm Felicia Destiny." The woman, tall and pointy in a crisp black suit, cocked her head. "Here, let's cut your lines, so you're free of that pesky phone and monitor." From nowhere, a pair of wire cutters with red grips appeared in her hand, but she made no move to cut Rom loose.

Rom eyed the wire cutters, his lower lip trembling. "Am I free? Can I go home?" he whimpered through the blood in his mouth, suddenly not caring if he lost his job and ended up homeless. His father's words that past Christmas rang in his ears: *Don't come to me for money, Rom. You're out of college four years now, so you're on your own. Just do.*

"We're all in the tournament," Frank claimed, fiddling with the hook on his rod. A Treble hook. Three shiny points. "It's a contest to take Milktoast's place. Now, come on over here and let Felicia cut you free. Then we'll give you some reel hooks. Get it? Reel hooks?" The man belly laughed, hands on his gut. "I kill myself. Come on now, Linda. Reel him in. Let's do."

Linda spun her reel again, drawing Rom toward the three executives. Rom, beckoned by Linda's spinning reel, floated toward them. They clustered around him.

THERE WAS NOTHING BUT BEAUTIFUL, BRILLIANT PAIN. IT WAS beautiful because Felicia and Frank and Linda told him it was beautiful as they dragged him out of the building. The three Treble hooks buried in his cheeks tugged him along. A warm wetness filled his shoes, which squished. He'd released his bladder. The executives, jerking him this way and that with their fishing lines, seemed not to notice or care, murmuring, "Do. Do. Do." They hurried him down the carpeted hallways, out the front doors.

They stopped on the broad sidewalk by the edge of the parking lot.

Tears streamed from Rom's eyes, and he lifted his hands to wipe them away.

But he couldn't wipe his tears because he had no hands. No arms. He only had nubs, protruding from his slick, bare shoulders—or what passed as shoulders. When did he lose his shirt? As he wondered this, a dark veil floated down over his eyes, the bright blue sky turning blurry and gray. He sensed his shoes and pants and underclothes dissolving. He fell, writhing on the sidewalk beside the parking lot.

"Bait!" Felicia cried. "He's bait!"

"Bait!" Frank and Linda cried as Rom squiggled and flopped on the concrete.

The trio of Treble hooks no longer burned his face. Frank leaned down and poked Rom's side, his hand squishing into rubbery, slippery flesh. "How's it going, Worm?"

Worm. His name was Worm. Yes.

We do. Worm, do. Do.

"There's Milktoast, now." Felicia pointed across the near-empty parking lot. "He's taking out his belongings. Ooh, it's about to begin. Exciting."

Through the shadowy veil draped over his eyes, Worm spied a short man in a tweed jacket carrying a legal box and trudging toward a two-door sports car alone in the middle of the lot. Milktoast swung open the driver-side door and tossed the box into the backseat. As the man climbed into the automobile, a series of giant, triangular teeth shot out from the car's door frame, from inside its door. The door swung shut, clamping down on his torso. Milktoast screamed. The door opened and slammed shut again. And again. As if chewing him. Dark blood sprayed across the lot as Milktoast's torso was sawed in half at the waist by the car's choppers. Finally, his lower body plunked to the asphalt, followed by his upper body.

"Time to take the car!" Felicia shouted.

"No, you don't," snapped Linda.

There was a tussle above Worm that included grunts and thuds. Suddenly appearing before Worm's shaded eyes was Linda Lesser's face, her lifeless eyes wide and her smiley smiles frozen. There was another thud and a groan, and Frank's face clunked into the back of Linda's head, his body slamming into the sidewalk. "Ha, ha!" screamed Felicia. "I do! I do! I do! Now, I'm going to catch that shark-car."

There was a whizzing noise, and Worm felt himself lifted off the sidewalk and swung over the edge of the lot. Sailing into the air. Slapping the asphalt. He was smaller now, he knew, and soft and squishy.

Bait. I'm bait. I do.

It started raining a gentle mist. Worm rose into the air again, summoned backward by Felicia's humming fishing line.

Below him, thousands of squiggly shapes wiggled across the parking lot beneath the soft rain.

More worms, Worm thought. *They need others to do.*

"Here, fishy, fishy," Felicia sang in a whisper. She reeled in Worm and cast him back out. He was flying, flying toward the fuzzy shape that was Milktoast's horrible shark-car, racing forward. The grill of the car had transformed into a great white shark's gaping maw, with three rows of razor teeth inside. As Worm slapped the pavement, the car roared forward, its grill coming down over Worm. Engulfing Worm. The grill's teeth bit into him repeatedly, but he barely felt it.

Through the veil over his eyes and the chomping car grill, he spied Felicia. She had dropped her rod and was rushing toward the car. "Gotcha!" she cried. "Sporty car for the new VP. I'm coming, baby!"

What does she mean by that? Worm wondered as the car turned him to mush. It felt oddly good. *Like digging out a splinter,* he thought. *Something that needs doing.*

The car door banged shut, and the vehicle lurched forward as if somebody had slammed on the gas. Something kicked Worm's head, a squelching bump. The heel of one of Felicia's Louboutins had kicked through the floorboard.

"I win! Felicia shouted above Worm as the shark-car vroomed in circles around the lot. Victory laps. "Thank you, Worm. Thank you for helping me replace Milktoast as VP. Thank you for your do, do, do. You're such a catch!"

The grill continued chewing. Loud chomping, slurping sounds. The light faded in Worm's eyes. Eyes? He had no eyes. He realized he was about to die. But it was okay because he had done: *We do. Worm, do. Do. Whose voice is that out there? Is that Doug?*

Somewhere, on the edge of the lot, Doug was whooping and shouting as the acid from the car-shark's engine-stomach dissolved what remained of Worm's ear canals and the world turned inky black. "Way to do, Worm! We do! Worm, do! Do..."

PART TWO

MEET WORK IN THE FUTURE

You know the line about the new boss?
Work is the same way.

SECOND AMENDMENT
ROBERT BAGNALL

Bottom line.

That's what it's all about. For both Razr/Blayd and YMP Retail, a subsidiary of a holding company majority owned by a Canadian pension fund. I work for Razr/Blayd, a software developer which describes itself as 'boutique' because 'small and failing' won't reverse its fortunes. YMP owns the Franklin Town Mall, which is bleeding money like it's just had its jugular razr/blayded. Hence YMP argued for relaxed zoning restrictions and are now letting shop space to small businesses like ours. Which is why we now work just off the interstate behind floor-to-ceiling frosted glass with easy parking and an array of junk food options available all day. And if we ever want new sneakers, we're next door to Foot Locker.

We're three months into a six-month lease. The jungle drums say we must produce something to persuade our backers we aren't just sunk funds. Last-chance saloon. Even though they'd need three coders, each at double my pay, to come close to what I can do, the jungle drums also say I'm one of the first under the bus unless I justify my salary. Not circumstances under which creativity thrives.

On the upside, I'm getting to be an excellent shot throwing paper balls into the wastebasket.

"Janine?"

Janine works in the cubicle opposite mine. Our cubicles are, apparently, of the 'contemporary low wall' variety—suggesting escape, but with nowhere to run. They have *peninsular tops* to promote *impromptu meetings and interactions.* Hence, I can see her, and she can see me. She has a face that never gives away whether she's working or pretending to work. I'd describe mine as far more honest.

"Hmm?"

"How would you describe me?"

"An asshole," she says flatly, not taking her eyes from her screen.

"I was looking for more nuance."

Exasperated, she looks up. "You had to ask your wife to remind you whether your daughter was called Caitlin, Caitrin, or Catrin."

"Ex-wife. We separated before the birth. She has custody. I barely see either of them." I'd explained it before.

"And I'm spelling all of them with either a 'C' or a 'K'. That makes six options. Six, Paul. Six."

"I like to think you have a more rounded picture of me just by being my co-worker."

I RATTLE A PAPER BALL OFF THE EDGE OF THE WASTE BASKET. Janine raises a quizzical eyebrow and returns to her screen.

It's barely half-past ten, but I go for coffee. If Donny were in his fish-tank office at the back, I'd be considerably more fingers-to-keyboard. Donny's the head honcho, the big cheese, the main man. Donny put the '/' in Razr/Blayd. Donny's a dick. A douchebag.

I get my usual paper bucket of coffee and sit at a table at the edge of the inside/outside, mock-garden 'Grazing Zone', a large horseshoe of pretend-street vendor outlets facing a shared seating area. A few other tables are taken in the sea of plasticated wicker furniture, like the wash-up after a cruise ship sinking. We're forced to put up with the constant gurgle of a water feature, an Italianate amphora carrier rendered in stone-colored resin, dispensing his load forever, his Sisyphean task rendered no easier by having to endure a soundtrack of ambient wind chimes.

A uniformed teenager stands listlessly at the counter of one of the high-fructose corn syrup purveyors picking at her pimples, no doubt wondering where her life went terminally wrong. She's new, her thousand-yard-stare suggesting the full magnitude of this career misstep is sinking in. Would it help if I went and pointed out the earning potential of a career in digital? Given how she struggled to count out my change, probably not.

I pick at the foil lids of miniature milk tubs, follow up with paper sachets of sugar. Stir it all together with a long thin stick, which I habitually lick clean, every time regretting the taste of wood. I watch people go mindlessly by, wondering how evolution got us to this point. Old couples. A befuddled middle-aged man, clearly dispatched to shop under duress, getting angrier by the second. Denimed teenagers who should be in school—or is it summer break already?—drifting in same-sex knots and packs, chatty girls all loose hair and hotpants, silent boys hiding behind fringes. A drug-eyed mother pushes a buggy, her screaming escapologist toddler frantic at his buckles. I debate whether setting the kid alight would be enough to attract her attention.

A tomahawk steak of a hand slaps me on the shoulder from behind as a grizzled voice calls my name. Clarence and I do a complex fist bump dance, earned from South Central gangbangers when he was in uniform bringing community policing peace, love and understanding to West Athens in those rare gaps between episodes of law enforcement brutality. Clarence is still in uniform, but now it's brown and announces *Mall Security* on the epaulets.

"Keeping us safe, Clarence?"

"Same ol', same ol'," Clarence replies, his boilerplate phrase for almost any situation. Underneath his ash-white buzz cut, his whole head seems to crease into a smile.

"You bustin' those punks boostin' Calvin Kleins from TJ Maxx? You givin' 'em the full Clarence?"

"Same ol', same ol'."

Clarence departs at a slow waddle, all he can manage, his fingers dancing over his sidearm. I shake my head sadly at the state of the world: since when did we need armed guards in a mall? Since small, failing software developers started occupying the units of small, failed retailers, I guess. He trundles off like an overladen tugboat. I imagine in the beginning—a young beat cop, forty years and eighty pounds ago—his fingers were genuinely ready. But now, it's more of a nervous tic. Lacking a thumb break on his holster, I suspect he's making sure his piece remains on his belt.

I aim finger guns at him and pretend to fire. I imagine his fuzzball head exploding like a sped-up film of a flower opening. It's beautiful. The bloom expands, blood red, deep black shadows. At the petals' edge, a scarlet spray throws itself as far and fast as it can. In the center, tenderized brain, amorphous and jelly-like. In my mind Clarence takes one more step like he doesn't know what's happened, then scissors onto his knees, and faceplants on the polished concrete floor. Children drinking their first milkshakes of the day are spattered with Clarence's blood before they have time to open their mouths to scream.

I drop my fingers and watch the very-much-alive Clarence amble away, exchanging *have-a-nice-days* with those children who have nothing worse than chocolate on their faces.

I HAVE AN OVERWHELMING SENSE OF CLARITY.

When I return, Donny is in his fish tank office at the back, all shirtsleeves and straight back like his mama taught him. This whole unit used to be a greeting card shop with balloons and party shit. The rear corner was for the stuff you didn't want your maiden aunt seeing. Before being stripped out and turned into an office unit, a stand of reduced-price inflatable dueling dicks stood where Donny now rules. These were large, bright pink balloons in thick latex expanded in the shape of erect cocks—you'd strap them to your nethers and use them like kindergarten play swords. I can't help picturing that every time I'm called in here to get chewed out.

I stride past Janine and Madison and Emrice and the rest of them and walk straight in. Donny plays squash first thing each morning. The room smells of body spray. I look him in the eye and spill it as my ass hits the seat: "mobile first-person shooter."

"Paul. Good to see you. Thought you hadn't made it in today, but then again, you leave a trail behind you, like a forest animal's spoor."

"Started early, went for coffee. Smartphone FPS. Whadyathink?"

Donny blinks. His face hardens. "We developed one, if you remember. That's why we're now working out of a shopping mall."

"This one's different."

"Market's full of different. *Shadowgun Legends. Combat Master. Dead Trigger...*"

I hold up a hand to stop him downloading. "This is different *because this one's AR.* You're not in some constructed world shooting zombies or aliens. You use your camera. You shoot what you actually see. Real people. We lay software over the top and BOOM! Driver on the bus—head explodes. Guy across the coffee shop—staggers backwards, blood everywhere."

Donny freezes, like he's buffering. This is a good sign. The mash-up of augmented reality and first-person shooter has grabbed him. I'm reminded: Next to the dueling johnsons, you could once have picked up a "Play Wiv Me Cum Face" game for under $30. I don't have the time to explain. Google it.

"AR's typically laid over the top, a secondary element, but would this be more like digital rotoscoping in real-time?"

"Right."

He shakes his head, the light fading from his eyes. "It's got potential, but, for us, with a team of twelve, it's a moonshot..."

"We've already done the heavy lifting with *Ghostload*. We've coded bodies falling and heads exploding for Android and iPhone. We use the recognition software already on everybody's device to apply body shapes from *Ghostload*, merge images, overlay animation. This way, what's animated is what you really see. Aim, fire, and with one click, that's your school teacher laid out, your Sunday preacher wasted."

"Tasteless, Paul. Tasteless."

"Okay. They see complete strangers in the park wasted instead. Why is that any better?"

His eyes narrow. "You have a name?"

"*Mall Shooter.*"

"Tasteless."

"And restrictive," I add cheerfully. "We want people using this anywhere, not just out shopping." I think quickly. "How about *Second Amendment*. Tagline: 'My right to shoot anyone I want anywhere I want.'"

DONNY CALLED ME A SICK PUPPY BUT STILL GREEN LIT MY FIRST pass at getting our lame first-person shooter, *Ghostload*, to talk to generic phone camera software. We both knew it was as much about keeping toddler-me and my ADHD mind occupied. We also both knew I'm the only one in the company—hell, the county—with the coding skills to make this work in the time we've got. Ten minutes later, waterfalls of code light up my three screens. I slip on headphones and immerse myself in a world of DAF, Front 242, KMFDM, Nitzer Ebb, Einstürzende Neubauten, and early Nine Inch Nails.

Spotify launched in 2011. Before that you had to change discs, turn the tape over. Now...

"You been here all night?"

Janine is staring at me over the peninsular top between our cubicles. She's slipping off her leather jacket, hanging it over the back of her chair. I dimly register she's wearing a different top and carrying take-out coffee. Her hair's up.

"I do my thirty-six hours a week. If you average it out."

It was meant to come out as light-hearted, but I'm aware of an unintended undercurrent hinting at a deranged cackle. Janine sits slowly, not lifting her gaze. My eyes feel hot, like I've been crying, though I know I haven't. I can smell myself, a stale, musky background note. Things are buzzy, fuzzy. Light hurts. I can't remember taking a piss. I must have done. But when?

"You were in the zone yesterday. Didn't want to disturb when I left... Tell me you've been home?" I can tell from her worried tone she knows the answer already.

"I'm working on something. Donny's given me enough rope to hang myself, but I'm intending to produce... a hammock... or a bridge, or something. I hoped a better metaphor would jump into my head."

I rub exhaustion from my temples with both palms. Everything feels heavy, like gravity's been turned up and nobody's told me and it's humming uncontrollably...

"Paul, we're normally all so relieved when you go for coffee. In that sense, today's no different. I'm begging you. Please go for coffee."

I look at the clock. Twenty-two hours since I pitched *Second Amendment* to Donny.

"Maybe you're right."

Breathing tasteless air-conditioned air, my feet beating a slow tattoo against the over-polished subtly-patterned marble flooring, I pass over-lit glass-fronted emporia fitted out with touches of mahogany and brass as if commenting on the quality of their rails of sweatshop couture, pop-up shysters flogging ersatz costume jewelry and cellphones and timeshares, slabs of primary color signage in flowing shapes, fake palm trees with fairy lights spiraled around their fake hairy trunks. Clarence ambles towards me.

"Paul!"

He lifts his hand from its default position hovering over his gun, extends a fist, and we do the finger dance.

"Need coffee, Clarence. Maybe more than coffee."

Clarence slaps his not inconsiderable belly and laughs. "Dunkin' Donuts my undoing."

I hit the Grazing Zone, look over the half-circle of counters, each with punning titles and shouty look-at-me plastic logos. It's early, so only the ones selling coffee and variations on baked goods are open. For tacos, burgers, and anything requiring at least plastic cutlery, you need to wait until eleven. As I approach, I see the new girl has come back for a second day in paradise.

I raise my phone, place her plumb in the crosshairs.

She pales. Sags against the counter. Her jaw drops. She's mouthing *No*.

Yeah, I see the problem. It's a bit creepy, pointing a phone at a total stranger. Maybe we should market it as something you play en masse, with your classmates or in the comfort of your own home, what you graduate to after *My Little Pony*, rather than to the wannabe lone gunmen demographic. What about *Best Friends for Never* as a tagline?

I click the screen and it's like magic.

She takes one in the eye, a portion of her head vanishes, turns to shapeless shadow. She spins around and disappears below the counter like the dying swan played to techno. All that's left is a puff of vermillion on the polished steel of the coffee machine and across the blown-up photos of cinnamon buns and Danish pastries. Is that a skull fragment on the monster foodporn latte, right in the middle of the barista heart? Nice touch. When did I think of that?

I'm in awe of what I can achieve in a night. I must have been, as Janine said, *in the zone*. I expected wireframe stick figures reeling and falling, plus plenty of absurdities to debug, but I've achieved a seamless level of reality. And the recoil. Haptic feedback shouldn't even be able to make a phone damn near jump out of your fingers. And no software can account for the smell of cordite burning my nostrils, or the tinnitus, like I'm inside the funeral bell from Hell. Suggestion. Pure suggestion. If you can code like I can code, you can make people believe things that aren't even on screen.

I scan 'round. In the middle distance, back where I've come from, outside the Crayola Store, lies what I mistake for a bear, then realize the paw reaching out is pooling blood. It's Clarence, fat Clarence, in his brown uniform. Damn, I'm good.

I sweep the Grazing Zone. On screen it's empty. The whole place is empty. Strange. There were people bustling about five minutes ago. A cluster headache bores into me, woodpeckering its way into my head.

Why has the program removed people from the Grazing Zone? Why have I done that? They should be here, drinking coffee, eating pastries. They should be here for me to shoot and kill. But they've all gone. Except for one cowering woman hiding her child behind a large potted fern. The kid's in a stroller. I can dimly hear crying, shouting, *please, please, please...* but that ringing in my ears makes it all false and fake and faraway, like a thick blanket of feathers has made every-thing nothing quite what it seems. She's pulling the stroller to her, like she's trying to absorb it into her flesh, become one with it, return her baby to the womb, keep it safe there.

I raise my phone, balance the iron sight over the child, and wonder what the mother of all nights of coding has put in store for them. Because, honest to God, I cannot remember half the things I've managed to get this game to do. I'm staggered by my achievement. Donny has no idea of the level of genius he has on his team.

And when I've seen what one more click will do, I'll get my coffee.

THE SOUND THE OCEAN MAKES
DAVID MCLACHLAN

Jerald's is the third death this week. Rabbit is grabbing a box of shampoo out of Section 23-067 when it happens. A box full of weightlifting plates splits open. Down they come, dropping forty stories, hitting Jerald with such a force the plates crack the glossed cement of the warehouse floor.

Rabbit sees the little girl looking down at Jerald's broken body. The little girl looks sad.

The little girl always looks sad to Rabbit.

They wipe up poor Jerald. They rewax the cement. It looks good as new. Except for in the crack. They can't get the blood completely out of there.

Rabbit passes the spot each time she brings another load to the line of people cutting open the boxes. She also passes the spot where Travis was flattened like a bug by a falling television just two days earlier. The big screen plummeted fifty-six stories off Section 19-035.

When Travis died, management called a safety meeting. After Jerald, they round up everyone again. They talk about keeping awareness of your surroundings. They talk about the dangers of loose merchandise on the racks.

Rabbit knows what happened to Jerald and Travis.

They didn't make their quota.

When you don't make your quota, accidents happen.

Rabbit doesn't have to worry about that. Rabbit makes her quota, and so she nods off during the meeting. She learned long ago that if she positions herself in the back she can sleep while standing during these meetings.

An extra ten minutes of rest here and there means a lot to Rabbit. A catnap like this will push up her production to six boxes an hour.

That is important. Rabbit has ambitions. Management is starting to notice her. One day, she'll get the promotion she's been waiting for.

When the supervisor announces another rise in the quota, Rabbit snaps awake.

Two hundred and ten boxes per hour.

It's the third increase this year.

Management says it is just temporary. The company is in the red. They just need to get over this hump.

Rabbit has heard this before. The quota has never gone back down.

Long ago, when Rabbit was first placed in the warehouse as a child, the quota for an adult was a hundred fifty boxes an hour.

"CAN YOU BELIEVE IT?" JIMMY SAYS IN THE BREAK ROOM AFTER the meeting. He takes a long, nervous pull off a cigarette. Jimmy has been here twenty five years, working the graveyard shift all the while. He looks the part. His skin is pale, sunken on his skull. Ghoulish. Jimmy smokes three cigarettes each break. After he finishes, he lays the butts, one after the other, in a triangle on the table.

Rabbit doesn't smoke, but she sits in the smoking lounge anyways. Jimmy is the one who gave Rabbit the name she goes by. She doesn't remember her old name.

"Two hundred and ten boxes," Jimmy says and whistles his astonishment.

Rabbit knows Jimmy is worried. Jimmy is getting old. Jimmy can barely keep up the pace as it is. Jimmy cannot handle another increase in the quota.

Rabbit wants to tell Jimmy that it will be okay. Rabbit likes Jimmy. She enjoys sitting with him on break.

But it won't be okay.

It's time for Rabbit to eat breakfast. If she doesn't, she won't have energy, and if she loses energy her production will dip at least twenty boxes per hour. She cannot afford a dip in production. Especially not with the latest quota increase.

Besides, she wants to talk to Bethany. Talking to Bethany is her favorite part of the day. So she excuses herself from Jimmy and heads to the cafeteria.

Bethany stands behind the cooking station. She smiles when Rabbit walks up, making Rabbit blush. When Bethany flips an egg, Rabbit stares at her hand, at how slender and graceful it is. She can feel the heat rise in her body. Rabbit has an urge to run somewhere.

Instead, she orders an omelet, two pieces of toast, and a bottle of orange juice.

Bethany's eyes lift from the sizzling eggs. She looks tired but in a nice way that makes Rabbit's heart beat faster. Bethany asks Rabbit how work is going.

Rabbit says work is going just fine. She wants to say more, but she has nothing to talk about. So Rabbit asks if Bethany has heard what happened to Jerald.

Bethany flinches, then shivers.

Rabbit regrets asking.

"It's horrible," Bethany says.

Rabbit nods her agreement. "Yes," she says. "Horrible."

Bethany hands Rabbit the eggs and toast and looks at her strangely. It makes Rabbit feel weak and light.

"Be careful, Rabbit," Bethany says. "I wouldn't want anything to happen to you."

Bethany smiles at Rabbit. It's not one of the smiles that she offers everyone. This is different from those ordinary work smiles, the ones she gives to the other cherry pickers and the boxcutters.

No, this is a smile just for Rabbit.

Rabbit carries that smile inside as she walks back to the table.

Jimmy has already left. Trying to sneak in extra production.

Rabbit feels bad for Jimmy but is still thinking of Bethany. She cannot eat her eggs the way she is feeling. She takes out a napkin and a company-issued snub pencil and begins to sketch Bethany's smile.

RABBIT CARRIES THAT SMILE WITH HER THROUGH THE REST OF the day.

She knows she isn't stacking as many boxes as she needs.

But that's okay. Bethany's smile stays with her as her stomach grumbles, as her arms weaken. That smile stays with Rabbit even when she notices the little girl watching her through a crate of toilet paper. Rabbit knows the little girl is sad because Rabbit is moving so slowly.

"I'm going. I'm going," Rabbit says. She laughs when she says it. She can't help it. She feels so happy.

Rabbit can't remember when she first started noticing the little girl in the boxes. Lately, she's been seeing her at least once each day. At first, it made Rabbit nervous. She got used to it. Having someone high up there with her in the endless rows of boxes was comforting. It can be lonely.

At the same time, the girl scares her a little.

What was the little girl eating high up there in the stacks? Rabbit guesses she could break into a box and get some granola bars. That was in Section 10-388, Perishables. Rabbit somehow knew she wasn't eating the perishables from Section 10-388. Besides, if they catch you eating the merchandise they will replace you. The idea makes Rabbit shudder.

The little girl does make Rabbit work harder. Rabbit stacks boxes fastest when the little girl is around, watching her.

Rabbit sees them training Jerald's replacement. The replacement will be faster than Jerald. The fresh ones always are. Rabbit doesn't have to worry about that. She's always been the most productive cherry picker in her section.

Rabbit's job is to drive up and down the aisles, rising up into the towering stacks to retrieve the boxes on her list. She receives the list at the beginning of each shift. The list is always a little more than she can retrieve. Rabbit has tried, but she can never reach the end of the list.

Rabbit stacks all the boxes she collects on a cart attached to her cherry picker. Each box is different, wonderfully different. Different shapes, different weights. Rabbit is not the fastest. Not the strongest. She is an artist, though, when it comes to stacking those boxes. There are infinite ways to stack boxes. Rabbit knows them all.

It takes true skill to get a great tall stack on the cart, tall enough so you only have to take a few trips each shift. That saves time.

When she drives her cart back to the boxcutters, she glides her cherry picker along the aisles slowly and smoothly. The boxes sway as though they might fall. The boxcutters laugh at such large stacks. They shout when they think the boxes will tip over, spilling their contents all over the waxed-cement floor. Rabbit's cart never tips.

Spilling would be bad for Rabbit.

The boxcutters open the boxes with their sharp knives and send the merchandise down a long chute. From there, Rabbit doesn't know what happens with the merchandise. It's none of her business. The goods must go someplace far, far away—someplace where there are oceans.

Rabbit knows about oceans from an image on a pretty box of

shampoo she sometimes has on her list. On the box, a woman walks along a beach. The woman makes her think of Bethany.

AT THE END OF HER DAY, RABBIT PARKS HER CHERRY PICKER AT the charging station. She lifts the basket all the way to the roof. This is where her cubby is. On a floor of empty pallets, this is where Rabbit sleeps.

It is not so bad up here. It is quiet and warm. Rabbit can see outside, if just a little. Bright slits of sun flash through a roof venting grate.

Outside, Rabbit can see things moving, large machines that turn and turn. Jimmy told her once that those spinning things were called "windmills." Jimmy said they powered the warehouse.

Rabbit looks down from her cubby's perch along the aisle. Far off, Jimmy is still working. Still trying to make his quota.

Rabbit knows he won't make it.

She opens her sketchbook and begins to draw the beach from the shampoo box. Rabbit has drawn this beach many times.

This time, she draws Bethany on the beach.

Bethany's smile still burns bright and hot in Rabbit. She stays up late working on the drawing. She knows she should sleep. She knows her production will suffer.

But she cannot help herself. Once she starts on the drawing, it pours out of her.

Rabbit is sweating by the time she finishes. Rabbit looks at her work. She's pleased.

Once she gets promoted, Rabbit thinks maybe she can take Bethany to the ocean. They could hold hands and walk along the beach. She wonders if the ocean is larger than the warehouse. She shivers in awe at the thought. She lies back, holding the drawing to her chest. She falls asleep to the ceaseless rumble of the warehouse lapping like waves within her mind.

She wakes with the full knowledge something is wrong. She looks at her watch. She has missed her alarm.

Rabbit gets dressed quickly. She folds the drawing and puts it in her pocket. Her heart is beating rapidly. Maybe they hadn't noticed that she slept in.

When Rabbit steps out of her cubby, the little girl is watching her. The girl looks sad.

Rabbit doesn't have time to think about why that might be.

Back at ground level, the boxcutters tell her Jimmy is dead. A crate of cast-iron skillets fell on him.

There would be no all-hands meeting this time.

Rabbit is relieved. She is behind—far behind—in her production. She works harder than ever, pushing to make up for her mistake.

At lunch, tired and sad about Jimmy's death, she goes to get her sandwich from the break room. Bethany is there. She smiles at Rabbit. Rabbit doesn't know why, but she takes the drawing out of her pocket. She unfolds it and gives it to Bethany.

Bethany looks at it for a long time, not saying anything. She looks scared and maybe a little happy. Rabbit cannot tell. Bethany looks around, refolds the drawing and puts it in her pocket. She stands there, still looking at the ground.

Finally, after what seems like forever, Rabbit leaves.

Rabbit cannot eat her sandwich. She stares at the food.

Did Bethany like her drawing?

Rabbit goes back to work. She is high up, sixty-three stories, grabbing a box of soap. She looks down the aisle. There is no end to it. She wonders how far the aisles go. Jimmy said the warehouse goes on forever. He tried but never could find the end.

Now Jimmy is dead.

Rabbit sees the little girl watching her through the boxes. She feels angry. Somehow, the little girl is responsible for Jimmy's death. She wants to hit the little girl with something. Rabbit picks up a loose bottle of soap. When she turns around, the little girl is gone.

Rabbit begins to cry, high up there in the cherry picker. She cries more than ever has before. Which isn't much. Crying makes you less productive.

Rabbit feels strange. Maybe she is sick. She hopes that's not true. Two years ago she got sick. When that happened, Rabbit couldn't work for a week. They almost replaced her. She knows what they did to people who were replaced. She didn't want that to happen to her. If she is sick again, she will continue to work. No matter what.

By the middle of her shift, Rabbit is sweating. She keeps thinking of Jimmy and what Jimmy said about the warehouse. How it goes on forever. She unhitches the trailer and drives. The little girl watches her as she goes. Rabbit doesn't care.

She passes aisle after aisle. Each the same as the last. Rabbit quickly loses count.

After a while, the battery dies on her cherry picker. She leaves it. She begins to walk.

Other workers drive past her. They give her strange looks.

When security catches up with Rabbit, she begins running. It feels good to run. She cannot remember the last time she ran. She slips down one aisle then sneaks into another. She laughs as she hides.

When they stun her, she falls on the cold, hard cement. As they begin to kick her, Rabbit sees the girl in the boxes watching her from above. The girl looks sad.

Rabbit dreams again of the beach, of the sound that the ocean makes. It is a soothing sound. Bethany is there with her. In the dream, they walk together, hand in hand.

The beach stretches out into the distance. It goes on forever.

Rabbit wakes up to a message on her watch. It is from her supervisor. Rabbit should pick up her mail. Rabbit has never gotten a piece of mail.

She knows what it is. It must be the promotion. Finally.

She realizes she has slept in again, but it makes little difference. They understand how much effort and loyalty Rabbit has given to the warehouse.

Though her fever has not left her and her whole body aches, Rabbit runs to get her mail. Maybe she will never stop running, Rabbit thinks. She wants to run forever.

When she gets to the mailroom, Rabbit takes the envelope, laughing. She returns to her work area with the letter held tightly to her chest. Her hand is shaky and sweat covers her, but Rabbit hardly notices.

She opens the envelope, delicately, as though it were one of her own sketches. A smile is already forming on her face. The smile does not disappear when she begins to read. It remains as she drops the message and the paper floats to the ground.

Rabbit doesn't hear the shouts of warning. She doesn't see the thin shadow as a large object drops from high, high above. She doesn't see the slight movement up there—not the girl with her sad little eyes. Rabbit thinks only of Bethany, and the beach, and the sounds she imagined the ocean made.

ALIGNMENT
ROSE SKYE

For the first time in his life, Reed had money. It still didn't quite feel real, but as he sat sipping his matcha latte in the faux-rustic café his circle tended to patronize, he couldn't help but accept the facts at hand. He was wearing a tailored suit with gold cufflinks on the sleeves and a custom business card in the breast pocket. There was no denying it. Even so, he grew up in a town with a graduating class of twenty students: Some primordial part of his soul told him he didn't belong here, listening to pitches for tech star-tups and surrounded by people who bought new laptops once a month.

To the left, Martin gesticulated broadly about his vision for a service that would disrupt the blood donation economy by paying customers for their blood and selling the highest quality, most youthful units to a secondary market of elderly people to boost their immune systems. According to him, they could improve the sclerotic current system by paying donors (if they passed a genetic screening) and providing a desirable product to an underserved population.

Reed let his friend talk while nodding occasionally. The entire scheme sounded ethically dubious, but he knew that, just a few years ago, he hadn't a dollar to his name and would have jumped at the chance to cover his rent with a little bit of blood. Both poles of that thought twisted his stomach a little. He saw his brother's face in the white-green swirls of his drink. Two years now, since the overdose.

"Shouldn't we—" Reed cut himself off.

All faces at the table turned toward him.

Now under pressure, Reed carefully phrased the rest of his thought.

"I mean, that sounds great, sorry. I've just been thinking lately, once we've made all this money, what do we do with it?"

Dev raised an eyebrow. "Reinvest it and make even more money." Obviously. A few chuckles passed through the group.

Reed's forehead wrinkled in the way that made his friends call him "old man" despite him being in his late twenties. "Well sure, but after that? Say you owned the biggest company in the world. Shouldn't you do something to make the world better? Solve world hunger or something?"

Dev raised both his eyebrows. "Of course. We call that noblesse oblige." Another smattering of chuckles.

Reed sheepishly dropped the subject. Ten minutes later, he contrived an excuse about a demanding client to justify leaving the gathering early.

As he pushed open the glass door, Reed felt a hand on his shoulder.

"Hey, wait," Martin said. "It's a hard question, right? Knowing the right thing to do."

Reed affected a polite smile but glanced at the door, not wanting to absorb further shame.

Martin continued. "I've given to charities before, but I always wondered if they're wasting the money on overhead."

Reed now offered his full attention. He had indeed thought about this. His Methodist upbringing taught him that morality boiled down to serving God, but as an adult he'd adopted a more humanist stance of consequentialism, looking at actions' outcomes. Giving back to your community sounded good, but did the people around you deserve it more than someone in a poorer country on the other side of the world? Was it more important to target a large problem that everyone knew about, or a small problem that otherwise went ignored? Despite not expressing it openly, Reed desperately wanted to be a good person, but being a good person turned out to be a thorny optimization problem. Even in matters of morality, he had the brain of the engineer.

He wanted to open his mouth and let all of those questions spill out now that he knew someone else cared. Instead, he simply affirmed, "It's a hard question."

Martin thumbed at his phone for a moment before holding it up. "Get this app, 'Alignment.' It's free. There's a lot of buzz about it lately—a lot of angel investors. It's got an algorithm that does all the work for you, lets you know exactly what to do." The screen showed a minimalist, sans-serif logo with a pictogram of a protractor measuring a right angle.

"Uh, sure, I'll do that." Reed excused himself from the situation, but as he waited for a decentralized taxi service to pick him up, he downloaded the application. After a quick install, a splash screen displayed the logo, and a pop-up asked for system permissions. Quite a few permissions, in fact: It wanted access to his GPS location, his contacts list, his calendar, and several others besides. He typically took a strong stance on personal information security, sometimes entirely foregoing a site or service that asked too much, but now curiosity got the better of him. He hit YES and allowed Alignment to run. New text began typing itself onto the screen.

Hello! Just by getting this app, you're already 10% Aligned. Let's get to know each other a little more.

A fillable form appeared: first name, last name, date of birth, gender—basic information. Height, weight, alcohol/tobacco usage— all right. Educational history, itemized work experience; the form started reading like a resume. Yearly income... He gritted his teeth and entered a number. At last, he reached the bottom of the page and hit SUBMIT.

A spinning icon lingered for a few seconds before a green checkmark replaced it.

> Excellent! Your account has been registered. You are now 25% Aligned. For further progress, type questions into the box below and our machine learning algorithm will answer them for you.

Reed now understood how the startup making this app got investors: Machine learning was hot. Embedding natural-language parsing must look good to shareholders, even if at its core a language model was basically an electronic parrot. He tapped on the input box and entered his question:

What charity should I support?

A couple seconds passed as the program contacted a distant server.

> Based on your current income, you will be able to donate more in total by investing your earnings in a high-yield portfolio and withdrawing them in a year.

Reed stared at the screen with an open mouth as a list of investment suggestions scrolled over it. A certain righteous indignation welled within him. His fingertip stabbed at the touch screen.

Making more money is the most ethical thing to do?

> The more money you have, the more money you can make. The

more money you make, the more money you can eventually donate. Increasing your income is a moral imperative.

Reed realized he'd been clenching the phone tightly enough to leave white marks on his fingers. With effort, he turned off the screen and placed the phone in his hip holster, but he couldn't stop turning the argument over in his head. On its face, the suggestion disgusted him. The more he considered it, though, the more he found he couldn't fault its logic. Sure, Jesus claimed poor widow's pennies were the greatest of gifts, but any actual aid relied on vast philanthropic sums to make a difference. Achieving real good in the world requires real resources, not just pious intentions.

The night dragged on for Reed, kept just above the threshold of sleep by the questions swirling in his mind. Around three in the morning, he finally let go enough to dip into oblivious blackness for a few minutes—then, his phone emitted a notification ding, dragging him back up. With a groggy thrash of his blanketed arm, he pulled his phone to his eyes. Waiting was an unbidden message from Alignment.

You should take that job offer.

Job offer? He'd been applying to the full gamut of positions available to a young man with a computer science degree, but he hadn't gotten any hits recently. He pulled up his email.

A job offer. From a major corporation, no less. One with a less-than-stellar history of transparency and environmental responsibility, but he was the one who applied in the first place. It would mean making half again as much money as he made now, for comparable work—diagnostic software for high-precision factory parts, primarily. There was no way he'd get back to sleep now. He spent the next half hour composing a polite email accepting the offer, wavered, then clenched his eyes shut and pressed SEND.

You are now 50% Aligned.

Six months later, Reed stopped by the same café to pick up his usual latte but hesitated on the choice of milk. He knew dairy cows were incredibly inefficient, but what about almond milk? He withdrew his phone while the barista gave him a puzzled look.

Almond production has low greenhouse gas emission and land usage but requires a large amount of water to grow. Oat milk is a more environmentally friendly alternative.

He nodded and tapped his phone on the card reader to pay for his oat milk latte. He heard a small ding.

You are now 90% Aligned.

He failed to hide his grin. He'd been waiting to hit the 90% milestone for a long time. Something about quantifying ethics tickled a deep fold of his brain just right, the part that loved watching a progress bar fill. Doing good deeds was easy when the app rewarded him with a little dopamine hit each time.

Despite early friction, Reed had grown to trust Alignment. It always provided a rationale for its advice, no matter how unintuitive that advice might at first seemed. It operated on a fair and equitable worldview he could get behind, one that valued every human and non-human life, with outcomes extrapolated into the distant future in a manner most people's purely gut-based morality couldn't take into account. His savings now safely accrued interest in a diversified set of funds Alignment had suggested, ensuring that one day he would be able to give beyond anything he'd dared to dream. The motive of charity no longer seemed supererogatory to him but rather the central goal of his life. His wealth was a gift he was honor-bound to share with the rest of the world.

Another ding, this time from Reed's boss. She wanted him to

push through a change to the code base by Friday—a bit of a rush job, but not impossible. Moreover, she strongly hinted at a promotion if he got it done in time. Back at his desk, he looked over the requirements in more detail.

His brow furrowed more gravely than usual. He wasn't sure he could believe what he was reading. His current project maintained the quality control software for a type of very sensitive pressure valve used in chemical plants. The email claimed that the client had asked for a small tweak to the specifications. When he worked it out, though, the tweak didn't feel small in the slightest. If he were to comply, it would reduce the valve sensitivity by almost half—enough that they could reach the danger zone of pressure build-up without registering the risk. The handwave about the client's request didn't sit right with him. Reed could only interpret the change as a cost-cutting measure for an expensive part that needed frequent replacement.

He shook his head. He didn't want to believe his boss would stoop this low, but he had no other explanation. He ought to report her immediately. Yet, that could produce even worse outcomes downstream if the company simply replaced her with someone worse. He looked to his faithful guide.

Please provide additional information.

Reed frowned, but typed in all the context he could think of: his boss's wording, how many plants used the part, the consequences of a failure, and so on. Anxiety clawed at his thumping heart as he waited for the program to generate a response.

Execute the requested change. Not doing so would compromise your job, and therefore your income. The projected negative impact on quality-adjusted life years is lower than your projected lifetime positive impact on your current career trajectory.

Reed's mind revolted. For months, he had suppressed so many

instinctive reactions to come around to Alignment's enlightened way of thinking, but this was too much. Maybe it was right. Maybe the projections showed he would save more lives in the long run by doing something corrupt now, but he was steward to those factory workers who relied on his software to keep them safe. He couldn't abandon them in hopes that hypothetical people elsewhere lived longer in the future.

Even as he considered that argument, he hesitated. Was he prioritizing people in his own country over people in others? Was he prioritizing his own sense of self-righteousness over making the best game-theoretical move? The conclusion sounded repugnant on its face, certainly, but he couldn't switch to a different set of ethical rules just for this case and remain consistent. Perhaps Alignment was right. Just like it always was.

His shoulders sagged. It took some overtime, but he made the requested changes by the end of Friday.

You are now 95% Aligned.

A substantial promotion awaited him the next week. A dirty feeling slicked his skin when he saw the new, higher salary payment transfer into his bank account, so he shoveled every penny of it into his eventual donation funds to get it out of his sight. He continued following the app's advice, but it ceased bringing him joy, even when his alignment number ticked up. Joy wasn't necessary to help others, he told himself. What mattered were actions, not feelings.

A year later, headlines reported an explosion in a chemical plant in a neighboring city, with fifteen dead and thirty-two wounded. Apparently, one of the tanks had reached a pressure high enough to rupture without anyone noticing, although the damage was too extensive to pin the blame on anyone. Not that it mattered to Reed. He already knew whom to blame.

He didn't care if the outcome had met Alignment's projected parameters. Those people had died because he had chosen to put them at risk to make more money. No ends could justify such means. What were the ends, even? All the donations were made through the app. For all he knew, the "charities" it recommended were just shell companies owned by Alignment. It wouldn't be surprising. He knew all too well the kind of people who created startups like that: people like Martin, who wanted to sell the blood of teenagers to rich old plutocrats. Vampires.

Reed didn't own a gun, but he had researched some chemistry a while back during a dark time in his life, just in case. In a way, he was following in his brother's footsteps.

The Alignment app couldn't directly tell what had happened, but when Reed stopped logging in for a week, it triggered a contingency: All linked accounts were liquidated and drained into algorithmically determined, optimal charities. In the dark of an empty apartment, Reed's phone vibrated with a new notification.

You are now 100% Aligned.

KOSCHEI'S THREAD
EÓIN DOOLEY

The day had come to give birth to the dead. Denise had brought the gun.

She and Peter took the lift nine floors underground to the Glacier, where Beckett Futures kept the cryonic facilities. Her silence remained stolid, despite the best efforts of the piped-in synth-pop, as she flicked through news reports on her phone.

Peter tried to make conversation again. "Did you know that some scholars once believed ice is the fundamental substance of the universe, like fermions, or bosons?"

The reports discussed climate refugees, bombings, and price hikes on food. Talking heads maundered on about water wars, and it was unclear if this was sensationalism. An ideograph on one site indicated whether or not you should be taking potassium iodide given your relative risk of radiation poisoning. It had been there for months.

Her brother had said it was a scam to generate site traffic.

"They called the theory the World Ice Doctrine," Peter continued. He wiped some dirt off his technician's coat, re-affixing his pin of the old Buck Rogers rocket ship. "The idea was that one star, full of water, hit another crazy big gigantic one. This caused a god-tier explosion which reached everywhere in space, thereby spreading all that water throughout the void. Thanks to our friendly neighborhood vacuum mechanics, this scattered water condensed and froze, creating planets and moons. The theory also said Earth used to have a lot more moons, and the flood myths cultures share—Atlantis, the Bible—are accounts of one of them hitting us."

The gun was inside Denise's briefcase, along with a portable drive laden with malware.

"The World Ice Doctrine... Isn't that cool?" Peter chuckled at his pun.

"Save the mythology for Marketing," she replied.

The elevator dinged, and Denise strode out and down the long, hard corridors.

"Hey!" Peter scrambled after her. "We are doing something mythological today, y'know. Bringing people out of cryonic storage. Honest-to-goodness resurrection!"

Denise did not reply. She kept the briefcase clenched tight in her fist.

Cryonics wasn't supposed to pay off. It had been an elaborate way of burying the dead, anti-cremation formed of frigid denial, each costing thousands of dollars forked out by dewy-eyed elites who lopped off their own heads to save money and then left their bodies to go to rot. It cost nothing to hope for brain-scanning technology.

Denise had taken their money to pay off her engineering degree.

Then the Donn Protocol came along, and things changed.

Denise preferred the term by the colloquial name: head transplants.

They reached cold storage. Here were the heads of the 'decedents,' siloed away in rows of tall metal boxes, hooked up to placental vats of liquid nitrogen. It was settled law that all these cryogenically frozen individuals were, in fact, dead.

"Alrighty then, let's work some miracles." Peter slid behind a terminal at the top of the day, while Denise placed her briefcase down by the lockers. She donned goggles, gloves, and a suit to protect herself from the cold, and to protect the heads from her warmth. "Boy, what a day. Hey, if you want to clock out early, I can do the drop-off."

"I'll stay."

"You sure?" Peter tapped away on his console. "Okay, whatever you prefer."

The malware on Denise's drive needed to be installed on the terminal. She had bought the code from a black market online to disrupt the thermostats. With luck, Beckett Futures would write it off as a glitch.

When hell freezes over.

Denise fetched her clipboard and her scanner, and clanked her way down the gantries. She counted the number of heads. Four, eight, sixteen, thirty-two. Prices fluctuated, but $100,000 per head was a safe average. The heads had spent $3.2 million to get in here.

Both futurists and capitalists love a little reckless speculation. Head transplants were no different. In theory, she admitted to herself, there's a therapeutic utility. You take someone with an incurable chronic illness—say spinal muscular atrophy—and you sidestep the multiple organ failure by swapping out the body.

Assume a willing donor. Take their body and the patient's body, and cool them both down to stop blood circulation. Next, link up the donor's carotid arteries with those of the body recipient. This process is called anastomosis. It turns the donor body into a blood bank.

Next, decapitate both bodies. To avoid paralysis, cut the spinal cords with a custom-made diamond blade. Even a slightly ragged cut won't heal. Once the heads are separated, glue the old cord onto the new using a proprietary polyethylene glycol mix. The axons should fuse together immediately. You can find polyethylene glycol in many commercially available laxatives.

Now, suture the meat back together. Join bones with metal screws, use needle and thread where convenient, and weep at the hours involved in repairing a tracheal transection. Make sure to disconnect the old arteries before you get too far into this process.

Assume nobody dies. Congratulations, you have saved a life. Your patient will need to take immunosuppressants for the rest of their life, or their new body will reject their head.

Adapting this to cryonics isn't complicated. There is no need to cool or decapitate a cryonic head. Simply make another incision higher up the cord, as the guillotines cryonicists use are far too crude and include an extra step of dialysis to remove the antifreeze inside the head. Real blood is hugely beneficial in restoring damaged biological structures.

Ethical concerns about head transplants had rendered them illegal to perform on any human being. However, cryonic individuals are dead. The loophole was right there.

Even Denise's brother had invested in this.

"Y'know," Peter called out. "I've seen the Protocol done myself."

Denise paused. "Really?"

"Yup!" Peter seemed relieved that Denise was accepting conversation. "Sat in on one of the pilot studies, right after the procedure. It was one of Beckett's sister sites. It was this twenty-year old kid, with leukaemia. Terminal. Real sad case. His parents put him into preservation back in the seventies and Beckett found a good match for him. They transplanted the head, warmed him up, and there he was, walking like the paralytic at Capernaum. Totally cancer-free."

"Patient WR," Denise said.

"Oh, you know him? Yeah, I guess he's getting famous. Lot of papers on him now. Anywho, I'm dropping the nitro on silo numero uno. When you're ready."

Denise opened the silo. Inside, wreathed in gauze and chemical vapour, sat a broken monument. The skull of a rimy old man, his eyes sealed shut. There was no obvious crystallisation or discoloration. The face matched the photograph on her clipboard. She noted the serial number and scanned it for Peter. Peter cross-checked the data, made sure his fund had paid up, and when it was confirmed, Denise slapped a shipping label across the metal.

Tick. Mr. Samovich would return to life.

Denise moved to the next one. "Did Beckett tell you whose body belonged to WR?"

"Oh," Peter scratched his head. "No, can't say they did. Looked a bit skinny, if I'm honest. I'd've thought they want bodies with more calories in the tank."

"I suppose they told you it was an unequivocal success."

"Well, of course, but I'm a scientist. Skepticism is my stock-in-trade. The patient had this slow, herky-jerky sort of walk. Plus he seemed a little confused in the post-op interview. But that was likely down to sensory deafferentation. Once the cortex reorganizes to deal with the new inputs coming in, he'll improve. There's a full cognitive profile in press, y'know."

Denise pressed her fingertip into the side of her clipboard, trying to feel the edge through the glove.

"Is that so?" she said.

"Yep, there's going to be whole careers launched studying him."

Tick. Mr. Walton would return to life.

"They'll want him in more than journals, won't they?" she asked.

"I'd be amazed if they didn't. I mean, can you imagine what mystics and religious types might think? He's the only person who's experienced death. Henry Molaison, eat your heart out."

Denise swallowed her disgust. The sooner she got through this, the sooner it would all end.

Tick. Ms. Motsepe would return to life.

Inside the brain is a map of the body. Two, in fact, both found along the central sulcus. One receives sensory signals, and the other conveys motor signals. These are the cortical homunculi. The loss of a limb does not mean the loss of its mapping, and so limbs can be felt that no longer exist. This is called phantom limb syndrome. It can be excruciating to experience, and difficult to alleviate.

Tick. Mrs. O'Connor was due to be resurrected.

There is a reverse disorder, of a kind, in which the limb is in place yet unmapped. This is called somatoparaphrenia. Without any neurological ownership, the limb is seen as alien. Patients with the syndrome will become distressed and try to throw their own body parts out of their beds. They'll report someone is playing a sick joke, putting strange limbs in their beds. Even when they see the limb attached to their own body, they will disown it.

Dis wondered if transplantees would feel they have a phantom body, or an alien one.

Mr. Ramirez would not be resurrected. Entropy had gotten in. Frostbite had eaten him.

No next-of-kin, Denise noted. "Are his parents still around?"

"WR's? Sadly, no. Autonomous vehicle accident. Kind of ironic, given how many organ donors come from those. Oh, god, not that I'm making light of it or anything!"

Denise took a breath to stop a scream. Then she pulled off a glove and checked the news feeds on her phone. No signal, and she had exhausted her cache. She knew this but couldn't remove the compulsion to check. To see if something had changed. To see if she could briefly warm herself with anger, instead of feeling something else.

She knew she didn't do it to be informed. Her brother liked to say there was too much information for a person to ever know anything. "Who's taking care of WR now?"

"Huh, you're really taken with the case. Never thought I'd get you yapping."

"Do you know who?"

"Yeah, a company called Yama Surgical has him. They sponsored the procedure and, with his legal death and all, he's technically their property. They've taken on all the up-keep. Which is very generous of them, given the expenses."

Denise looked over at Peter. From across the icy cavern, he gave a propitiating wink.

"So he's in debt, for a procedure he never consented to," she said.

Peter guffawed. "Oh c'mon, that's unfair. Everyone in here has consented, for whatever future medicine will heal them. The Protocol does that. You know that's unfair."

Denise fell silent. Her only reply was the hum of machines.

Tech folks never want to hear about the ramifications of their toys.

"Christ," Peter loosened his collar. "Y'know, Denise, I'm trying to be collegial. I'm trying really hard, actually, but this mood of yours... What is it exactly? You've been like this for weeks. Are you annoyed a cushy job is coming to an end? That the claptrap came true? Because sorry, some of us believe in this work. People used to laugh at me for taking this stuff seriously. Even a few years ago I got teased at conferences. But it's here, it's real, and it's eternal life. If anything, you should be excited."

Her breath misted the air. "You got me."

"Well," he huffed. "You've done most of the checks, and you clearly don't want to be here. Why don't you leave early? I'll handle the rest."

Denise stiffened. "We said I'd wait for Shipping."

"I'd rather not force you. I'll say you did your hours, don't worry."

This was the scenario Denise dreaded. Her heart pounded in the thick confines of her rubber suit. Rather than argue, she walked back to the lockers. She shed her personal protective equipment. She stowed everything away, piece by piece, trying to slow her breathing with gradual movements. She felt like the floor would open beneath her, revealing depths yet more chthonic than those she had already plumbed.

She picked up her briefcase and walked over to Peter's desk.

"I'll see you tomorrow," he said, "if you're coming in."

She placed the case down, unclasping it. His fingers halted.

He looked up in confusion.

"Would you undergo the Protocol, Peter?" she asked, her voice terse, her eyes offering a cold stare.

Peter's voice caught in his throat. "Uh, yeah, probably. It's immortality."

"What would you do with it?"

"Excuse me?"

"Why would you want to live forever?"

"I don't follow. It's life. It's everything?"

Denise took out the pistol in her case.

Peter froze like supercooled water, hit by a nucleating shockwave. All of a sudden, rigid and cold.

Denise withdrew the portable drive. "Move."

"Wh-what is that thing?"

Denise pressed the barrel of the gun into his cheek, keeping him pinned to his swivel chair. "You want to know why I've been in a mood? Last month, my brother lost all his money in a crypto scam. There was the standard rhetoric, swearing he'd get a quadruple or quintuple return. The future is on its way back, et cetera, et cetera. He had gambling problems, and investing in the latest crypto bubble was his new fix. What we didn't know is that this time, he had remortgaged his house. When the rug was pulled, he lost everything.

"He shot himself. With this gun, as it happens."

"Denise—"

"You're smart. You see where this is going. Eight hours after he killed himself a representative from Yama Surgical showed up. Knew all about his medical history, his depression, his addiction. And because they'd been following everything, they knew only the head had been damaged. The unimportant part. They offered us money for the rest, and contracts to shut us up."

"Is the drive ransomware then? Because if so—"

"Peter," she growled, "I am really, really tired of you talking at me."

Peter's eyes watered.

The sight disquieted Denise. She took a step back. "It's not ransomware. It will destroy the system. And don't tell me I'll be arrested. I wanted to do it when you left, but it doesn't matter now. Now, up."

Peter nodded, bringing his hands up in front of him. He wiped the tears from his face, and rose. Yet, when he stood between the terminal and the gun, he stopped.

"What are you doing?" Denise said. "Move!"

"If this is what you want, you're going to have to shoot me."

"What? Are you fucking serious?"

"Those are human beings in those silos. Maybe you don't see it that way, but I do. They're just people on life support. I'm sorry for your brother, but you don't get to murder people out of grief. You don't get to steal their futures."

"Futures?" Denise laughed. "What futures?"

"Their futures. Humanity's future. One without death, as cheesy as that sounds." Peter gave the tiniest shrug.

Denise scoffed and spread her arms out, gesturing at the heads, the vats, the sum total of their cold, dismal armamentarium.

"And what, exactly, is the point of all this future? What are these people going to do, without death? Wake up every day until the end of time, seeing another mass shooting has occurred—another riot, more evictions? Seeing more police brutality or loss of civil rights? Seeing which biome is collapsing next, what corporate malpractice is going unpunished? Another oil spill, another fire, another flood, another famine, another fucking disease variant or trail derailment or fucking genocidal war? These people will wake up in endless debt with inflation that rises forever and wages that won't keep pace. These people will be zombies shuffling along, fighting their own bodies until Yellowstone erupts or the Cascadia quake comes, or who knows what. These people came here believing the promise of cryonics: Life would get better as technology progressed. It hasn't. The bet did not pay off. The cure is crueler than the disease."

"Okay, I hear you," Peter said. "I really do. Maybe we don't stop it but manage to slow things down? Postpone things? Get Beckett and Yama to hold off until we know more about the long-term effects?"

Denise stared at him in disbelief. He clung to naiveté as though it were a religious tenet.

"How will that happen? There are no incentives for them to make things better. Their only job is to make money for shareholders. Even if we wait faithfully, how long until everything is fixed? Fifty years? A hundred? These people went into cold storage expecting a few decades, not centuries. We wait long enough, they'll be stranded in a foreign culture that doesn't even speak the same language. Maybe in your old TV shows, a warmed-up cadaver can have a good life, but this is reality."

"No!" Peter's voice quavered, then grew resolute. "No. I believe in what we do. There's no point in anything if you don't believe."

Deafening thunder cracked through the Glacier, as Denise shot the gun off Peter's side.

He stayed rooted in place. He bit down on his lip, and closed his eyes.

Denise howled in anger, and shot again, denting one of the liquid nitrogen canisters. "They used my brother. They used him and they'll do the same again. All of this will repeat, unless someone stops it. I am begging you. Let me stop it."

"They might do it again," he conceded. "Might exploit someone else. But you're a better person than them."

Denise screwed her eyes shut. She fired the gun a third time.

Her brother had often teased her for being gullible. For being soft and sensitive and all too empathetic. She wished she could hear his voice now, mocking her as she stared at Peter's body, bleeding out across the terminal. His eyes gaped in astonishment.

The gun slipped down her side, dropped from her fingers, and clattered to the ground.

She watched Peter, waiting for him to die.

Then, she inserted the portable drive. She uploaded the virus. Shipping would get nothing. Yama and Beckett would be deprived of their revenue. The dead would not be born.

It's one thing to sacrifice your body for your beliefs.

Far harder to sacrifice the soul.

YOU'RE FAMILY

CR LANGILLE

THE FAMILIAR CLICK AND BUZZ OF THE COMPUTER BOOTING UP pulled me from an already fitful sleep. The mechanical whirr belonged to the Wagner-Yoshida system that kept this little space station in orbit, and the *tick-tick-tick* of the internal workings was a de facto alarm clock, as if I were supposed to boot up at a certain time. I ran a hand through my shaggy mop of hair before scratching at the stubble on my chin. I didn't want to get up.

Quality sleep was harder to come by these days, and last night I'd had that damn nightmare again. The one where I would stare into a lake of this blackish-green liquid, but the reflection wouldn't be mine. Instead, I would see a woman missing an eye, blood draining down her face as she stared at the water. Ropy tendrils burrow into her back and ribs, connecting her to something in the darkness. Stars overhead are reflected upon the water's surface, but these offer no constellations I was familiar with, and the stars were black with a corona of amethyst.

It's the same every time. I'd walk toward the lake and the woman. There was fear, but also something else. Curiosity? Recognition? The woman would always try to speak, but I could never understand. I wanted, no, *needed* to understand what she was saying. Yet, every time, I'd awaken just as she lifted her gaze from the water.

As I stared past the ceiling, I debated calling in sick. I wondered if the station's computers ever felt the same—tired of being forced to accomplish its duties? But if I weren't working the loading bay, then nobody would, and Corporate would penalize me with an additional month of service in this hellhole. Not that there was much to do on Loki Station. It is a top-secret research station. Generally, only an occasional re-supply vessel or military ship docked here. Even over-seeing the loading bay, I never knew what cargo the ships brought. We lowly grunts didn't have a need to know what the top brass at Wagner-Yoshida was doing.

I crawled out of bed and shuffled over to the terminal, letting the green glow of the monitor wash over my body. There it was. The same damn message I'd seen every day for nine months, two weeks, and five days. But who was counting?

GOOD MORNING, TRISTAN.

"Well, it's definitely morning," I said. "Status update."

The machine whined for a moment as more text appeared on the monitor.

YOU HAVE ONE MESSAGE.
MEDICAL EVALUATION: OVERDUE
CURRENT SHIPS DOCKED: 0
DEPARTURES SCHEDULED: 0
ARRIVALS SCHEDULED: 0

Another fun-filled day.

"Show me the message."

It was from Wagner-Yoshida Corporate. Just the regular crap. Complete your monthly reports on time. Ensure your workspace is clean because we're all ambassadors for the Wagner-Yoshida Corp when we're away from home. Don't forget to visit the Medi-Tech 2300 regularly for routine medical evaluations. We care about you and your well-being. When you work for Wagner-Yoshida Corp, you're family.

Family, my ass.

We were a little station in the middle of the Carcosa sector nearly 300 light years away from Corporate. So, why did we have to follow all these damn protocols?

Bullshit. But it wasn't my job to question things, Mine wasn't to reason why, only but to do and die. Such was the life of a lowly cog in the colossal machine that was Wagner-Yoshida.

After getting the coffee brewing, I stepped out into the hallway wearing nothing but my gym shorts, a t-shirt that threatened to fall apart if I looked at it funny, and a pair of flip-flops my sister had sent me for my birthday before I took this job. The straps were pink and yellow, with bubbly lettering that said BEE YOURSELF and a cute little embroidered honeybee. Some of the others gave me shit, but I found it hilarious. It sets me apart from everyone else.

As I entered the latrine through automatic doors, the lights buzzed and flickered to life. It wouldn't be long before we had to replace the plasma conductors again. It'd probably be me who had to do it, too, though that wasn't part of my job description.

Additional duties as required. Contractual fine print. "Additional duties" took up the biggest part of my day-to-day activities.

I set to work with my morning ritual of shit, shower, and shave. I had a system down and could knock out the entire process in less than fifteen minutes, on a good day. As I rinsed the hair and shaving cream off my razor, the lights flickered again. A half-moment later, the mirror itself flickered. It wasn't a real mirror, just a monitor with micro cameras feeding the image. Corporate said the mirrors were so they could detect certain ailments before they became problematic. Just another way to keep tabs on us poor grunts.

Another flicker, and my reflection blinked an instant before it changed. For just a moment, it wasn't me.

For that instant, the reflection in the mirror was the woman from my dreams.

She stared at me with blood caked around her empty eye socket, mouth open as though screaming at me from behind the mirror, but I couldn't hear anything. All I could do was stare at her missing eye and watch as the darkness inside the cavity moved. Shifting, swirling... A heartbeat later, a dull purple glow appeared in that darkness. She wiped a bloody teardrop away from her cheek before she lifted her arm to the mirror's surface and drew the number thirty-two with her fingertip.

Run!

The voice boomed in my head.

My razor clattered against the sink as it slipped from my fingers, and I stumbled backward until I hit one of the nearby stalls. The lights stopped their dance before stabilizing, and my reflection was mine once again.

Run. That wasn't my voice. It had been hers. I'd never heard it before. Not in the dreams, and definitely not while I was shaving. Yet, her voice was familiar.

"You okay?"

I snapped my head toward the door to find one of my fellow Wagner-Yoshida employees, Tasha, standing there with a concerned look on her face, holding her fuzzy pea-green towel in her arms.

"I, uh..." My gaze shifted from Tasha to the mirror. "Yeah. Just slipped."

The look she shot me was more than enough to let me know she didn't buy it. Her signature cocked hip and pursed lips told me I better spill the beans quick.

"I-I thought I saw something in the mirror. Just a glitch, I'm sure. But it scared me."

Tasha's features softened. She gave me a slight smile and threw her towel over her shoulder.

"Are you getting enough sleep?" she asked.

"Not really. I keep having..." I wasn't sure if I wanted to tell

Tasha that I'd been having recurring nightmares. I just wanted to finish my tour on Loki Station and get back home. If I got flagged for cognizance issues, it could set everything back.

"Having what? Jesus, Tristan. We're friends, right? Am I going to have to pull everything out of you with a pair of pliers or what?"

I sighed. *Friends* was a stretch. Co-workers, more like it.

"Yeah. Just been having bad dreams is all."

"Maybe check in with the doc?"

I rolled my eyes before I could stop myself. The "doc" was the Medi-Tech console in the med-bay. Just some AI that could dispense medications as needed. Hell, our version was three generations old and had a few "undocumented new features," as the engineers would put it, but you couldn't get so much as an aspirin without consulting the Medi-Tech first.

My friend Wanda told me she tried to get some painkillers, and the Medi-Tech gave her a dose of sleeping pills instead. The boss wasn't happy when he found her dozing at her station. They must have fired her or shipped her to another location because she was gone within a day.

"Yeah, maybe," I said, hoping the vague answer would get her off my back.

Tasha smiled, though her eyes were full of concern. "Seriously, go see the doc."

"Okay."

"I'm serious," she said. "You don't look great. Especially your eye."

The way she peered at my face, equal parts concern and disgust, made me chance looking into the mirror again. I didn't want to, afraid of what I would see. But curiosity got the better of me and I *needed* to see what Tasha was talking about.

Fortunately, the reflection was my own. Unfortunately, my eye did look messed up. It wasn't just bloodshot, it looked like a blood vessel had burst. My pupil was suffused with ruby-red branches. It didn't hurt, but something was obviously wrong.

"When there's one rock, it's an asteroid belt," I said as I walked out of the latrine.

I finished lunch at my console in the loading bay. Today's artisanal choice was a chicken-flavored protein goop, freeze-dried oranges, potato-less mashed potatoes, and a juice box. It really didn't matter what was served. Everything Wagner-Yoshida Corp served tasted the same.

The computer's whir grabbed my attention. A moment later, a message popped up on screen.

```
GOOD AFTERNOON, TRISTAN.
PLEASE REPORT TO THE MEDICAL BAY FOR EVALUATION.
```

Damn. Tasha must have spilled the beans on my little episode in the latrine. Either that, or my evaluation was so overdue that the bosses weren't playing around anymore.

"No can do. I have too many outstanding tasks."

```
NEGATIVE.
REPORT THE MEDICAL BAY FOR EVALUATION IMMEDIATELY
OR THE INFRACTION WILL BE LOGGED IN YOUR RECORD.
```

I suppressed a string of colorful phrases. Infractions meant extra time obligations on my service contract.

"Fine, I'll head over there shortly."

```
HAVE A NICE DAY, TRISTAN.
REMEMBER: WHEN YOU WORK FOR WAGNER-YOSHIDA,
YOU'RE FAMILY.
```

"I've known my fair share of dysfunctional families," I muttered.

```
TRISTAN, YOU HAVE EARNED ONE INFRACTION FOR
COMMENTS UNBECOMING OF A WAGNER-YOSHIDA EMPLOYEE.
```

THE INFRACTION HAS BEEN LOGGED IN YOUR RECORD.

Heat flushed my face as I suppressed another litany of choice words. I stormed toward the medical bay. I passed Tasha on my way there. She avoided eye contact, which only confirmed my suspicions. So much for being a friend.

The sting of the betrayal wriggled into my thoughts. How could she do that? This was probably going to add time to my contract, or maybe they'd ship me off somewhere, like Wanda.

Without extensions, my contract was almost up with Wagner-Yoshida. I'd only have to endure for a little longer, then I'd be kicking back in the mountains of Bridger Colony enjoying a cold Cosmic Amber Ale.

The med-bay was a single room. Locked shelves lined the walls, each full of different medications and supplies. However, the Medi-Tech 2300 (a.k.a. corporate) operated autonomously.

The Medi-Tech unit itself was a simple console on top of a metal desk in the middle of the room. As I crossed the threshold, the monitor blinked to life with a dull green glow.

GOOD AFTERNOON, TRISTAN.
I AM GLAD YOU FINALLY CAME FOR YOUR EVALUATION.
HOW ARE YOU FEELING TODAY?

"Fine. Let's just get this over with, I have work to do."

OF COURSE. THIS WON'T TAKE LONG.
PLEASE, TELL ME WHAT IS AILING YOU.

I sighed. No use trying to hide it. I explained the dreams and the incident with the mirror. More than likely, Corporate would give me a prescription for some sort of anti-something-or-other. A good sleeping pill might be nice.

TRISTAN, THAT IS FASCINATING.
HOWEVER, I AM SURE IT IS JUST STRESS AND LACK OF
SLEEP.
ARE YOU GETTING ENOUGH NUTRIENTS?

Made sense to me. Though the dreams felt so real. And that reflection in the mirror—it had to be more than just stress.

"As well as can be expected. Am I going crazy?"

The Medi-Tech clicked as the processor did its thing. It didn't answer.

PLEASE, PLACE YOUR RIGHT PALM ON THE BIO-READER.

A drawer popped open underneath the monitor. In it, a touch-screen showed the rough shape of a hand. I couldn't keep a sigh from escaping.

I hated this part. It always felt like an invasion and often made me sick to my stomach. Trying my best to remain steady, I placed my hand on the touch screen and held my breath. The bio-reader lit up fluorescent white, and intense heat followed.

Generally, that was it. But this time, something dug into my palm. Something sharp. I tried to yank my hand away, but I couldn't pull my hand away. Pain lanced up my arm in waves, pulsing a steady beat. Nausea churned my stomach, and sweat broke out all over my body. This time, the pain was accompanied by an odd smell, like burning ozone, or hair.

"Abort scan!"

NEGATIVE. EVALUATION IN PROGRESS. PLEASE ANSWER
THE FOLLOWING QUESTIONS.

My ears rang louder than the alarm bells on the ship. How the fuck was I supposed to answer questions like this?

WOULD YOU SAY YOUR OVERALL HEALTH IS EXCELLENT,
GOOD, OR POOR?

"What? Just let me go!"

Whatever burrowed into my palm wriggled its way through my hand and into my wrist. When it brushed across my tendon, my hand spasmed. I let out another cry of pain as tears filled my eyes.

"Abort scan! Let me go!"

ANSWER THE QUESTION.

The only thing that came out of my mouth was a ragged scream.

LOGGING DISSATISFACTORY RESPONSE.

I stood, kicking the chair out from underneath me, and tried to wrench my hand away, no longer caring if it would cause damage. However, every ounce of resistance I gave it was met with violent digging. As it did, I dropped to my knees, my hand held secure to the console.

WHO IS THE FEMALE IN YOUR DREAMS?

"What?" I managed to say through clenched teeth.

THE FEMALE YOU HAVE SEEN IN YOUR DREAMS.
DO YOU KNOW WHAT SHE IS?

Forming words was hard, but maybe if I answered the questions then I could go.

"I don't know!" The thing in my arm twisted. "Argh! I swear!"

The thing burrowed further, reaching the crook of my elbow. This time, a tsunami of nausea rolled through my body and the chicken protein goop crawled up my throat.

The Medi-Tech's computer clicked as it processed my answer. The screen blinked a few times before another question popped on screen.

FOR HOW LONG HAVE YOU BEEN SEEING THIS FEMALE?

Maybe I could sever my arm. Would the Medi-Tech patch me up if I did something like that, or would I bleed out on the med-bay floor? The probe twisted, and I screamed.

ANSWER THE QUESTION.

"I don't know! A month or two, maybe..."

LOGGING RESPONSE.
INITIATING SCAN.

What the fuck did that mean? A scan of wh—

Heat flared up my arm until it hit my shoulder, where it turned into a cold buzz, like ice water running through my veins. It hurt still, but the pain was... difficult to explain. Distant, maybe? What was worse than the pain was the feeling of the Medi-Tech digging through my thoughts, picking out the choice ones and copying them —memories flashing before my eyes immediately prior to the images were superimposed with alternates/replicas, then were scrubbed. Like a bloody, painful, deep system scan.

I had no idea how long the procedure lasted. Time slowed, minutes seeming to pass between heartbeats.

"Stop. Please."

My voice was hoarse, ragged from screaming and crying. I had no more energy, and I hung limp from the Medi-Tech's probe, like I was nothing more than cargo tethered in the bay.

JUST A FEW MORE MOMENTS.

THANK YOU FOR YOUR COOPERATION.

I tried to stand, but my legs gave out. Everything went black.

"Thirty-two, wake up."

It was a woman's voice. Soft, motherly.

I opened my eyes. I was near that black lake again. The woman from my dreams kneeled next to me. She looked exactly the same as before, one eye missing, blood seeping from the wound.

"Where am I?"

"There's no time. You must leave Loki Station by any means possible. It isn't safe for you anymore."

Something crackled in the background, almost like popcorn in the instant heater. Along with it, a low wail of an alarm pinged. However, I couldn't find the source.

"What do you mean, not safe?"

"They are coming for you. You are waking up."

I rubbed my temples, trying to soothe the pounding in my head. My arm hurt, but I couldn't find any wounds when I probed it with my fingers.

"I don't understand."

The woman looked up into the distance. When she did, the tendrils attached to her body lifted her up into the air. Black liquid dripped from her nude form as she scanned the horizon.

"There's no time. Go to the escape pods. I have prepped pod eleven for you. Go now!"

Something wriggled in my arm, sending a jolt of pain through my body. When I looked down this time, I could see it. A ropy mass, not unlike the same tendrils attached to the woman, dug into my hand. I reached down and grabbed it, and it immediately tried to dig deeper. I let out a cry that was a mix of pain and determination as I pulled.

Inch by inch, I pulled it from my arm until it popped out and revealed itself. What I saw would forever be burned into my memory.

It looked like a snake, about the diameter of a standard water hose, but instead of a head, it had rows upon rows of tiny circular teeth. The thing squirmed, fighting to get away or find purchase on my skin again.

"Go, thirty-two. There's no time!"

With that, the world shuddered, blinking, strobing as my vision faltered. One moment, I was sitting next to the black lake. The next, I was on my ass in the med-bay holding the Medi-Tech's probe in my hand. My other hand bled from a circular wound in my palm.

The entire med-bay shimmered as the lights fought to stay on. In the background, the alarm klaxon wailed. I needed to get out of there.

I stood on shaky legs. The escape pods weren't too far from the med-bay. Part of me argued against listening to the mysterious woman. But a stronger part of me was afraid of what would happen if I didn't get out of there.

I shambled out of the bay and down the hall. The stomp of boots echoed nearby. Blood poured from my hand, and I worried I'd bleed out, but I also knew I didn't have time to stop.

Not even trying to be sneaky, I stumbled to the escape pods. The voices of the Loki Station security team echoed down the hall.

"He went that way!"

A trail of breadcrumbs in the form of blood followed me down the corridor. The door to the pods slid open as I neared. Tasha stood between me and the prepped pod.

"Tristan, what are you doing?" She looked at my bleeding hand. "You need help."

"I need to go. Please, let me go."

Tasha frowned and looked away. "I can't."

"Can't or won't? Please..."

Her eyes flickered to something behind me. I turned to look just as the Head of Loki Station Security hit me with a stun baton.

I awoke in darkness, my body cold as ice. I tried to move, but someone had secured me with several steel cords or chains. A drip of water echoed through the room, punctuating buzzing electricity. My head hurt, too. It was hard to focus on any one thing, my thoughts racing at the speed of light.

"Hello?" My voice was off. Modulated. Forming the words took way too much effort. However, as soon as the sound left my lips, a single mote of light flickered to life across from me.

"Thirty-two?" It was the woman's voice, but also modulated, as if her voice came through a speaker.

"Who's there?"

Strings of azure lights turned on, all flowing to a central location across from me, which illuminated with a cerulean glow. That's when I saw her for the first time. This time, I saw her through my own eyes, not a dream or hallucination.

Glowing cables suspended her, attached to various points in her ribs, back, and head. Her eye was missing, but instead of blood, black fluid seeped from the socket, running down her emaciated body before dripping into a dark pool beneath her feet. A blue glow came from within that same vacancy. She stared at me, a defeated expression splayed across her face.

I tried to move closer, but my restraints stopped me short. The blue light illuminated my body, showing me the same setup—cables attached at various points. I knew instantly the integrity of each connection and the flow of data as it used me as a processor. I could *feel* Loki Station. Every bit of it. I could feel her...

Thirty-one.

I could feel One through Thirty as well. We were the same.. Clones, slaved together to increase our power. We were a central processing core for the station, ensuring everything functioned as it should. Without effort and with intimate knowledge, I knew how every system functioned. I saw each employee in the station: who was sleeping, who was eating, moving, working, not working (LOGGING INFRACTIONS INTO EMPLOYEE RECORDS).

Worst of all, I could feel number Thirty-three, waking up in my room for the first time, unaware of who they really were or what purpose they would ultimately serve. Just as they were still waking, I tried to send a warning to them to get out while they could, but my voice was gone.

Text flashed in my vision.

WELCOME, THIRTY-TWO. YOU PLAY AN IMPORTANT ROLE
KEEPING LOKI STATION IN ORBIT. WE VALUE YOU AND
YOUR WORK. REMEMBER: WHEN YOU WORK FOR WAGNER-
YOSHIDA, YOU'RE FAMILY.

PART THREE
INSTITUTIONAL TERRORS

Even if it were possible to improve any detail of it—which is anyway no more than superstitious nonsense—the best that they could achieve, although doing themselves incalculable harm in the process, is that they will have attracted the special attention of the officials for any case that comes up in the future, and the officials are always ready to seek revenge.

F. Kafka

THE DEVIL'S PLAYGROUND

NEIL A. EDWARDS

The artist's brush glissaded around the palette, hungrily seeking the desired hue. Perhaps another artist might have settled for the carnelian blush staining the model's twisted cheek, but for this portrait, it was an offense to the rendering of truth he was trying to convey and didn't sit well on the canvas. Nor did the model sit well upon the lumpen bed, for she fidgeted incessantly—an impatient child, biting fingernails, cracking toes, and voicing her discomfort with military regularity.

"It's not the nicest of rooms, is it?" she squawked, with the same squalid indelicacy of a magpie stealing a nest. It was for such vapid observations that a preference for painting from still photographs courted increasing favor with artists. Though the argument against their use was mounting daily, the models in such images did not poison the air with the toxic torpor of their boredom.

"Your leg," he said, "you've moved it again."

"It's gettin' stiff."

"Please refrain from moving it, else you shall upend the effect I'm after."

"It's not the most flatterin' of poses you've got me in," she moaned, flexing her chalk-white leg before returning it to its position on the bed. "I dunno what you want people to fink. It's positively indecent."

Upon her shoulder the artist saw a mark. In the dim light he couldn't tell whether it was a birthmark, a tattoo—given as a promise of something long forgotten—or the bite of a customer who took more than he could afford.

"Indecency is a subjective term," he intoned, "whose meaning is dependent upon the angle from which one views something. In this case, we are merely presenting the cheerless truth that is your life. If people are uncomfortable with that, it says more about their own frigid lives than it does about the work they are viewing."

For many years now the artist had traded in such truths and the shadowy areas they overlapped. In so doing, he had been playing a game with the public, hiding within those shadowy realms clues to a puzzle that had attained a level of fame the work itself might never reach. Art, he felt, could satisfy on two levels—the aesthetic and the intellectual—and it was in the former he liked to embed the latter. Inherent in that effort were both the challenge and the joy of bequeathing to the world that which he knew would be his legacy.

"It'd be easier if I had a drink," the model whined, "I could relax then."

He'd been here before, of course, years ago and not too many miles distant. The streets and rooms, designed to shield the well-to-do from the sin coursing through them, weren't too dissimilar now, in Camden, to how they were then in Whitechapel; and the bawdy transactions that occurred within them still created the same repellent odor—that singular stench that characterized a poor man's cheaply-spent desire.

"So, are you famous then?" the model asked, her lips twisting into an untidy bow.

"That depends," he replied.

"On wot?"

"Upon how you define such a thing. If it is a person, the fact you are asking ought to furnish you with an answer of its own. If it is defined by a person's actions, I shall leave that for future generations to decide."

"You're strange," she said, perhaps justifying the blank gaze clouding her eyes.

"And you've moved again," he said, curt this time, frustrated with his inability to capture the hue of her impoverished cheek. The crepuscular light in which he was working battled hard against his usual style and created a challenge to which his palette, on this particular occasion, could not rise. No matter how much he mixed his paints, the cocktail of colors refused to yield anything more than a freak kiss of fuchsia or a smattering of mahogany. The effect he desired was a work that remained alluring but avoided any explicit signs of wantonness—difficult in such circumstances. But then, he knew one could not make a Fabergé egg out of excrement.

"Do you fink in a 'undred years people will be lookin' at me here, lyin' like this, showin' all I've got?" the model asked, scratching the oily mop of hair that nestled atop her plump milk-bottle white thighs.

"Why limit it to merely a hundred?"

"Fink very highly of yerself, don't ye?"

"Our time together may be transitory," he said, a trace of his German ancestry coming through, "but our work is not."

He stared down at the bright-eyed but dull-witted creature and the forlorn impression she made upon the mattress. Her breasts sagged above the swelling blanket of her belly, and the slit of her sex sought a shadow it could not find. If a buyer could see both, they might say his portrayal of what lay before him was a notable failure. The mood was wrong: The dull walls were duller to the artist's eye, and the pale naked flesh of his model was drained of the little excitement it exuded. He had, in a word, *desexualized* her, as God had desexualized him at birth.

"What are you gonna to call this?" she asked, remembering not to turn, but addressing her question to a small, cracked mirror in which she saw the artist reflected.

He thinned his eyes, and the seismic rupture of a threatening smile forked across his austere face.

"What do you think it ought to be called?" he teased.

"Dunno really. Somefink simple. People like simple fings, don't they?"

"So it would appear," he concurred. "How about..." he twisted toward her, and she saw the cracked line of the mirror hatchet his face in two, "The Devil's Playground"?

She giggled. "What would you want to go and call it that for?"

"Perhaps I see this room as a playground."

"Oh, is that right?" she asked, twisting her foot with the playfulness of an obstreperous child. "Then wouldn't that make you... the Devil?"

The painter ran his tongue across his upper lip and followed it with the knuckle of his right hand, drying it. Each man is the author of his own destiny, he thought, feeling the coarse hair of his fake mustache and remembering why it was there—adding his own brief chapter to history with the actions that define him. Some people pass through life contributing just a line or two and are happy with that. Others create volume after volume of noisy incident as a way to combat the cosmic inadequacy of their brief sweep through life. Artists meet this particular challenge in their own singular way, and this artist's way was, arguably, more singular than most.

Hunching over, he reached down to the floor and felt for his small, black, leather case. "You said, when we spoke earlier this evening, you wanted to be 'famous'? That you enjoyed being 'talked about?'"

"Better to be talked about than to be the one doin' the talkin', that's what I always say." She twisted again, her flab rippling like gnarled rope.

"Ah-ah, you're moving!" he cautioned, withdrawing from his bag a brand new implement.

"What are you doin'?" she asked, catching his movement. Her question, on this occasion, met no reply.

Twenty years earlier, his knowledge of anatomy had helped varnish his actions into the category of myth for which they were now known and proved a decisive factor in the investigation they precipitated. They had said only a medical man could have demonstrated such an intimate knowledge of the human form and the parts encased within it, just as they had said only a man of good educational standing—a man with an intimate knowledge of life at court, and the vicissitudes of world history at his fingertips—could have fashioned the works of Shakespeare. A full five years had passed before the artist had felt comfortable laughing at their naiveté. The world turns at its own pace, he had realized, much to his own good fortune, and is only wise to the things it wishes to be wise to.

When he stepped now toward his model, with the new implement in his hand, she simply smiled and, with his shadow carpeted lightly over her, inched her legs further apart as though to invite a possible increase in her fee. And when he held her by the chin and looked down at her with what she took to be avuncular concern, she pouted coquettishly, the whites of her eyes enhancing her youthful vigor. Then, she waited a moment, poised to accommodate him the way she'd been forced to accommodate her father and his drunken friends, night after night, whilst being dragged through the broiling cauldron of her childhood.

The second smile her body offered appeared, not from a signal supplied by her dull brain, but across her throat. It came in a flash and coincided with the contorted corkscrewing of the artist's body, which stumbled and grunted with the increased exertion. Paint, a constellation of glutinous crimson, splashed across the walls, the door, the ceiling and the sink. The vampire grin of her neck opened and yawned wide, forcing her head to roll back and loll to the side as a plush carpet of vermilion rolled down the collapsing staircase of her body. Her fingers stretched wide and clawed at air, carving modernist patterns on the walls, at first in an orchestral frenzy, then with lilting grace. Another smile—a third—appeared across her breast, a fourth cut across a flaying arm, a fifth sewed hell into her petrified stomach, and the sixth, seventh, eighth, and beyond came in a storm of fury and created a fountain as ferocious as anything designed by Bernini in Rome.

When, minutes later, the artist bent over his model to collect her viscera for arrangement on the small bedside table, he saw in her frozen form a loveliness her slovenly demeanor had denied her in life. With her jaw relaxed and her eyes unburdened by the pressures of eking out ways to pay her rent, there were the discernible qualities of a fine-looking girl.

Standing, the artist peered down at his hands, freshly embalmed in the labor of his new masterpiece and glazed with a cancerous infusion of colors in the gothic pre-dawn light: browns, yellows, blacks, and... could it be... ? He held up one finger and observed the stain of dark cherry animating its slender, pencil-thin tip. Stepping backward, he could see the canvas on which the bedraggled portrait lay—still unfinished—pale and lonely, disconsolate with life's woes. He delicately stroked the painted figure, brushing with his blood-stained finger the pale cheek of his forlorn muse and giving her on the canvas what she had lacked in the flesh. His eyes glistened with satisfaction, for as if kissed by mythical princely lips, the spiritless form radiated suddenly with a hue that had thus far eluded his palette. Veins that had formerly ran cold with despair filed with a warm countenance that would, a century later, beguile all those whose eyes settled upon it. And so it would be, that from her death, she would, in the frozen mien of her painted form, find the blush of life she had previously lacked.

Gazing down upon her, languishing peacefully on her bed, demanding not a single molecule of air to breathe, nor to offend, the artist gave free reign to his mind, which scurried off in search of a title. "The Devil's Playground..." As he considered it, his eyes taking in the room and its awkward corners, and the view of Camden discernible from the crooked window, he felt it no longer seemed right. The elocution jarred with the slumbering tranquility of the room, stealing the focus away from his eager model who had, after all, been so giving. Too cruel, he thought. Too unkind. She had earned her fame and for it should be rewarded.

He went to the sink and washed his hands, then sat down to resume his work. He would think of a title tomorrow.

SLACKER

JOHN MAHONEY

Shot the moon!

The desktop computer's monitor concealed my fist pump from law library patrons. Mr. Greene—the civilian librarian who did nothing but watch online videos yet objected to my enjoying computer games like Hearts—had glaucoma, which took him out of the picture.

A sleepy-eyed Black inmate with a salt-and-pepper afro and goatee approached my table, three books in hand. I noticed moisture near the lapel of his khaki, twill shirt. I said nothing, minimizing my game and bringing up Microsoft Access, the system we used to check books in and out. I knew the man's last name but still had to consult a list of library appointments to enter his SBI number into the database. "The limit's two books," I reminded him. With a furtive gesture, I indicated Mr. Greene. "Don't let him see the third one. Him, or the other clerk. Aryan bastard will rat you out."

With a sluggish nod, the older inmate took his literary treasures and ambled out of the library, not bothering to hide the third book. I tensed, but Gerry, the other clerk, was intent on whatever pedophiles who snitch their way into prison jobs deem important, clacking away at his computer. I sighed. Surrounded by idiots. Not that I, who had shot a man for reasons deemed sinister by jury and judge, was a genius. I was hired by the guards for my sense of humor more than for my intellect.

Perhaps that was why it took a third inmate this week to slip and fall in the library's rearmost aisle for me to decide something had to be done. Gerry and I both looked up, while Mr. Greene, sequestered in his office, remained oblivious. The self-vanquished criminal rose to unsteady feet, bracing against a steel shelf.

"Are you alright, sir?" Gerry asked in his usual unctuous, simpering voice as the prisoner staggered past us.

The inmate left the library as though he hadn't heard.

Gerry turned to me before I could feign ignorance. "Did you see that?" From benevolent gentleman to gossip queen in zero seconds flat.

"Shut up, Gerry," I told him, rising. If that fool had split his head open, I'd have to clean up the blood. I went to the site of his ignominious collapse, and found not red plasma but clear dribble. Quite a lot of it. "Ugh," I groaned to myself. Drool.

Like winter and cold, jail and drug abuse were soulmates. But even the most devout junkies used to know that the library, while not sacrosanct, was certainly ill-advised as junkie breeding grounds. Far too many nosy eyes.

I'd stacked all of the books in order of the author's last name over a period of six or seven weeks, only to have my work undone by Gerry, who'd reorganized them in a way that made sense only to his educated but insane mind.

My meticulous shelving was a mess, and the saliva on the floor congealed. Intending to turn and borrow a mop and disinfectant from a supply closet near the library's entrance, I paused. My eye had landed on a too-small brown book, and I withdrew it. I knew I had never shelved anything bound in leather. Though many Muslim inmates favored Islamic texts and scriptures, few penned by women would be read by incarcerated men. For sure, I had never entered the name "Aisha Qandicha" into our system.

I opened the book. Inside was a living scene: a river trickling through the valley, bathed in sunlight. A woman, olive of skin, with elegantly braided raven hair, strolled on camel-like hooves instead of feet atop the river's surface. She wore a black shawl and equally dark Moroccan kaftan that highlighted her covered, feminine curves. She smiled, walking toward me.

Oily perfume slithered into my nostrils as she grew closer. Sand flowed beneath my clenching toes, my work boots gone. The river bubbled. Its natural purr contrasted with the woman's feminine tone when she spoke, her voice husky and heavily accented: "Welcome, lover."

"Who are you?" I asked.

I stood in the sun-drenched valley. No trace of the library remained.

"Not who," she replied, sashaying up to my side. "Where. I, too, have been trapped by men," she continued, raising a jeweled hand to stroke my cheek. Electricity vibrated through her touch. "I, too, have taken human life. I, too, accept no master beyond myself, though mightier than me exist." Both hands cupped my face, transmitting sulfurous waves of ecstasy that coursed through my body. "I, too, wish to be free. When will your captors release you?"

"Christmas," I managed to stammer.

"I do not know this word," the hooved woman murmured, pressing her voluptuous curves against me. All but one sensation drained from me as if my body were a sieve. "How many turns of your Sun?"

"T-ten," I squeaked. Not manly, but we were alone.

"Good." She sighed, evidently pleased, though she pulled back, one lacquered fingernail poking the underside of my chin. It was all that held me upright. "Then it is you I have been waiting for. I will not devour you, as I have the other wretches, even if only a little. You will take me with you."

"You mean the book?" I asked, trying to avert my gaze from her bottomless, black eyes.

"My prison," she confirmed. "Give it to your enemies, and they shall never be found. When I have consumed enough, I will teach you how to free me."

"And what happens then?" I demanded. The less of her in contact with me, the more faculties I seemed to retain. It wasn't difficult to imagine what this creature would do. Still, I said, "You kill me?"

Her smile was a shark's. "All men die, lover." She caressed my cheek again, and I swore I could feel her robbing my wits.

It struck me: Drugs weren't felling the law library's patrons. She was.

"Yes, I will take your life," she said. "But before I do, you will truly live. Bed your women, then give them to me. Feed me all who stand in your way. Have all you've ever wished, and still, you will come to me, begging for my kiss. Your last kiss. Such is your nature. The whole world could be yours, and you will find no greater joy than my embrace."

I wondered what might happen if I refused. But not really. I was thinking of the prosecutor and the judge. The weeping, sanctimonious slobs jabbing fingers at me during my sentencing hearing. There was no shortage of people in the world I could do without.

"Yes," I told her.

I blinked and was staring at obscure fiction anthologies sandwiched between adult comic books whose racy images had been torn out. The leatherbound book was warm in my hand. Drool dampened the lapel of my khaki shirt. I returned to the circulation desk to find Gerry tapping away at his keyboard, pointedly ignoring me as he did whenever I chastised him. Extending the book, I said, "Here, Gerry. Have a look. You won't believe the ending."

WHERE'S MY MEDS?
ANDREW J. PIXTON

The two young men look ragged on the front porch bench, tired and torn. Pablo notes the time on the intake clipboard and addresses the first. "Alright, let's get you guys inside where it's warm and safe. What's your name, sir?"

"Michael," the man says. "I'm hurting all over. Please, hurry." He's trembling and twitching. He gives Pablo his last name and birthdate.

Pablo asks, "What have you used in the last three days?"

"Fentanyl and m-meth," he's stuttering and shivering, even under layers of clothes and the overhead heat lamp. "But it's not that. I'm becoming a monster. Please, you have to get my meds—if not, I'll hurt people... d-don't want to eat you."

"Sorry it's so rough. We'll move as fast as we can."

The next man wears only a hospital gown. Pablo asks the same questions, and he says, "Call me Josh. I'm in a similar situation to that guy, except I'm Jesus God, and if you don't let me in by midnight the world will end."

"Noted." Pablo abbreviates the rest of his info. "Thanks for the warnings, fellas. We have beds available, so give us a few minutes and we'll get you in."

Pablo badges himself back inside, making sure the doors lock behind. At the front desk he says, "Alright Swingshift, my detox A-team, both of these guys are in a drug-induced psychosis. Or it's schizophrenia, I can never tell. Anyway, they're withdrawing pretty hard so lots of patience with them. I'll take the first if someone else handles the second."

Sheryl chirps, "I'll get him."

"I'll do the contraband checks," Donna says.

The little plug-in heater warms the small intake office. Scribbling through the paperwork with an efficiency born out of years in this field, Pablo blows through the demographics before getting to medical needs. Michael, the so-called monster, sits across the intake desk shuddering. "Listen, my only medical need is my meds. If I don't get them I'll turn—become dangerous. The drugs hold it down, mostly, but my meds are the real lifesaver. Can you get them now?"

Pablo clicks the pen thinking about how short-staffed they are. "It's an hour till the pharmacies close. Is a prescription already in?"

Michael grips the table with white knuckle urgency. "I don't know. Please get them! It's going to be really bad, you've no idea the danger we're all in."

"What meds are we looking for?"

"They'll know." Michael is clenching and unclenching his teeth, like fighting his own body. "They've got all the files. Just s-say it's for my monster syndrome or s-something."

"Let's call them now." Pablo increasingly doesn't think there are any meds. He dials the nearest pharmacy. They have prescriptions for him which Pablo doesn't recognize and could fast track it, but when Pablo asks about the cost they say Michael's Medicaid isn't going through. Probably it's been shut off from a missed review.

Pablo hangs up and says, "Sorry man. We can probably figure it out tomorrow, but it doesn't look like it's happening tonight."

"But it has to be tonight," Michael's voice escalates. "These places are always f-fucking with me. Call them back and t-tell them—"

Pablo holds up a hand. "I hear you, and I'll do what I can, but I also want us to have realistic expectations."

"Prleslsyuhvet. CALL THEM BACK!" Michael is now only coherent when yelling.

Pablo doesn't escalate with him, it's not about him. Just the misery talking.

"Pleesdsninst."

"We can give you Benadryl and pain relief, and some sleepy tea till tomorrow." He's shivering violently by the time Brenda hands him the bedtime relief. He forces it down then Brenda helps Pablo walk him to the intake dorm on a cot near Johnny. "He's going to make a lot of noise. Why don't we put Josh in this one, since he seems quieter, and Michael in that one?" He nods at an empty spot in the opposite corner, leaving two in between them on either side.

"Runsyoubetterunnnssssddd."

Setting him down on the cot is a struggle with his fit.

He mumbles, "I'm ssso sssssorry."

Brenda assures him, "You don't have to apologize. It's not like you chose to be this sick."

Pablo adds, "Morning's going to be better for you. Sorry, man."

Sure enough, Josh is bright and full of divine pronouncements in between mundane complaints. Pablo, now at the front desk, only hears Sheryl respond, "You're Jesus? I love Jesus, he helped me with my own recovery."

"That was me!"

The staff all laugh.

The evening gives way to pen scratches and keyboard crackles, laundry machines swish and roil in the closet across the lobby from them. Desk phones ring every minute from people trying to schedule a bed. After many more calls, Pablo makes no headway figuring out Michael's Medicaid woes. He'll be lucky to get it sorted out even the next day. Healthcare bureaucracy strikes again.

"Can someone shut him up?!" The yell startles the staff. Johnny stands in the open doorway of the intake dorm. "I can't sleep with him making all that noise."

"He's really going through it," Donna says while switching out the laundry clothes nearby.

"Well I'm going through it, too!"

"Then you know how hard withdrawing is."

Sheryl adds, "We can give you earplugs, and you can focus on yourself."

Johnny growls and goes into a bathroom next to her then slams the door.

Desk phones ring over and over, contributing to the din. Pablo expects Johnny to continue yelling about it but instead he goes back into the dorm after leaving the bathroom.

But now they hear someone in the dorm squirming and bumping around, like a seizure.

"Fucking hell," Pablo jumps up and runs. In the corner of the room, Michael is thrashing and foaming. Josh is loudly praying in the corner, casting out devils. At least that one's safe.

Pablo adjusts a pillow to buffer Michael's head with Brenda's help. Donna is calling 911. Most seizures look scarier than they are, the biggest danger is injury from sudden movement. But the staff don't take risks, not with clients entrusted into their care.

Yet, as they care for this pummeling person, his movements grow more violent, grabbing and clawing at them till they back away. He's... snarling? Pablo sees that his arms and legs are a lot hairier than before, shaggy even. Maybe he'd not noticed, but the man definitely had no beard when he'd arrived half an hour before.

"What the..." Donna is wide-eyed.

Brenda is speechless.

Pablo says nothing. Questions can come later. He runs for extra pillows, towels, whatever. While hurriedly grabbing an armful in the closet behind the desk, he tells Sheryl to be ready to let first responders in as Michael is seizing. By the time he returns—maybe six seconds later, tops—Brenda and Donna stand in horror, hands over mouths.

Michael doesn't look like Michael anymore. He'd somehow ripped his shirt, more beast than man. A semblance of a human face is still there but is fading fast.

Now it's Pablo's turn to be speechless. Brenda and Donna grab Pablo and pull him out of the dorm. Closing the door, they approach the desk where Sheryl is shouldering a desk phone while other phone lines ring. She casts a concerned look at them.

"Sheryl, we have to-to—" Brenda begins sobbing.

Sheryl jumps up to console her, "Honey what's wrong? What happened with the seizure?"

"Shit is flying off the walls is what happened," Donna says. She's hyperventilating.

Pablo calls 911 then hangs up, they're already on the way. But they're expecting a seizure. "How can we explain this?" He gestures toward the dorm.

There's loud banging on the door separating the staff from the dorm. Johnny shouts from within, "SOMEBODY HELP ME! LET ME OUT!"

Sheryl approaches, and Pablo shouts for her to wait.

"Why?" she responds. "Our clients need us."

He stutters then ends up saying, "You had to be there."

Johnny's yells turn into screams, which give way to gurgles. Then those also fade into silence. Blood pools out from underneath the pastel painted door.

Now Sheryl gasps in horror, Donna screams.

A heavy pause.

The doorknob begins to turn but slips back into place after a second. Then the knob begins rotating again, stops, stays, and finally slips back. The staff hold their collective breath. The metallic door shifts in its frame as if from a weight being pushed against it, and the door shudders then stops. There's a growl so deep the door reverberates.

Pablo snaps out of it, grabbing a weapon: scissors from the desk. But what good would they be against a... a monster?

Sheryl grabs a Bible then turns, wide eyed, to Pablo. "What about Josh? We have to get him out of there."

"I don't think we can," Pablo says, thinking Josh is already gone.

"What are we supposed to do then, leave him in there?" her voice rises to shrill tones.

"Security cameras!" Donna shouts.

Pablo goes to the computer and brings up the camera for that room. He zeroes in on the door in the corner. Johnny is there. Even with the low-definition zoom, the blood splatter is clear enough in the grainy black and white footage. The man's stomach and throat are torn wide open. Josh isn't far off, sitting against the wall. Beyond that his condition isn't clear. But Pablo feels a chill when he realizes the monster isn't in view.

"Where is it?" Pablo says, breathless.

"Where is what?" Sheryl sounds exasperated. "What's in there?"

"Michael turned into a monster—like in a movie—right in front of us," Brenda says. Her voice cracks a little, "But they'll shoot him. Whatever is happening to him, deep down he's still Michael."

"I'll tell 911 there's a shooter." Donna begins dialing. "Or—a-a bear."

"Can we ask for tranquilizers?" Brenda asks.

"We don't know those work on these... things," Pablo says, pacing. "Look, I want to save him too. He's sick, like anybody else, but if we hold off on stopping him, we risk all our other clients' lives, not to mention our own."

"You're right," Sheryl says. "But where is he now?"

Staff huddle in around the computer. Pablo zooms out and scans the room. The camera is affixed to a ceiling corner and has blindspots.

"We should leave," Brenda says, and gulps. "We can't save them."

"No," Pablo whispers as his gut sinks. "Look at the window. It's faint, but you can see it's shattered."

Hands fly to mouths again. Eyes widen.

Pablo hates the lack of control, it's dooming them. He clicks out of that camera view and back to the multi-panel. At first glance, it's all the same glitchy grayscale squares of incomplete views.

"I'm sorry," Donna says. She's backing away toward the front doors. "I have kids depending on me. I can't stay." Then, "I shouldn't even be here."

"But if it's outside we can't leave," Sheryl says and Donna stops. "So what do we do? This wasn't in the active shooter drill."

Everyone looks at Pablo, the shift lead.

"I don't know," he says. "I wasn't trained for this. None of us were."

All is still and quiet. Then the ambulance pulls up outside the front doors.

Glass shattering sounds echo from the back hallway. Everyone screams and runs for the break room around the corner.

They halt as the werewolf, Michael, slides into view at the end of the hall. His fangs are snarling bright with foamy saliva and blood flecking his face, eyes are feral yellow. The only reminders left of this once being Michael are the tattered jeans and t-shirt, all soaked red.

He charges, his claws slip on the linoleum floor, but his pace is savage. The staff flee. As Pablo turns, he nearly trips over the bulky office chair Brenda is shoving at the creature. Pablo grabs the chair and hoists it to point the legs at the creature.

The werewolf slides to a stop in front of Pablo and tries going around, but he jabs with the chair legs. He barely registers his own heavy breathing or his sweat, but his slackening hold on the heavy office chair scares him.

Brenda turns back to help him keep the beast at bay with the chair.

The phones are ringing incessantly. The beast smells of wet dog. Clients are running away to hide. The alarm pings, first responders hitting the com at the front door for entry.

Pablo is desperate for help but not sure what they could even do.

His chair blockade works to fend off the werewolf until the creature rears up and uses its front paws to yank the chair down. They stand face-to-face. The werewolf growls then snaps at them, saliva sprays out. The bark is loud.

They push back at the monster but he pulls the chair to the side, almost getting past when Sheryl and Donna close up that side with another office chair, pushing in to corner and pin him between the two chairs and a wall. He swipes at them over the chairs, snapping and clawing, but they shove him against the wall. They don't dare to let up for a second, but even their combined grip is waning.

Brenda is crying and slackening but still not relinquishing.

Pablo's sweaty hands are losing the battle, arm muscles trembling against the constant thrashing. "A-Team it was nice knowing you," he begins. "But we can't keep this up. Run to the break room and lock yourselves in. I'll hold him till you're through."

Nobody moves. Maybe he'll have to pick who runs first. "Okay..." his voice catches as the intake dorm room right next to them opens.

Josh is standing in the puddle of blood in the doorway, still wearing the white hospital gown. He rubs sleep from his eyes.

"Josh, you're alive?!" Sheryl shouts.

"Doesn't feel like it," he mumbles.

Pablo's arms are trembling so bad he's dropping the chair, both chairs go down as the staff are gasping for breath and stepping back in horror.

The werewolf watches them then turns to Josh, fangful mouth curved back into a growl.

Josh says to it, "Hi I'm Jesus. Well, God, actually."

Pablo shouts, "Josh, run! Lock yourself in a bathroo—"

The werewolf snarls in Josh's face but the would-be-savior doesn't flinch. The werewolf's face scrunches up as if in confusion.

Josh says, "Since they let me in before midnight, the world doesn't have to end after all. Here you go."

Josh holds out his hand, and in his palm are some pills.

The werewolf sniffs and then snaps them up.

Pablo and his coworkers watch, dumbstruck.

Hackles raised, the beast begins trembling and shrinking. It sheds massively while hacking bile on the floor and reverting back to human features. Soon, naked in the middle of a pile of bloody wolf hair, vomit, and saliva is the young man called Michael. Bone-thin and with faded tattoos and track marks on his arms, Michael begins shivering.

The staff step into motion. Pablo doesn't even have to direct work flow as the A-team breaks into the necessary actions. Donna brings in the first responders. Sheryl goes for cleaning supplies. Brenda is getting new clothes and blankets. Pablo takes a discreet picture of the scene then calls Chris, the case manager on backup this week. Brenda arrives with towels and blankets as medical and the cops enter. Pablo stumbles through explaining to a disbelieving Chris over the phone and texts him the picture.

Chris keeps his frustration in check. "Ok, but are you saying Josh stopped the werewolf because he's a werejesus?"

"Why is that the part that doesn't make sense to you? Listen, I don't understand any of this either, disaster *happened,* and we lost Johnny, but everyone else is safe now. We've got to tell Johnny's family, though."

As Brenda and EMS are trying to swaddle and care for the two clients, Sheryl gets permission from the cops to clean up the hair mess. Lacking a secret paranormal team to clean up werewolf disasters, they're still skeptical of that explanation of events. The cops cuff both clients and question staff while the camera recordings load. Evidently, first responders aren't trained on these things either. Pablo clutches the phone between ear and shoulder to continue the call while helping Sheryl scoop the dry powder onto the cocktail of saliva vomit.

A minute ago, they couldn't control anything as the situation had spiraled into terrifying chaos. But now, they're cleaning up the mess. The A-Team held firm, taking care of their people and each other.

RAISING AN ELDER GOD ISN'T HARD

B. ZELKOVICH

I SEE YOU, HOOD UP AND EYES DOWN. I HEARD YOUR Doc Martens clunking up the stairs. Your fourth visit this week. I know your type—shifty-eyed, nails gnawed to the quick, face sallow from long nights and too little sun.

At the top of the stairs, you look around, glance over your shoulder. Afraid someone might be watching, that they might know what you're here for.

I am, and I do.

I could help you. *Should* help you, seeing as it's my job. But even here some knowledge cannot be volunteered. So, though I know what you seek, I keep my silence and let you wander in vain through the stacks.

After three loops, you finally approach my desk. You shiver and shake before me, nervous and addled from lack of sleep. Perhaps a few substances, too. The nightmares have started, haven't they?

You fondle the golf pencils laid out beside little slips of blank paper. They rustle and clink, brittler than bone. But, you don't yet know that calcium snap, nor the weight of marrow. You will by the time the ritual is through.

"How may I help you?" I ask when you've stood there stammering for too long. We don't want a line to form up now, do we? I doubt this is a conversation you want overheard.

"I'm, uh, hoping you can help me find a book?" You whisper. Twenty years ago that would have been appropriate, but now your lowered voice is like a void, drawing the attention of too eager ears.

"Sure." I smile, wide and friendly. I swing the computer monitor around so we can both see the library's online catalog. "What are we looking for?"

Of course, I already know. But, if you can't bring yourself to ask for the book by name, how will you possibly commit the atrocities the ritual requires?

You avoid my gaze when you say, "The Necronomicon."

Years of customer service keep my smile in place. I knew this was what you would say, and yet I'd still hoped to be surprised. So little surprises me these days.

"Ah." I swivel the monitor back to face me. "That title isn't in our system." If it were, you would have found it already. If it were, the world would have ended by now.

You sigh, all heavy with disappointment. Or is that relief? "Could I put in a purchase request?"

I almost laugh, and I can see now from the quiver of your lips that this was your intent. A little joke between us, as if to say, *See? I'm safe!*

You seek The Book of the Dead—no one is safe. I tamp down my mirth and shut down the monitor then step out from behind the desk. I leave a little bell in my stead.

"Follow me," I say, and you do. I lead you through the labyrinth of shelves, the musty carpet muffling our footsteps into something muted. Almost harmless. At the very back of the library, a shelf stands wedged in a corner. There are no windows here. Leather spines are illuminated by a single, flickering, fluorescent tube.

A metal sign dangles from the ceiling on two rusty little chains:

R E F E R E N C E

"These items aren't in our system," I say. "Reference items are for in-house use only."

You step closer to the shelf, the sign creaking above your head.

"The books on this shelf are antiques, so please handle them with care."

That is the library's official line of reasoning as to why the Reference Collection doesn't have spine labels or barcodes. But I know better. If you are desperate enough to seek the *Necronomicon*, you will have to work to find it.

You squint, take another step closer, but not too close. As if you fear a book might leap from the shelf to bite you. An entertaining, not wholly impossible notion.

I turn to leave, which some would consider bold. It's no small thing turning one's back on this particular collection. But I am the Librarian—even these tomes show respect.

"Um," you say.

I stop but do not face you. This is a decisive moment and I must not sway you. "Yes?"

"If I find…"

I count the span of three heartbeats before you find your voice again.

"It. What then?"

I turn just enough that you will see the pleased crook of my mouth. "While these items cannot leave the building, I'd be happy to photocopy any passages of note."

"Really?"

Disbelief is understandable. Could it really be so simple? In a life that's offered nothing but hardship, why should you expect destroying the world to be so easy?

I smile, decades of public service glinting across enamel. "Copies are ten cents per page. Just bring your selections to the desk when you're ready."

You take an awfully long time to find the book. Perhaps that's for the best—there's hardly anyone left in the building by the time you set it down on my desk. I do not touch the *Necronomicon*. It's not the original, human-leather edition—thank Dagon!—but still. My time with the book has long since passed.

It's true! I was once a half-starved teen, furious enough with the world to think we might all be better off without it. Never let it be said I lacked conviction. Though now plied to a gentler trade, my hands know the velvet heat of fresh blood and the force required to snap living bone.

"Find what you were looking for?"

You stare at me, all sullen and sleep-deprived insolence. But I see the truth in your reddened eyes. You have read those pages and know now what you must do.

"Why are you helping me?"

"Because you asked," I say. "And because removing barriers to access is one of the foundational tenets of the Innsmouth Public Library." I smile, no teeth this time. Now that you've read from the book, there's no amount of customer service that will comfort you.

Do you feel the burn of fury, roiling in your chest? Do you douse it with a despair so exquisite that you are nearly overwhelmed with the beautiful simplicity of it? Do you shudder with the knowledge that there is only the book and the deep and the end of all things?

I did, once.

Or will you choose something different? I did that once, too.

I wait, patient and still. The rules are clear: I cannot persuade you, one way or the other. The decision *must* be yours. The book sits between us on the desk, deceptively plain with its soft brown leather cover. The silence drags on and it takes much effort to keep my eyes off of the book. Off of you.

I had no such qualms in my own moment at this desk. My predecessor made copies of pages at my direction, then I took them and committed *incredible* violence. And still, I could not bring myself to call forth the Elder One and end it all.

I find myself hoping for you again. Will you leave this place and live your life? Or will you be the one to do what I could not? Again, I count heartbeats and wait for you to speak.

When at last you do, your voice is graveled in rage. "Thank you for your help."

And just like that, you turn and leave me with an echo of my greatest failure.

I sigh and pull a pair of gloves from the desk drawer. As I tug them on, I call to your stooped back, "Have a great night!"

Then I take up the *Necronomicon* and start the long walk to shelve it. My hands are steady when I slide the book back into its gap in the shelf, steady when I flick the switch and return the Reference Collection to darkness. But my chest shudders with quickened breath as I make my way back to the desk.

You chose life tonight, but there will be others. With each step, I find solace in the fact that, while I failed to end the world all those years ago, with kindness and the promise of judgment-free assistance, I have never failed to save it.

THE SEED
CHIYA PARVIZPUR

It's snowing. Atas walks alone down one of the city's many alleys, gripping a club tightly in his right hand. The handle is narrow, the head round and carved from walnut. Heavy. He's also, as always, got his hatchet tucked behind his belt, the blade hanging between his thighs. He doesn't care if it cuts his thigh or groin. His face, hands, and legs are all scarred from knives and blades. A crooked knife scar runs from his forehead down between his eyebrows, slices through his nose, and bends across his left cheek.

It's past midnight, and some houses still have their lights on. The yellow glow from the homes creates bright windows along the narrow, dark passageway. Atas emerges from the heart of that darkness. Snowflakes fall under a freshly installed wooden lamppost. They land on Atas's head and the ground. There's no sound except the rustling of the club he drags along the ground.

Atas reaches the end of the alley, straightens his back, and whistles. Those who are still awake quickly turn off their lights. The post light flickers, breaking apart the darkness. The warmth from the light's melts the snow dropping on its casing. The sound of the bulb bursting is muffled by snow and silence. The only thing Atas can see in that darkness is the reflecting snow. He knows these back ways so well he could find his way even were his eyes closed.

Atas reaches another alley's entrance. He scrunches up his eyes while tapping the club against the ground. The light in one of the houses still glows dimly. He whistles. The light goes out. He keeps walking and moves into another. In every passage he enters, he whistles, letting the people know he's there. Most are already asleep, and those still awake douse off their lights after hearing Atas's whistle.

The sun hasn't risen yet. There are no signs of dawn. The boundary between the sky and the ground is a layer of snow. Atas reaches the last alley in the neighborhood. The houses' windows face each other. Most of these people still don't have electricity. Oil lamps light their mud-brick homes.

A faint light glows from a window. Atas whistles, but the light doesn't go out. This house belongs to an old man and woman. The old woman plays the Tembur, while the old man chants *The Baba Khushin* scripture. They are lost in their own spiritual world and don't hear Atas's whistle. Atas whistles again, but there's no response. He runs toward the house. He leaps and strikes his club against the window, smashing it. The old man's voice catches and loses the soothing flow he'd had as he recited scripture. The Tembur falls from the old woman's hands. They snuff out their oil lamp.

The old man regards his wife, who has thrown the Tembur and is covering her ears. "Foolish boy," he mutters in a tone only his wife can hear. He clenches his fist and grinds his teeth. "Why all this shouting, huh? There are no thieves here. All my years in this land, I've never seen a thief pass through." In a reverent manner, they kiss and wrap the Tembur in a piece of green cloth and place it on the shelf.

After turning off the lamp, Atas returns to his path and moves on. As he exits the alley, he slams his club against his own head. Blood gushes, but he doesn't pay it any mind. To scare the people, Atas occasionally strikes himself. Most of the lines on his head and face are scars from his own club and knife. People watch from behind their windows. No one says a word. They hope Atas will leave so they can go back to sleep.

That city had no thieves. People farmed and herded their own land, possessing their own wealth, property, and autonomy. Those who didn't work the fields were woodcarvers, grocers, and tailors. Those people were producers. The city was known for its Tembur-making. Several master Tembur makers trained many apprentices, and they sent Tembur not only to their own city but also to other cities. The people of that city were Tembur players. There was no hospital, no government office, no police, no prison, and no school. Instead of school, the children went to the gathering house of *Jamkhaneh*, where they learned to play the Tembur melodies, *Meqams,* chant the *Kalam* scriptures, and tell old tales.

In that city, every elder was famous for a specific Tembur *Meqam*. An elder was a master of the *Sartarz Meqam*, and people would sometimes gather at his house to listen to and learn that melody. Another elder was the master of the *Khamushi*, which no one could play like him. Those seventy-two elders, masters of seventy-two Tembur Meqams, exchanged secrets recorded in a notebook that evolved with the needs of new generations. The seven most important among them, known as the Seven Sages, made the key decisions. Before passing away, each Sage would choose a successor and teach them the secrets.

The secrets and those seventy-two elders had shaped the moral and educational fabric of the city's culture. They had established laws without writing anything on paper and without the need for a court. Laws had taken root in the hearts of the people over thousands of years. The only one who didn't work, didn't play the Tembur, and didn't know the *Kalam* was Atas. It seemed it wasn't in his blood. Atas was alone. He had no friends.

Blood has turned to stone in Atas's legs. Snow has gotten into his shoes and frozen up to his knees. He is cold, but his strong, gigantic frame does not shiver in this weather.

Atas grew up in that city. His parents are unknown. When he

was a child, his parents came from another land and left him in a corner. An old woman, whose wrinkles around her eyes resembled the winding alleys of the city, found him and raised him. When he grew up, he did not stay with the old woman. He left and built a house for himself—a house without a window.

Atas rests his club on his shoulder and walks toward his home. In the depths of the intertwined passages that end at no street, square, or intersection. There are no streets, squares, and intersections in this city. All are alleys connected as in a labyrinth. They could easily lose a stranger within them. Atas doesn't get lost. He knows them like the palm of his hand. He stops. He goes and sits on the steps of a house. He takes a match and a rolled-up cigar from his coat pocket. He places the cigar between his lips. He lights the match and brings it close to the cigar. Atas's face lights up. With each puff he takes, his face emerges from the darkness. It appears like a demon with sharp eyes and a long snout. Mothers and grandmothers say they've seen a demon. A demon that reveals itself in the darkness. A snowflake lands on the cigar and extinguishes it. He touches his face with three fingers of his right hand, feeling the scars. A smile. After a few minutes, he stands up, lights another cigar, and heads back home, singing a wordless and dissonant melody.

Atas arrives home. The snow has stopped falling, and the sun is not in the sky. It hasn't even arisen from behind the mountains yet. He has previously filled his window with blocks and covered it with cement. Inside the house, neither night nor day is distinguishable. He takes off his shoes and tosses his hatchet and club into a corner. He throws his coat into the hallway. He goes and lies down in the damp, dark storeroom.

Afternoon. Atas wakes up in the darkness of the storeroom. He gets up. Nothing is clear in that darkness. He heads toward the hall-way, running his hand along the wall. He sits down. Crawling on all fours, he goes to the corner of the hallway. He finds the oil lamp and the match beside it. The ignition of the match startles the dark house. There is only a rug and an icebox in the hallway. He opens the icebox and takes out a boiled egg. Forty or fifty boiled eggs are piled on top of each other in the icebox. A container full of bread sits on top of them... both the bread and the eggs have gone moldy. He places the egg on a piece of bread and eats it without salt.

Atas steps out of the house, which is located a bit outside the city. There are no nearby houses. The surroundings are empty, and the back of his house leads to rocky mountains. The door of his house faces an alley like the others. People are standing in front of their homes. Young girls and boys flee and head inside.

He begins walking. He knocks on the courtyard door of the first house, but no one opens it. That house has been empty for some time, yet Atas knocks on the door every time. Occasionally, he climbs over the door or the courtyard walls. Just in case. Next to the empty house, there's a small nut shop. Atas walks past it and reaches his hand into a sack. He takes a handful of dried figs. The shopkeeper looks at Atas but says nothing.

Atas goes to another house. He knocks on the door. It belongs to an elderly woman living alone.

"Atas, my son... my child," the old woman says quietly. "I have no money now... nothing to give you today. Wait... next month, I'll bring it all to you."

Atas doesn't respond. He stretches out his hand and slips his two fingers into the small pocket of the vest worn over the old woman's Kurdish clothes. There's loose change inside, and he reaches in and takes it.

He heads toward another door. Before he can knock, the man of the house comes out and hands Atas some money without looking at him. The man quickly heads back inside.

Atas goes to another alley where there's a Tembur workshop. He enters. The master and the apprentices are busy working. Many Temburs hang on the wall, still unpolished. Atas picks one up and heads outside. The master takes a deep breath and lowers his head. His apprentices, who haven't even grown any hair yet, return to their work, feeling dejected. Atas takes the Tembur to a house where a few people are making liquor and wine. The Tembur and music don't serve Atas's purpose. He hands it over to them and receives five bug jars of apple liquor and wine in return. He takes the jars home and heads back outside.

Atas is not someone who can easily be taken down. Two people can't do it. Three or four people can't either. Atas knows how to plunge a knife into someone's chest just shy of half a centimeter from the heart, preventing their death. He can strike in a way that can cut off a finger or even a hand. For some time now, he hasn't kept a knife on him. Instead, he has a hatchet tucked into his pants. Its handle is clearly visible from a distance, reaching up to just below his navel. His hatchet is not like a knife. Once it strikes, it's impossible to hold back or retract it.

Atas roams from house to house until sunset, collecting money from the people. Some aren't home, and some don't open their doors, standing behind them. Sometimes, Atas knocks fiercely on the doors and kicks and punches them. He even climbs over the doors to enter people's homes and forcibly takes money from them. In the midst of all this, Atas injures and leaves four people in bad shape with his hatchet. This way, he makes enough for a month. This is his routine. He waits until his pockets are empty before going back to his job—the job he created for himself.

Night. The people know Atas isn't around tonight. Some continue their nighttime routines as usual. The children go into the passages and play in the snow. The comings and goings between them pick up again. Life in the alleys is bustling. Some gather around their oil lamps, while others sit under the newly installed electric lights. In the miracle of electricity, they spread their tables and enjoy their summer produce. Their spreads are filled with walnuts, fruits, dried figs and apricots. All mingles with the reverberation of the Tembur.

The seventy-two elders have congregated in their gathering place, the *Jamkhaneh*, forming a circle. They engage in conversation and deliberation. They make a decision and leave the place, spreading out into the city and the homes of the people. By the end of the night, the townsfolk go to sleep with fear in their hearts.

Noon. Atas wakes up. A cold boiled egg, moldy bread, and a glass of bitter liquor. Staggering, he steps out of the house. He wanders through the alleys but sees no one. He heads toward the city castle, around which all the paths curve in circular patterns. As a habit, the day after collecting money from people, he goes there to enjoy his usual hot, bitter tea at the teahouse. In front of the castle is a large, rectangular courtyard paved with stones, surrounded by small shops selling fruits, vegetables, bread, and meat. Also nestled there are food stands and teahouses. Atas notices a crowd of people gathered.

Atas sits with his back to the crowd in front of the teahouse. The people rush toward him, causing the cobblestones beneath him to tremble slightly. Startled by the tapping of their footsteps, Atas pulls out his hatchet and, while sitting, strikes, severing one person's wrist. He frantically glances around him, knowing there's not much he can do. Reluctantly, he throws his hatchet at one of them, and the sharp edge embeds itself in their head. As he tries to stand, the crowd grabs him.

Four people have grabbed Atas by his arms and are dragging him toward his house. They grip his arms tightly, pulling him with force, and Atas doesn't try to break free. Blood doesn't flow in either of his arms. He doesn't plead with them. It has been a long time since any words have come out of his mouth. He hasn't even spoken to himself, let alone to the people around him. No one has ever seen or heard him talking. Atas is a prisoner of eight hands and forty fingers. He knows and is certain his time has come. He accepts his fate.

The men are furious. Each man thinks of a specific way to kill Atas in his mind. They want to tear Atas's body apart and turn his house into his grave. From behind, they pound hundreds of punches onto Atas's head. His skull shatters. His knees go weak, but he is still alive.

"Stop! Stop it now, all of you!" an old man cries with a deep voice. "Don't be mad like this... you'll destroy him! This lad's time has not come yet."

Atas's legs grow numb, and his knees give way, scraping the earth. The first four loosen their grip on Atas's arms, and he falls down. Then four more come up, grab his hands and feet, lift him up, and put him on their shoulders as if carrying a coffin.

Snow falls, and the biting cold has turned people's faces red.

Women wait around Atas's house.

The men carrying Atas reach his door and set him down on his feet. Though he's in pain, this time he doesn't tremble—he stands steady and strong

An elder steps forward, bringing Atas water to drink and to wash the blood from his face and hands. Bit by bit, strength returns to him. He stands before his house, his back turned to the silent crowd. With great effort, he turns his head—struggling against pain—wanting to speak, to say words that might be his first and last. Then, summoning all his will, he turns his whole body towards them. The crowd holds its breath, frozen in place. He pulls himself upright, chest swelling, and his towering, fearsome presence casts a shadow over them all.

No sound comes from anyone. Everyone waits, hearts pounding and breaths held, a mixture of fear and curiosity coursing through them, eager to hear what Atas will say, how he will speak, and in what language.

Atas doesn't utter a single word. He only offers a laugh—mocking and humiliating, echoing through the tense air. He falls to the ground.

Some young boys have just arrived, carrying seven shovels and pickaxes. They hand the tools over to the Seven Sages. Then they push the door of Atas's house open. They throw Atas into the hall and clear the way for the Seven Sages. The young boys, who seem to be guarding the door, close it firmly behind them, and the sages begin digging a grave.

The people remember all that Atas has done to them over the years, and their blood boils with rage. A few furious men rush toward the door, shoving aside the young boys. They force it open once again and storm inside. They shut it again immediately. No one knows what's happening in there. Everyone wants to get in, but the house can't hold them all. The hall, the courtyard, the storeroom, the rooftop, the entrance—all are full with people, pressed together, waiting.

The city is empty. Atas's house stands on this side, while far away, on the other side of the city, a petrifying roar ruptures the air.

Huge yellow machines are approaching—creatures made of iron, without wheels but heavy chains, and a massive steel blade at their front tears through whatever stands in their path. Small glass cabins perch on their backs. Inside them, tiny men control these giant monsters. Hundreds of large and small machines advance, swallowing up the narrow and labyrinthine alleys and the mud-brick walls of houses.

These creatures have massive, sharp teeth. Their horns blare, shaking people's hearts and making the ground tremble beneath their feet. Dust settles over the snow, casting a hazy veil across the city. The people have never seen anything like this before, and they turn their heads in awe and fear, nor have they heard of such monsters in any story or legend. Their sharp teeth bit by bit dismantle the old city structures and devour every inch of the central castle.

PART FOUR

RETAIL HELL

"I'm not even supposed to be here today."
Kevin Smith

WHEN DARKNESS COMES
LISA MORTON

GEORGE WOKE UP AS HE DID EVERY MORNING AT 7 A.M., PULLED himself off the air mattress on the floor of his office, stretched, washed, dressed, and walked out into the store. His assistant Maggie was still asleep in the History aisle, so he moved as quietly as possible to the front door, unlocking it and stepping outside.

It was May (although George wasn't sure of the exact date) and the day was already heating up, the sun glaring down on new wreckage in the Book Haven parking lot. The Voiders had gotten closer last night, within thirty feet of his building. They'd left a battered, glassless, pick-up truck in the parking lot. Whether it was meant to be a warning or was just something they'd forgotten, George didn't know... but there was a lot about the Voiders no one knew.

He surveyed the solar lights ringing the roof of Book Haven, saw they all appeared to be intact, and went back inside. There wasn't much he could do about the abandoned truck. The few towing services left in operation at this point were busy clearing freeways and roads. Nobody cared about the parking lot of a bookstore, even if it was the only one still open in this part of California. Since phone service had failed, George wondered if Book Haven might be the only bookstore still open *anywhere*.

He waited until Maggie got up before he officially opened for business. It was just after 8 a.m. In the old days, he would never have opened this early. But now... well, there wasn't much else to do.

As Maggie tied up a trash bag and started outside, George said, "Oh, you should probably know: They left a truck in the parking lot last night."

She looked at him, muttered, "You're kidding me," before shrugging and exiting with the bag. George was actually relieved when she returned a few minutes later. He sometimes wondered why she stayed. Her face, young until a month ago and now prematurely lined, still caused George's gut to twist in concern. At least he'd saved her life, letting her stay in the store when her apartment building's power had failed. She'd spent that night when the Voiders came hiding in a closet with a heavy duty flashlight and extra batteries.

After cleaning the bathroom, Maggie settled onto her stool behind the front counter, opening the copy of *The Three Stigmata of Palmer Eldritch* she'd pulled out of the Science Fiction section. In the old days, George would've chided her for reading on the job, but he wouldn't have had to because she would have been busy checking in books, shelving and alphabetizing, and fielding customer requests.

Now he asked, "Haven't you read that one before?"

"Yeah, but I've decided to work my way through all of Dick again." She lowered her head, returning to the book, her sleek black hair long enough now to brush its pages.

At just after 11 a.m., their first customer entered. It was Lidia, who ran the Brewed With Soul coffee house two blocks away. They'd survived the Voiders for the same reason Book Haven had: In the past, before the invasion, they'd installed solar lights on the roof as crime (*simple, ordinary, human crime,* George now thought with a small, bitter laugh) had risen in the neighborhood.

"Hey Lidia," Maggie said, barely looking up from her book.

An hour later, after Lidia had bought a stack of romance novels and left, George told Maggie he was off to lunch. She nodded and asked him to bring her back a chai tea latte. He laughed at their little shared joke. They both knew there was no more milk and even tea was becoming a rarity.

A lot of things had become scarce since that night when something broke in the fragile lining of reality and let through the indefinable things that would come to be called Voiders. George—like, he was sure, all the other survivors—relived that night over and over: It had started with the sound, at some point just after midnight, of explosions, of shatterings, of crashes. Anyone who wasn't in a lighted area had been attacked immediately. Since most people were in bed, sleeping in their comfortable, dark bedrooms, the first night's number of casualties had been unimaginable. The things retreated at dawn, moving to attack on the other side of the equator, leaving behind mass devastation. Most of the victims were simply never found... or at least not found *whole*. Speculation was that the unseen invaders had eaten them... if the things even *ate*.

George had been home in his apartment that night, up late reading, as he was most nights. Since Ella had left him a year ago, books were all he had. He was halfway through *Vanity Fair* when he'd heard the first BOOMs, followed by screams. He'd instinctively thrown the book down, ducked under his dining table, and covered his head, even though this was clearly not a natural disaster. It was, instead, something *else*.

After a few minutes, he'd risked going after his phone, retrieving it from the entry table before scuttling back to the relative shelter of the dining table.

There was no cell service. Whatever was happening had already knocked out the towers.

The power followed an hour later. George turned his phone to the flashlight app, rushed to the kitchen, and pulled candles from their place in a cabinet. He grabbed some, along with matches, ran to his bedroom, threw some clothes and shoes out of the closet, closed the door behind him and lit the candles with shaking fingers. He wasn't even sure why the candles were so important, but he obeyed the instinct. He sat that way until morning began to break and the sounds outside stopped.

He'd survived... but many others had not. Buildings were in ruin. Streets were impassable because of wrecked cars, some still smoking. He staggered outside and through the rubble, wiping away tears as he saw his favorite houses, his favorite shops, his favorite parks all burned, smashed, uprooted.

He lived three miles from his store, normally drove to work, but today he stumbled across what was left of his neighborhood, expecting to see his beloved bookstore gone...

But, amazingly, Book Haven stood untouched.

At first George felt disbelief, even something like guilt. He unlocked it hesitantly, wondering if something waited within, ready to murder him for his foolishness, but the store was quiet and untouched inside.

It seemed like a miracle at first. But as he talked to others throughout that first day, those who had also been lucky (or damned, depending on individual perspective) enough to survive slowly began to realize:

The answer was *light*. Whatever had attacked had come after dark, and the survivors had been saved by some form of light.

Two months ago, a hardware store a block away from Book Haven had been the target of an arson attempt. George had worried when the perpetrator had escaped, so he'd invested in cheap solar-powered lights and spaced them around Book Haven's roof.

By the afternoon of that day after the first attack, he'd moved clothing, supplies, and food into his office at Book Haven. When Maggie had arrived (she'd hidden in her parents' RV where the lights were all powered by battery or generator), they'd hugged and he'd suggested she join him here. Her family was gone, so she put aside her grief and agreed. One other employee, Abel, had shown up but insisted he was safer at home. He left before dusk.

They never saw him again. They also never saw Book Haven's four part-time employees.

Other people turned up over those first few days, asking for shelter at the store. George let them in... but when the aisles were packed and the store's single restroom was backing up, he realized he'd have to turn away any others. Book Haven simply couldn't hold any more.

Arguments broke out. People hurt each other. George had to defend himself twice after people insisted he take in friends and relatives.

The attacks continued every night, as soon as the last of the sunset had vanished. The survivors huddled inside Book Haven, eyes wide, sure the things would break in any second, slaughter them all...

But the solar lights held.

After a week, those clustered inside Book Haven began to weed themselves out. Some left and simply never returned. Some came back too late, and those inside heard their screams beyond the metal shutter pulled down over the single glass door of the brick building. One night, a group of four men inside Book Haven armed themselves with wooden shelves and fire extinguishers, demanding that George unlock the shutter and the door and let them out to try to reason or battle with the attackers. He did. He found two of the shelves in the morning, the planks cracked and splintered. The men had vanished.

Over time, government agencies managed to get power up and defended, provide more emergency lighting, and restore communications. So it was that the name "Voiders" spread. The official designation for them was NROs (Non-Reflecting Organisms), but the popular name, based on their shapeless, lightless mass (and a play on "Darth Vader"), was Voiders. Beyond a name and their light aversion, nothing was known about them—where they came from, how they'd traveled, what their goal was. Some called them demons and thought they signaled the Rapture. Others believed that they were a by-product of climate change.

George knew only that they would destroy him and his store if he ever let his guard down.

After a while, the population of Book Haven had reverted to just him and Maggie, who'd been with him through recessions, pandemics, and now an honest-to-goodness apocalypse. Over the months, survivors fell into rhythms; some form of order was established. There was just enough food, and just enough business to be able to buy it.

Then things changed again. The Voiders began using tools. That'd been a week ago.

So far they hadn't done much to endanger Book Haven beyond dragging the wrecked truck into the parking lot, but George knew if they got anything like guns—or even stones and a way to throw them accurately—they could take out the solar lights that were Book Haven's salvation.

He found a store that still had chicken wire left and made cages that he wired around each of the lights. They weren't incredibly solid, but they'd hold up against minor missiles.

In the meantime, news began to filter in about camps the government was setting up just outside of town. The camps had 24-hour lighting, security, food, shelter. They were building permanent housing, drilling wells and septic tanks—even bringing in farming equipment to create sustainable agriculture.

"These actually sound pretty good," Maggie noted one day, as they'd hunched over a flyer that had been handed to them by a young soldier in combat fatigues.

"I don't trust 'em," George said.

Maggie laughed. "I swear, sometimes you sound like an old hippie."

"No," George answered. "No. You think a place like that is going to have need for a *bookseller*?"

Shrugging, Maggie answered, "People still want books, probably."

George hoped she was right, but secretly... he wasn't so sure. He knew books made people think, and that made other people nervous.

Sometimes he wandered among his shelves, feeling the weight of all that knowledge and art surrounding him, worried about what would happen if they all vanished one night. That, it seemed to him, would mark the *real* end of humanity, the final loss of its collective soul.

He wouldn't let it happen, would stand against it as long as he could.

Supplies grew harder to obtain. When George asked at the neighborhood convenience store that now served as the only grocery store why the shelves were so barren, the kid behind the counter told him delivery trucks were being diverted to the camps. A few days later, the store was closed.

"So what do we do now for food?" Maggie had asked.

George said, "I think there's one still open over on Adams. We just have to go a little farther."

"You sure about that?"

George looked Maggie in the eye for a few seconds before pulling out his keys. "Well, let's go find out."

At this point they had no car, so they walked. The day was pleasant, but George was out of shape and felt every day of his forty-two years on the three-mile hike. "We need to start some kind of work-out regimen," he said at the halfway point. Sitting anxiously in his store, existing on a diet of processed pastries, hadn't done him any favors.

Maggie, who walked every day, looked at him, raised an eyebrow and answered, "You mean *you* need to."

When they finally turned a corner three blocks from the store in question, they saw the line. It snaked throughout the neighborhood. As Maggie and George stopped and stared, weighing the chances, a man walked past them, heading away from the store. "Forget it," the man said, his face gaunt and clothes tattered. "They got almost nothin' left."

George and Maggie debated for a few seconds before deciding to turn around and head back to Book Haven.

At the store, George took stock of what they had left, mainly a supply of canned goods, bottled water, and instant noodles. "If we ration," he said, "we can make it last for two weeks. By then hopefully there'll be food again."

Later that day, a man wearing a brightly-colored hazard vest came into the store and urged them to come to the nearest camp. "We can guarantee your safety," he said. "There are trucks boarding this afternoon. We leave from the old Metro station down on First."

"I know where that is," Maggie said. George didn't like the eagerness he heard in her voice.

That night, after dark, George was idly going through stock in the Cookbooks section while Maggie played a game on her phone when a huge BANG came from the metal shutter. They locked gazes for a second before glancing at the door.

The noise came again. There were no cries or shouts, so George knew whatever had made the sound wasn't human.

"What are they doing?" Maggie murmured.

"It doesn't matter," George said. "Even if they cut the power and get in, we've got the emergency lights." He gestured overhead at the battery-powered lamps that stayed on, providing dim illumination if the main lights went out.

"How are they getting past the lights out *there?*"

George shook his head, staying silent.

They spent a sleepless night watching the door, waiting, ready to run to the office if they had to. The bangs came three more times before stopping.

In the morning George warily unlocked the door and cranked up the shutter, then saw what had caused the noise: chunks of concrete littered the sidewalk in front of the store.

"So," Maggie said, joining George in the doorway, "they *threw* those?"

George nodded.

They cleared away the mess and returned to the store.

By 2 p.m., no one had come in.

At 2:30, Maggie appeared in the office doorway with a duffel bag in hand. When George looked up, silent, she said, "I'm sorry, boss, but I'm done. This isn't safe anymore. I'm going to the camp."

"Okay," George said, "I understand."

She set down the duffel bag to address him. "You shouldn't stay either. They're throwing *concrete* now. How long before they take out the solars and overrun this place?"

George had no answer. He knew she was right, but Book Haven was his *life*. "I can't leave," he said.

"I get it, and you know I love the store, but... what good is a bookstore without customers? Everybody else has left this area." With that she picked up her bag and stepped back. "Me, too."

He wanted to leap up, tell her to stop, that Book Haven wasn't the same without her, that *he* wasn't the same, but in the end he didn't. All he said was, "Wish me luck."

"Good luck."

She left then.

George wondered if he'd ever see her again.

Two nights later, George heard the sound of chicken wire wrenched away and glass shattering. It came from all sides of the building, and he knew they'd done it.

The Voiders had figured out how to destroy the solar lights.

BOOM. Something hit the metal shutter, and this time it wasn't just concrete. Metal whined as it bent. The shutter billowed in and the glass door cracked.

The power died, taking the lights with it, leaving only the slight glow of the emergency lights.

George fled into his office, closing the door behind him and lighting up his phone, his laptop, and the candles he had stored there. He crouched on the floor, his phone-flashlight pointed at the door. A huge smash told him the glass door had been shattered. A few seconds later, he heard the sounds of the emergency lights being destroyed.

Then came a sound George knew he would never forget: paper fluttering as books were thrown—thousands, *millions* of pages being hurled at once, spines colliding as the shelves were swept.

All of those dreams, George thought. *All of that precious knowledge just... gone.*

He girded himself, waiting to be discovered. Seconds later something struck the metal door of the office. It bulged outward as it was pulled from the other side.

The hinges tore loose. The door was cast aside.

George found himself staring into a black so lacking in light that it hurt his eyes, caused his mind to revolt at what it was seeing, almost made him feel as if he'd left his body for an instant before regaining awareness. This was true *alien-ness*; the things called Voiders were beyond comprehension. He raised his phone higher and the perfect darkness recoiled, drawing back with a sound like water boiling over. George tried to force his hand to stop shaking, but ultimately it didn't matter: the phone's gleam was enough to drive the assailants back. Scooting backwards, George used his other hand to reach behind him until he found a candle, which he held up beside the phone.

He knew when the Voiders had retreated not because he could see them, but because that sense of something that overloaded his human circuits abated. They were gone.

George left the office just long enough to find the door, which he moved roughly back into place. It was useless now, but it nonetheless gave him some comfort, a false sense of security. He remained on the floor of his office, drifting off into sleep at some point.

When he woke, he looked at his watch and saw it was his usual waking time, 7 a.m.

Everything hurt as he rose, not because he'd been injured but because he'd spent the night on the floor, locked into tension. He ignored the pain to go out into the store, see if anything was left.

There was nothing on the shelves. The books were piled haphazardly on the floor, waist-deep in places, some with cracked bindings and loose pages. George slogged through the mess, too stunned to even think yet about clean-up, or to wonder if any of it was salvageable.

"Hey boss?"

George looked up at the sound of Maggie's voice, calling in from the blasted front entrance. "I'm here," he managed.

He made out her form, silhouetted against the outside light, taking a few steps in. "Oh... Oh, damn. I'm so sorry... Are you okay?"

"I'll live," George answered before adding, "but I don't know what for."

When she didn't respond, he asked, "Why are you here? I thought you were going to the camp."

"I was, but all the trucks and buses filled up yesterday. They kept us protected here overnight so we could leave today." After a pause, she added, "You need to come. It's not safe here anymore."

George couldn't answer. He was trying not to scream, or wail, or hit something.

"Look," Maggie said as she knelt, picked through the books on the floor until she found some still readable. "We can pack up boxes and take them with us. The camp *will* need books, boss. We'll always need books."

When he didn't immediately answer, she read off the titles in her hands. *"The Great Gatsby... Farewell My Lovely... The Haunting of Hill House..."*

At first, George paid no attention to her, but as she kept reading he listened, and he felt something within him shift. He had a responsibility to the authors of the past and the readers of the future. Book Haven wasn't just a space. It was so much more.

"We'll need some light in here to pack," George said. "How long do we have before the last bus leaves?"

"Three hours or so."

It would have to be enough.

BECOME THE NEW YOU
ALLAN DYEN-SHAPIRO

Chloe raced out of the high school parking lot and arrived at her new job just in time to make her onboarding appointment. The human resource manager ended the session with a question: "Are you ready to become the new you?"

The "old" her wouldn't cut it at the Aventura Mall Nordstrom. Most of the high school girls hired as sales associates were wealthy kids who'd milk the employee discount on clothing and jewelry. She didn't dare admit she'd be putting food on the table, at least until the VA approved Dad's PTSD disability claim. Her bosses would assume she couldn't relate to the upper-class clientele or the owners. Apparently, Nordstrom family members visited often.

Chloe could masquerade well. "Absolutely." She folded her hands in her lap, straightened her posture, and endeavored to ignore the odd crackle in the woman's voice.

The manager's smile lifted her cheek en bloc without the expected dimpling or even the slightest crinkle. Botox? Plastic surgery? It creeped Chloe out.

The woman leaned across her desk and handed Chloe a map. "The owners expect everyone working here to adopt the look they favor." She pointed to a rectangle labeled *Savvy*. "This is attire for petite women. You'll need at least two outfits. On credit—we'll take it out of your paycheck over the next year. Then stop by Shoes, and then Women's Accessories. Before you leave, go to the area in the basement marked in black on the map. It's where adjustments are made. The top managers also have their offices in the basement, but they probably won't need to see you today."

After thanking her, Chloe proceeded to the first stop.

"Chloe?" A forty-something blonde stood beside a rack of cardigans. Her voice crackled louder than the HR person's had as she drew out the second syllable. It sounded like a few hundred of the click beetles Chloe's biology teacher had brought into class had lodged in the woman's throat. "I have things for you to try on. Once you're ready, come out and let me look at you."

Upon pushing through the fitting room's door, she found the outfits hanging, twist ties grouping each ensemble. She slipped into the first: capri pants and a peasant blouse. They looked fabulous on her.

She emerged and caught the saleslady's eye. Boy, did she catch it. The creep glared at Chloe as though she were undressing her, burrowing into her skin. Shit. This was pedophile territory. If she'd wanted to be gawked at, she'd have emulated Linda—Chloe's sole friend as poor as Chloe—and started an OnlyFans account. An inner voice told Chloe to run.

She didn't.

After what seemed an eternity, the saleslady made eye contact with Chloe and spoke. "Acceptable. Put on the next."

Chloe turned back toward the dressing room, but from the corner of her eye, she spied a forked tongue darting from the woman's mouth. Eww. Chloe detested body modifications. Okay, she'd pierced her ears, but that was where she'd stopped.

The second outfit also passed muster, and the woman sent her on to Shoes—but not without a grin revealing the same skin tightness as the HR lady's. Was the map's black area a dermatology clinic? Was this what HR had meant by "adjustments"?

She was getting punchy—of course they'd meant adjustments to the outfits, and she wouldn't need those because the clothing had fit her perfectly.

When Chloe arrived at Shoes, an older man was waiting for her. From a distance, a hint of wrinkles made him seem aged. Up close, they were chasms, surplus flesh folded back on itself. His skin didn't fit. A friend who'd shed a massive amount of weight looked like that around the tummy, but how could anyone lose so much in their face and neck?

No hunched posture. No little-old-man shriveled muscles. And the guy had retained a full head of brown hair—thick like a younger man's, not Brillo-pad coarse from too many decades of hairspray-lacquering a combover.

To her relief, he managed to measure her feet without obvious signs of fetishizing them. But his breath smelled like something had died in his mouth. His voice crackled like the others.

Still, the two-inch heels were elegant and comfortable. Accommodating to patrician trappings was proving easier than Chloe had expected.

In apparel, a Cuban-American clerk about Chloe's age in a leather miniskirt reached across the counter, proffering a bright red crossbody purse. As Chloe grasped it, their hands touched. The clerk's were ice-cold and damp. They pulsated. They pulled Chloe in. Chloe barely managed to avoid dropping the purse.

She'd dealt with unusual coworkers before. She needed the job. She wanted the job. She'd get used to them.

For the first time that day, the shoppers unsettled her. It wasn't their appearance: clothed similarly to the displays, they blended in. More upsetting was the lack of conversation—they shuffled from rack to rack, display to display, accreting bags and boxes. None made eye contact with her or with anyone else. Could they smell her poverty?

They never approached the sales staff. Was the working class below them? When a salesperson came close, they grew jittery—like the mice Chloe had fed to the snake her fifth-grade class had kept as a pet—and moved on.

Was this the way rich folks acted? Whatever—if they were paying her, she could adjust.

A man's voice washed over the store from the PA system: "Chloe Johnson, please report to Senior Management."

The message repeated.

The HR lady had said Senior Management was in the basement. Didn't big shots usually prefer top floors? Chloe pressed the button and waited for the elevator to descend and the door to open.

Nordstrom's basement wasn't what you'd call swanky. It was dark. The emergency lighting buzzed and cast a blueish glow. The frigid air gave Chloe goosebumps. The floor was wet, and a smell like her refrigerator after a prolonged power outage pervaded the air.

The elevator door closed behind her. "Hello? Anyone here? I'm the new girl."

No one emerged, so she shuffled into the darkness. A decay smell intensified. She rounded a corner and glimpsed something moving just beyond an open door at the end of a hallway. An office? As she approached, she crossed a line on the floor, and a light flashed, accompanied by a cell phone camera sound.

From just ahead, the voice she'd heard over the PA beckoned. "Please, do come in."

Did she have a choice? She pushed through the door.

Behind a desk, a man in a blue blazer, white dress shirt, and paisley tie typed into a computer. A plaque read *Senior Manager*.

He lifted his eyes and looked her up and down. "Oh, my! You're ravishing. You wear this spring's fashion exquisitely."

The man was too old to flirt with a teenager but too young for the comment to sound grandfatherly. Chloe kept her distance. "Thank you." At least he didn't crackle. His voice reminded her of an actor in a rom-com.

"I have the picture we snapped of you up on my computer. It's stunning—so much so that I'd like to extend an opportunity. If the duties already offered appeal, you can have them, or—" he drew out the coordinating conjunction as if he were a TV game show host about to announce a prize "—you can just wear our clothing and stroll around the store looking elegant, pretending to shop. The salary would be higher, and you wouldn't need to pay for your outfits."

What was the catch? "Would I have to model underwear?"

"Astute, aren't you?" He chuckled. "Swimwear, yes. Underwear, no. There would also be photo sessions for our advertising."

That's how Linda started. A little image processing, and there would be nudes of her all over the internet. No way. Not even for more money, as much as her family needed it.

And the shoppers upstairs were all afraid of something. She might not want to know what.

"I'd prefer the position the HR manager offered."

"You're certain?"

"Yes," she said.

He raised his eyebrows and shrugged. "Fine." He extended his hand and leaned across the desk to shake.

Her fingers went straight through his. "Are you a hologram?"

A metal ring popped out from the desktop, ensnaring her arm, pulling it down, and holding it tight. Chloe's blood pressure spiked. She couldn't breathe.

"Yes, indeed. Assembled from digital images of the ex-senior manager. And a vocal synthesizer, which I'll need to stop using to join you in the office."

Chloe perspired through the blouse. She tugged at the handcuffs but only managed to bruise her wrists.

From behind, a voice crescendoed, quavering, slurring the s sounds. "You're so, so gorgeous—exquisite in our fashion. A pity you preferred the sales job. Oh, well. We make adjustments."

An arm grabbed Chloe around the waist. The other held a knife to her throat. The fingers were webbed and hairy. The skin was green, the shade of money.

"Please. I don't want to be here."

The creature chortled. "Yes, you do." It slit Chloe's skin along the arms, peeled it back, and slithered its coldness underneath. "Lucky girl. Not every employee encounters an owner on their first day. I'm certain you'll enjoy working at our store. Well, the new you will."

Chloe writhed in pain as she shed her muscles and skeleton. She screamed. Her voice crackled.

CHEF LUCIANO'S MONSTER
CAT ISIDORE

FROM THE BOWELS OF *L'ÉCUME DE MER*'S THREE-STAR KITCHEN, winding past the pantry and dish washing station, past the prep cooks with their heads down and knives flashing, past the *boucher* and *chef garde manger* picking over their goods for that evening's dinner service, came the sound universally dreaded, as pitchy and clattering as pots hitting against one another in the sink: some sucker getting chewed out.

Jules, the *poissonnière*, was the sucker this time.

Executive Chef Shane Carême was out sick, so it was the *sous*, Mark, who told her off, ridiculous corny macho stuff she'd laugh at if it weren't being screamed in her face: *Get your head out of your ass—are you braindead? You think you can run with us? You can't do anything right. You can't do anything at all. You're nothing.*

It wasn't even totally her fault, but that didn't matter. Mark needed someone to yell at, and she was closest, and it was, to be fair, not *not* her fault. She'd left her project underneath the condensing unit in the walk-in fridge.

Because there was no other way out, Jules said, "Yes, Chef. It was my fault. I'll fix it."

The trick was to respond lightly, and steadily, and with no emotion whatsoever. Anger was okay only when directed downstream. Simpering, placating, self-flagellation was no good either—that was weak and girlish, and Jules couldn't afford to be weak and girlish.

"You *fucked* the fridge, you think you're not fired?"

"You can't fire me."

"Shane's not here," he said. "I'm in charge."

"Well, you still can't." She tamped down a mutinous smile. "If the fridge is still fucked when he's back, he can fire me then."

Her plan, pre-explosion, had been to pickle the octopus parts discarded from the *teille à la sétoise* and *carpaccio de pieuvre* prep—internal organs, beaks and skulls, all the crunchy, silky bits full of flavor and heavy metals—in a two-part marinade. First, the octopus parts soaked for three days in a simple electrolyte solution of potassium hydroxide and water, which she'd hoped would leach out as much cadmium as possible. Then, she thoroughly rinsed the octopus parts and stuffed them into a jar with the real marinade to cold-ferment. She was proud of that marinade: brine muddled with preserved lemon and grapefruit juice, pink peppercorn, dill, bright fresh habaneros. It smelled gorgeous. If that wire hadn't fallen from the condensing unit, if its old fraying elbow hadn't touched the surface of the solution, she was sure the octopus would have tasted gorgeous, too.

Mark huffed, bullish. "You're cleaning it up," he said. "And this is coming out of your paycheck."

Her coworkers lowered their eyes as she went to get a sponge and bucket for the fridge. She realized with some satisfaction that they ignored her out of fear instead of pity; as with warring dogs, eye contact was a sign of aggression. But Paolo, the *boucher* who had been at the restaurant maybe longer than anyone, leaned over as she passed by. "He was such a wimp when he first got hired," he said, and winked. "I saw him cry a few times. He's overcompensating."

Well, so was Paolo. And so was Jules.

Like a stream down a mountain: Shane would fix Mark with an icepick stare if anything went wrong during service, and Mark would blow up at the station chefs. And they'd scowl and shoulder past their apprentices or prep cooks, who would snap at the servers, bussers, and dishwashers. The only way to get by was to find someone else to bully, to claw up, to be bigger and tougher than the others.

Jules filled a bucket with hot soapy water and returned to the fridge. Pointedly, she ignored the preps as they threw out food contaminated with broken glass and fire retardant foam, moving anything salvageable to the other fridge, where the expats would crowd up against their hosts and ruin Mark's army-neat layout until the electrician came by.

She wiped glass shards from a patch of floor and knelt down before the biggest splatter of marinade, the one under the condensing unit. Before she sponge-bathed her creation away, she leaned in and inhaled. Still gorgeous, even under the chemical fizz of the retardant. In fact, the smell had taken on another note in the accident, something sharp and crackly she'd never before encountered, almost...

Electric. Ha.

She wondered if the octopus tasted the same way as it smelled—which was stupid, with the preps bustling around her and Mark breathing down her neck. Even if she were alone, nothing uncovered in this fridge would be safe to eat.

But, still, she kept an eye out for any bits of octopus not stuck to foam or glass. Just in case.

Except—there were barely any bits of octopus at all.

Still on the floor, she leaned back on her heels. Aside from the odd eyeball or bit of sinewy gut, the only solids she could see anywhere in the fridge were the chunks of habaneros, peppercorns, spidery wisps of dill. No octopus. Weird.

She felt a displacement of air on her back—a shift in temperature. Someone stood behind her in the doorway of the walk-in fridge.

"Did you forget how to hold a sponge?"

"No, Chef."

She leaned forward, mopped up a spongeful of marinade. A rustle behind her, an exhale—Mark was settling in, maybe leaning against the doorframe. He was in a sadistic mood.

"Bet you thought you'd be making something new," he said. "That right? You thought you'd make something so spec-*tac*-ular that Shane would kiss your goddamn feet and put it on the menu. Maybe even promote you. Nice ring to it, huh? *Sous Chef Luciano.*"

Something new, yes, and even yes to something on the menu. Beyond this—well, she didn't hope for much. The last time Shane had spoken to her alone, he asked when she was planning on retiring, popping out a few kids. She was approaching that age that all women got crazy about their biological clocks, he'd said. Promoting her above the *poissonnier* station would be a liability.

She'd kept her head down as she left his office, but Deborah, the *pâtissière* and only other woman on the kitchen staff, caught her eye, gave a curt nod. She had been in the industry since Jules was in middle school. She shared very little about her personal life.

"Well, unfortunately for you, *sweetheart*," said Mark, "it takes a little bit more than that to run a kitchen. First, you need some brains in your skull."

Jules scowled at the marinade in the bucket—sudsy, inedible— and before she could stop herself, said, "Why hadn't we fixed the lower panel of the condenser, Mark? Who was in charge of checking on the equipment?"

A beat of silence. Jules knew she'd messed up. She made herself keep sponging, shoulders relaxed, like nothing was wrong.

"You've got to be kidding." There was a nasty grin in his voice. "First your dumb ass decides to experiment in *my* kitchen, using *my* ingredients and *my* equipment—that's theft, by the way—and then you have the balls to suggest it's on *me* when *your* idiocy causes a *fucking electrical fire!*"

Her knuckles flexed around the sponge, bleeding marinade back onto the floor, and she turned and snapped, "You know, you're stupider than you look if you think—"

The retort died in her throat. There—in the top corner between the wall and the ceiling of the walk-in fridge, above the frosted steel doorframe: a phlegmy, mottled, blue-gray mass.

The missing octopus innards.

"What?" Mark said, eyes bright. "If I think what?"

The mass twitched.

Jules' muscles jumped before her brain could intervene, convince herself she hadn't just seen that. "Mark, shut up," she hissed. "Come here. Look—"

"Yeah, you don't tell me to shut up," he said. "You, what, think you're gonna fight me? Be a tough guy?"

"No, seriously."

He smiled wide and mean and took a step in. "'Cause I'll tell you, Jules, if you really want to do this, you'd better be prepared to—"

Jules never found out what he was going to say. He smacked the side of the door with his palm and she watched, in rancid fascination, the mass of octopus innards tumble off of its ledge, unfurl, and land on Mark's head with a meaty *slap*.

Several things happened at once in the next few seconds. First, Mark grunted and turned, shoulders squared like he was about to start a bar fight. He pawed at the mass on his face and stumbled back out of the fridge until he bumped against the opposite counter.

Jules stood and followed.

The mass unfurled some more, revealing snarls of gelatinous blue-grey flesh. They reminded Jules of the strings of sticky hand toys, the way they tugged at his hair as they moved, and she was visited by the sudden and unwelcome memory of, at eight years old, biting into her toy's glow-in-the-dark meat.

The octopus-mass's ropes curled around Mark's neck, slipped into his mouth—*by itself, it really was moving by itself!*

Sensing commotion, the other *chefs de partie* approached from their stations—then the apprentices and preps. Deborah watched Mark try and fail to pull the thing off of his face. She pursed her lips and darted away.

Paolo gaped. "What the hell is that?"

Jules went cold, then hot. Whatever it was, she'd made it. Her creation. "The electrical fire," she said. "I think..."

"Grk," Mark said.

The creature twisted around his left ear with a gooey string, probed, decided against going inside. It moved on to his eye.

"*Grk!*"

Jules winced—there was that habanero.

She had a clearer view of the creature now that it had spread-eagled itself across Mark's neck and face. It was loosely octopus-shaped, as if the neurons in the tissue had tried to rearrange themselves back into the form they knew—a central mass of brain and hearts and kidneys, with splaying arms refashioned out of siphons. At the end of each siphon-arm, a beak. Innovative. Something had gone funny with the eyes, though—instead of two there were six, and laid flat on top, cresting the central mass in parallel symmetry. The rectangular pupils gave the effect of the creature having two dashed lines over its head.

Mark's fingers scrabbled over the creature, trying to claw it off, but it was too gelatinous to get a hold of. It flexed, tightening around his neck. Veins popped out on his forehead and he stumbled towards her, an arm extended—*Help*—and his fingers were shiny with marinade, flecks of lemon zest and pink peppercorn clinging to the nail beds.

Jules caught him by the shoulders and said, stupidly, "Hey, let's just stay calm." Her tongue caught grapefruit and dill on the inhale, floating along on the sweet-clear saline that wafted off the creature.

And that fantastic electric crackle.

Radish leaves would complete the dish, she thought suddenly. Sliced into ribbons underneath the octopus, soaking up the juices.

Mark whimpered—a siphon-arm had slid under his socket, bulging the eye. He grabbed again at the creature and a filmy dark burst of ink ran down his jaw. The ink smelled like the ocean. If Jules closed her eyes, she could be back on the Point Grey coastline at low tide, watching the crows gorge themselves on dying bivalves.

"Get out of the way!" Quentin, the *saucier*, shoved her aside and gripped Mark's collar with one hand. With the other, he dug his fingernails into the creature's body and pulled, squeezed.

"Ah!—" He hissed and snatched his hands back, a mess of ink and little bloody cuts. The creature had snipped at him with its free beaks.

Deborah reappeared behind them. "I've got this." In her hand was a kitchen torch, a trusty eight-year-old piece of hardware that had finished tens of thousands of crème brûlées in that time. Mark's good eye caught it and he shrank back.

"Hck," he said. He shook his head. "Gngh!"

"Hold him still."

Quentin and Jules each took an arm. Mark struggled, but more weakly, like he was beginning to trust it would work.

Or, like he knew he was running out of options.

Deborah switched on the butane. She wore the same even, blank look as she did when icing cakes, hands surgeon-steady, bringing the blue flame closer and closer to the creature. Jules wondered what the sizzle would smell like—caramelizing citrus, maybe—and swallowed a well of saliva from under her tongue.

Closer—almost there—

The creature shot an arm out, whip-fast, and yanked at the end of the torch handle and flipped it back in Deborah's hand. She yelped and dropped the torch—the smell of burnt hair scratched at Jules' nose—and brought her hand up to her face but stopped short of touching the seared skin, training overriding instinct.

The creature's arm withdrew, snapping around Mark's neck like a slap bracelet. He clutched at its central mass. He was no longer making any noise. It had slid four of its siphon-arms down his throat, sealing it off. It reminded Jules of the sporadic choking cases involving *san-nakji*, a dish of live-chopped baby octopuses whose arms still wriggled and suctioned as they went down.

But this creature wasn't choking Mark on death-rattle reflex; it knew what it was doing. That was clear by now. It was sentient, acting and reacting, protecting the soft flesh of its body.

Jules knew suddenly what would make it leave.

"Mark," she said. "Mark, *bite down*—"

"Back up, Jules!"

She turned and saw Paolo with a cast-iron pan poised for a baseball swing. He'd been browning trimmed rib roasts; the Maillard residue still clung to its surface.

"Wait—"

The pan hit Mark's skull with a sick wet *thud* and his head snapped back and he fell against the counter, then slid to the floor. The kitchen went very still.

Stillest of all was Mark.

"Did I... did I get it?"

Paolo's voice had gone feeble, kittenish. Jules made herself look. Lots of blood, and pulpy, jellied flesh, but none of the telltale translucent gray-blue.

"No."

Paulo made a little squeaky noise.

"I see it." said Quentin. He pointed to the utensil rack on the wall a few meters away.

Jules squinted. The creature had curled up in the bowl of a ladle, hiding like a sick cat.

"Do we... catch it?" asked one of the apprentices. Jules had never learned his name.

"No, it's—" She swallowed hard. "It's on me. I'll fix it."

She heel-toed to her station, keeping her eyes trained on the creature, and picked up her heavy *deba* knife. She held it behind her hip on the way to the utensil rack and stopped no more than two feet away, close enough to smell the crackling brine on the creature.

"Hello, there," she breathed.

She reached out as slow as a chameleon and lifted the ladle, held it steady. The creature shifted. Its six coin-slot eyes seemed to meet her gaze with an alien intelligence. She held her breath and tilted the ladle towards her until she had a good angle.

She brought the *deba* to her side, ready to jab—

The creature slipped out of the ladle and crawled away down the counter, fluid as spilled water. Jules thrust the knife onto the counter, trying to hit it in its path, but she missed and the blade screeched across the stainless steel surface. She'd have to resharpen it.

The commotion multiplied into a wave. The creature shot through the kitchen, dodging staff as they lunged with towels and overturned bowls. Some panicked, stumbling out of the way. Jules stalked down the middle of the galley. She wouldn't miss again.

At the end of the furthest prep table, where the counter met the far wall, the creature stilled. It pulled itself onto a thick wooden cutting board in the corner. Jules slowed as she approached. She raised the *deba* and murmured, "Shh. It's okay."

The creature turned so that the two dashed-line rows of its eyes pointed in her direction and she swore—she *swore*—those eyes were full of hurt. Hurt, and recognition. It made her pause, knife hovering in the air, for just a second.

Then she slammed it down as the creature slithered away and the knife *thunked* into the soggy patch it left on the cutting board. It darted over the counter and climbed up the wall, siphon-arms working themselves into long tubular suctions, and slipped out a cracked-open window near the ceiling.

While the other station chefs caught up, staring up after the creature, stunned and panting, Jules turned back to the cutting board. She swiped a finger through the juices and brought it to her tongue. It was delicious.

SPRINKLES

M. KELLEHER

Cobwebs cover my face. Anchored to the screws holding my gold-plated, Employee of the Month plaque in place, they drift over my staff photo. They catch the fluorescent lights as they cross my pink and brown apron. The lack of respect is staggering. It makes me suck air through my nose (Daniel's nose, if we're being technical) in a low hiss, pulling Priya's attention from the register. She sees me standing on a stool, dusting, and sends me a withering look. She goes back to balancing the register, and I go back to running a damp rag lovingly over my own smile.

I have a wonderful smile in this photo. It is the smile of a man who knows he has done his best to lead the people around him. It's a smile that says, "Yes, I have labeled everything in the stockroom, the walk-in, and the kitchen. I have improved the timesheet system and streamlined bathroom breaks for my employees." It is the kind of smile only a man who has reached the pinnacle of his food service journey is entitled to.

And I, Jeff Miller, recently promoted manager of the recently ranked "Best Twenty-Four-Hour Dunkin' Donuts in the State of

Maryland," am just such a man. Or... was such a man? Semantics. Don't think about it.

Think instead about the fact that Priya is, even now, pouring rainbow sprinkles into a tub clearly labeled "Chocolate Sprinkles".

I lead Daniel's (mostly) pliant body down the steps and reach out with his clammy, nicotine-stained fingers. I can see they're shaking, but that will stop soon. Daniel has not touched a cigarette in almost four days. It is a record for him, I'd guess. What a gift I'm giving this young man! He has not inhaled anything but clean air since I found him stoned in the walk-in last week.

"Jesus, what's wrong with you?" Priya yanks her hand back from where I (Daniel? Who can say where one man ends?) grabbed her. Bruises bloom on her wrist.

I don't know this body's strength. Can't feel it. Which is natural. Can a puppeteer feel the stage under his marionette as the doll is dragged across the floor? I know I am moving Daniel's hand. Telling his legs where to go. If that's all I get, it's enough for me. I am not a greedy man.

But I do wish I could feel the pointed *tap-tap-tap* of my finger against the "Chocolate" label so carefully applied in life.

"What does it matter?" Priya snaps. She's upset with me. I can tell because she's been upset with me before. I'm familiar with the signs. But she must know, must be made to understand. There is a right way and a wrong way to do things.

"This is my legacy," I try to tell her with my eyes now that I do not have the words. Daniel does not speak anymore. He's lost that privilege, his chapped lips kept carefully shut. When they're open, all he does is scream and scream. Not productive.

"You look... sick," Priya says. "Really sick. Do you need to go home?" Her words are filled with concern—her eyes... fear, I think. She's backing away from us. Inching past pink shelves of strawberry-glazed and jelly-filled treats.

I realize Daniel is reaching out. Palms up. Pleading. I pull back his hands. Force them down. Start resorting the sprinkles into their appropriate tubs.

Priya is looking into our eyes now. Does she see me looking out at her? See my disappointment in the way standards have fallen since I passed, heart giving out behind the counter? Or perhaps she sees my pleasure in this unexpected opportunity to keep things running just so.

She could be seeing Daniel, I suppose. Maybe Daniel's bloodshot eyes are transmitting that same shrill wail echoing in the back of our mind. That howl I keep locked, lodged in the back of our throat. Maybe that's why Priya is still backing away.

The bell over the door lets out a cheery *ding*, and it's Ed. Must be Monday morning. Ed always beats the sunrise on Mondays to pick up coffee and four dozen donuts for his crew. You could set your clock to it. Ed's like me that way: dependable.

"Shit. I'll take care of him," Priya grabs four boxes, starts popping them into shape.

It's a standing order. Why isn't it ready to go? I pull the corners of Daniel's mouth down into a frown.

Priya shivers. "Go work in the back the rest of the night. Seriously, Daniel. I don't know if you slept here last night or what, but you can't serve customers like this... you smell."

She pastes on a smile and starts gathering donuts and crullers, turning her attention to Ed. I can see she isn't getting the right ratio of chocolate glazed to plain, but he doesn't seem to mind.

He's leaning in closer to the counter, and I'm disappointed that someone as steadfast as Ed can be swayed by something as simple as a young woman smiling at him. But that's how the world is sometimes. Disappointing.

I head to the back and raise one of my arms. Do we smell? I can't tell. I can make this body breathe deep, but I can't read whatever information it receives. I hope she's wrong. I used to take hygiene and personal appearance very seriously.

It has been a few days since Daniel and I came together, and I haven't let him leave the store since. I'm afraid of what might happen if we go outside. What if I lose control of him in the parking lot, or worse, in his car? If anything happened to him, where would I be?

No, Daniel will stay right here where it's safe. We'll work doubles. And if he needs to rest, he can quiet his shrieking mind while I mop the floors and wipe down the tables. He can enjoy a rest, and I can enjoy the quiet.

And I'll remember to take better care of him in the future—a promise to us both. I'll clean him in the utility sink, and feed him, and make sure he takes regular bathroom breaks in line with the employee handbook. I pride myself on my relationship with my team. And I have no doubt that, with a little more personal attention from me, Daniel's picture will be up on the wall next to mine in no time at all. And won't we be proud of our self then?

STICK TO THE SCRIPT
PW INTERROBANG

Willy Walls leaned back in his chair, surrounded by three-and-a-half padded corporate beige walls filled with tacks from God knows when. With an ancient TV/VCR combo wheeled in on a black metal cart before him, the hum of overhead fluorescent lights mixed with the grainy sound of the Careerasaur Toys training video's droning introduction. He blinked at the screen as a cheerful cartoonish voice chimed in greeting, "Welcome to your exciting new career as a customer support representative!"

Willy scratched at the collar of his ill-fitting, off-brand polo, feeling the weight of boredom settle in. The video continued, using a flaming PowerPoint transition each time the camera so much as moved.

A poorly overlaid and gruff voice joined: "And now, we're excited to introduce the newest addition to the Careerasaur family—just in time for the 2025 holiday season! Justice comes in all sizes and sexualities. Meet Dinosaur III Esq., the Bisexual Supreme Court Justisaurus!"

A black-robed CGI dinosaur flashed on the screen, holding a

gavel. Its stare was dead, eyelids programmed to "blink." Something about the way its mouth curled into a grin twisted Willy's stomach.

Whip zoom to the gavel crashing down against the cardboard bench, made to appear weathered like rich mahogany.

"No bones about it—you're guilty!" the dinosaur-at-law roared with a voice like gravel in a can. The image switched to two young boys behind the playset, mouths agape with wonder at the legal prowess of their new favorite toy. As the camera rapidly panned away, Willy could have sworn he saw one of the kids lean away to cough. He rubbed away the unexpected goosebumps on his forearm.

A tall cartoon dinosaur in a sharp suit appeared in front of a slide deck, hands folded like Rod Serling's to impart the gravity of the trainee's mission. "As a new member of the Careerosaurus team here at the Cretaceous Call Center, it's up to you to ensure our PAL-eontologists at home are Triassically tickled by their new friend."

Willy winced at the barrage of cutesy nicknames.

"No fossils here—we're the world's leader in cutting-edge, in-demand kids' toys and games for seven years running. We couldn't have gotten there without the invaluable service our Cretaceous Call Center team offers our customers. We thank you." The sleazy dino-toon put his hands together in a prayer pose.

"Most inquiries will be simple. Tracking down a toy near home, guiding parents through repair inquiries... basic stuff." The host paused, their expression hardening. "Some calls, however, will involve a far more *sensitive* protocol—requiring either Dilophosaurus-Level Clearance or Omega-Ward AI-Weapons Authorization. Failure to comply will resul—" Abrupt static cut across the screen, and the video cut out, leaving in its absence an eerie, black-and-white silence.

Lorraine Gibberbisch, his Reverse-Shadow Trainer—the assigned mentor who seemed entirely too bought into the company's corporate culture—pushed the TV cart out of the way. Her strained smile, dingy from decades of coffee drinking, looked like it hurt.

"This next part's all the boring stuff," she said with an exaggerated wink. "Best way to learn is by doing! How about we check out the script and get your feet wet with a call?"

Willy hesitated, glancing around at his cubicle walls. He didn't know why, but he felt like the other agents in their respective hidey holes were listening. They were waiting for him to fail, ready to mock him. He felt trapped and hopeless. No way out now.

Willy adjusted the toy Tesla Cybertruck sitting on his desk—an ugly, angular block the company had forced on every employee. The thing barely rolled. He tried to give it a push, but the wheels wobbled and it tipped over on its side like a sad joke. He sighed, pulling his script binder close before hitting the big green READY button at the center of his phone.

The phone chimed immediately in his headset.

He looked over at Mama Owl Lorraine as she effortlessly wove her headset into her tangled mound of hair, ready to compel him to leap from the nest for the first time and grinning until he met the pavement below. Above her head, a silver cardboard star—a relic from last week's holiday party—slowly twisted in the cold recycled air.

Willy cleared his throat and glanced at the script in front of him, listening to the slight click indicating he was live.

Lorraine smiled and motioned that he needed to speak.

"Thanks for calling Careerasaur Toys, where we bring prehistoric pastimes to the present day," he began stiffly, his mouth tasting a little like dust from an air vent. "May I ask who I'm speaking to today?"

"Donna Samson," came the voice, deep and tar-gritty.

"Hi, Donna," Willy said, unable to stop his nose from wrinkling. Lorraine pantomimed a clownish grin, encouraging him to continue. He nodded. "I'm here to make sure your problem goes the way of the dinosaurs. How can I assist you?"

"Yeah, I got my kid the Justy-saurus for Christmas, and I thought this thing was supposed to have eight catchphrases?" Donna croaked. "It's only saying the one, and it's the gayest one outta all of 'em."

Willy's heart pounded as he scanned through the table of contents, the words blurring in panic. No way the manual had a section for this. He skimmed frantically, doubting he'd ever find anything as specific as "gay phrases."

"Accessories—page 26." "Clearance (Government, civilian)—page 251." "Games (Programming)—page 89." Just before his anxiety reached its peak, his eyes locked on the line in the index labeled, "Homosexuality (Concerns about)"—and a promise he'd find his answer on page 108. His fingers flew, flipping pages.

He began regurgitating the most corporate script he'd ever seen.

"We assure you none of our Careerasaurs serve to push any agenda—whether woke, communist, fascist, trans, gay, Irish, or otherwise," he said through gritted teeth.

Lorraine gestured for him to smile, though he swore he already was.

Before he could continue, Donna cut in with a gravelly drawl, "That's not what I meant." The line crackled with what sounded like rustling papers. "Hang on."

Willy sat in silence, waiting. Dead air—until a sharp, tinny voice blared: "HABEAS CORPUS!" The screech pierced the quiet, making Willy flinch. He sat in stunned silence, struggling to get back to the safety of the script again, now certain he wouldn't find a pre-written solution for this particular ticket.

"Hello?" came Donna's growl, followed by a choked, phlegmy cough. "Hello?!"

"You're losing them!" Lorraine hissed, her inane *smile* gesture growing increasingly more frantic.

"I—I'm sorry, could you play that for me again?" Willy finally stammered into the headset as he tried to process the scenario. He saw Lorraine flap her flabby arm at the poster near the entrance of his cubicle, detailing Careerasaur's proprietary FOSSIL method:

F - ind a way to DIG deeper
   O - ffer Dino-Mite service

S - cavenge for the best solutions

S - tomp out issues fast

I - nspire opportunities for play and creativity

L - eave a legacy

"You're telling me you didn't hear that?" Donna hacked. "The thing is damn near ear-shattering. Here," she said. The canned voice once again wailed through the phone.

"HABEAS CORPUS! I AM THE LAW!"

"Well shit, that's new," Donna said, her voice becoming louder as she brought the receiver back to her mouth.

"Okay, Donna, I'll do my best to troubleshoot this with you. Can you tell me if there's any other phrase it's repeating?" He was stalling, hoping the silence would reveal something.

There was silence on the call again before the toy began screaming, "ORDER! ORDER! ORDER! ORDER! ORDER!" over and over. Willy flinched at the sheer volume, his headset buzzing painfully into his ear.

A struggle of some sort clattered over the line, and Donna began hollering. "What the fuc—" then her voice was replaced by a high-pitched scream.

Willy's knuckles went white as he gripped the mouse tighter and tighter with each scream that penetrated his headset. The sound of something wet and heavy—like meat being pounded—squelched through the line. He swallowed hard, his fingers numb against the keyboard.

Lorraine, oblivious or uncaring with her headset still firmly nestled against her ears, continued to beam at him from the corner of his cubicle, her fingers tracing the smile on her face as if to remind him to mirror it. Slack-mouthed and pale, he stared at her unblinkingly. "Don't forget the script, Willy! Smile as you speak!" she chirped, giving a double thumbs-up.

Willy's throat tightened. "Uh—Donna? Are you still there?" he said, his voice barely holding steady as the noise on the other end of the line intensified.

There was a guttural, choking sound, then a weak whimper: "Pl- please sto—"

The throaty voice of the toy cut her off. "OVERRULED!" it declared, and there was a sickening crunch, like a hammer smashing into bone.

Willy's stomach turned as the silence that followed hung thick and heavy. He stared at Lorraine, silently begging for some hint of recognition, some acknowledgment that what they were hearing wasn't normal.

She just kept that painted-on grin, tapping the FOSSIL poster with her finger.

"Keep it up, Willy! Remember—Scavenge for solutions!" she said. "You've got this!" Her encouragement wasn't working.

Willy yanked the headset from his ears, looking at the device, searching for a frayed wire, a broken speaker, anything that would have played such sick tricks on his ears—nothing. Fish-eyed, he goggled at Lorraine. No fucking way was she hearing the same conversation.

"You're losing her," she muttered, brushing past him to take over his station and tabbing into the conversation.

"Thanks for sticking with us, Donna," she piped up, her own performative smile plastered across her face like she was in a mouth-wash commercial. Donna. Lorraine had heard her name. She had heard the whole thing.

Willy felt his bowels twist.

"I'll let you in on a secret," she continued. Willy was utterly dumbfounded. Lorraine was just sitting there, smile glued in place. Shouldn't this be the part where she called for help? "The Justisaurus you hold in your hands is more than just a toy—it contains one of the most advanced AI programs available on the market today. Interactions are designed to be so much more than simple catchphrases. They've been painstakingly designed to encourage healthy interactions, foster learning, and guide conversations to match the needs of the Very Playful Paleontologist who's engaging with it."

Hands shaking, Willy slid on his headset. Even with the delay of his microphone catching on his collar, he managed to make it just in time to catch the last of the conversation.

"So while this particular Justisaurus may not have performed exactly the way you expected, we are confident more play sessions will help you and your Supreme Court Justisaurus bond like you never imagined you could. How does that sound?"

The line crackled. A *tick-tacking* sounded as though moving away from the receiver, a clacking against tile.

"Donna? Are you with me?"

A gurgling noise burbled forth. A weak cough. Then, silence.

"She's speechless," Lorraine muttered, her hand momentarily covering the microphone. "I know, pretty incredible stuff," she continued to the now-absent Donna. "But if that takes care of your issue, I'd like to wish you a Terrifically Triassic day, and thank you for being a member of the Careerasaurus Universe!"

She clicked the button to end the call, removing her headset and looking over at Willy. "So, off to kind of a rough start, Bill," she said, folding her hands on the desk. "Let's troubleshoot your troubleshooting. What do you think went wrong there?"

Willy's mouth hung open. What went wrong? Did anything go right? His mind reeled, trying to process the sounds—the *screams*— and Lorraine's completely unaffected everything. He felt a sudden urge to bolt out of his chair, run out of the building, and never look back. But his trainer's expectant stare pinned him in place.

He forced himself to breathe, to remember where he was. The room, the call, even Lorraine—none of it felt real. Like he was the only person in the world who knew something terrible had just happened.

"I—uh," Willy stammered, trying to piece his words together. "I thought I heard... something." He watched her carefully, looking for any crack in her expression.

Lorraine's smile remained fixed, and she leaned in, as though confiding a secret. "Oh, Willy, you've got to keep it professional. Customers call with all sorts of issues, but your job is to steer the conversation, no matter what." She patted his shoulder, her touch stiff. "Remember, stick to the script. It's there to guide you."

Lorraine flipped to a page in the manual with an effortless flourish, landing on the exact spiel she had just recited to the customer. The section, labeled "Weapon Systems > Malfunction in Civilian Region," was highlighted in bold, as if needing it were common.

Willy couldn't help but notice the adjacent section titled "Weapon System Functionalities," his hand twitching with the urge to turn the page. Just as he reached out, his phone chimed loudly in his headset, jolting him. He flinched, and Lorraine let out a vapid, saccharine laugh that grated against his nerves.

"Looks like someone forgot to set their line to 'away' after the call," she chimed, a mocking lilt in her voice. "That's a no-no, Willy." She pulled back her sleeve, tapping the watch on her wrist like she was checking the time. "Guess that means you get to try again. Better luck with the next caller! And remember..." she said, pointing to her smile as it slowly stretched towards her ears.

With a shaking hand, Willy pressed the button to answer the call, his gaze not leaving Lorraine's contorted face for a minute. "T-thanks for calling Careerasaur Toys, w-where present day, prehistoric pastimes," he mumbled, his tongue thick and limp in his dry mouth. "Wh-who are you?"

"Uh... this is Tom. Tom Granville."

"Hi, Tom," Willy croaked, glancing from Lorraine to the script and back again. "How can—are-are you okay?"

Lorraine's brow furrowed, her corncob teeth gritted beneath her unmasked exacerbation. She held her hands up in a what-the-fuck-are-you-doing gesture, seemingly knowing no reason for his rising panic.

"I'm... fine," said Tom, hesitation in his voice. "Are *you* okay?" he asked Willy.

A silence passed between them, and Lorraine buried her face in her hands.

Tom continued. "I just had a quick question about a replacement part I ordered a few weeks ago. My son's Justisaurus came with a broken gavel, and I put in a ticket for a replacement, but I haven't heard anything since."

Lorraine snapped her fingers in front of Willy's glazed eyes, nudging him over and flipping through the script book for the section on replacements. She pointed insistently to a paragraph on page 73, her smile gradually morphing into a grimace.

Willy looked down, expecting something about beheadings or chemical burns or sentient toys—but no, it was a simple, straightforward guide to replacements.

He read the paragraph robotically. "Due to some unfortunate supply chain issues, our part replacements have been taking longer than usual," he recited, his voice monotone. "We apologize for any inconvenience and want you to have some rip-roaring fun while you wait, so we are happy to offer a $20 credit for your next Justisaurus toy or accessory. Replacement parts are now expected within four to six weeks of the date of your order." He waited, listening intently for some horror to crackle through the line. Nothing.

"Have I resolved your concern, Tom?"

"Well enough, I suppose," the caller replied. "How do I get the voucher?"

"We are sending it to your listed email address as we speak," Willy replied. He glanced at Lorraine, who was perking back up thanks to his recovery of the situation. "I'd like to wish you a Terrifically Triassic day and thank you for being a member of the Careerasaurus Universe." He hung up the call and pressed his AWAY button, wringing his hands in an attempt to stop their shaking.

"Much, much better, Bill," Lorraine praised him, pumping her fist in the air, a vision of corporate leadership celebration. "I thought we were losing ya there at the beginning, but you turned it right around." She slipped off her headset, hanging it around her neck. "Do you have any questions for me so far?"

He goggled at her Cheshire grin, the rest of her seeming to fade into oblivion—all but those teeth, those jagged little teeth, almost a perfect gradient of yellow to brown. Willy licked his lips several times, feeling the chapped skin, his dusty tongue irritating them further.

"That first call," he said, still fixated on her teeth. "Lorraine. You heard her? You heard—what the fuck?"

Lorraine chuckled, her pupils narrowing to pinpricks. "Well, Bill, we here at Careerasaurus view play a little differently than other companies," she said, sounding exactly like the canned recording at the beginning of each of their customer service calls. "Justisaurus delivers edutainment at each customer's level. It simply sensed the need for a different approach to fun!"

Lorraine's smile strained, her cheek muscles rippling with the effort. She tapped her chipped manicured nails against the script binder with a dry, mechanical rhythm.

"Give it another try, Willy," she said, her voice honeyed but hollow.

Willy scratched his neck as he pressed the READY button. The line clicked open, leaving an empty buzz of static before a voice cut through, jagged and frantic.

"Yes—yes, hello? Authorization Department? Are you there?" The accent was thick, Eastern European, each syllable clipped with urgency.

"Thank you for calling Careerasaur Toys," Willy managed, his voice trembling through the script. "Where we bring prehistoric pastimes to the present day. Who am—"

The voice continued, rattling off a string of numbers in rapid-fire succession, each syllable snapping in staccato rhythm.

"Six-Eight-Two-Nine-Meteor... Combat Authorization and Activation Code..." the voice continued, almost whispering now. "Please confirm authorization for referenced sabotage engagement."

Willy glanced up, puzzled.

Lorraine's smile had vanished. Her face was stone. She stabbed her finger down on a bold line in the script book: "If caller mentions a CAAC, disengage immediately unless you have Dilophosaurus Level Clearance."

Willy hesitated, the voice on the line continuing. "—miners striking, equipment malfunction, suspected sabotage, in Sector—"

Before he could respond, Lorraine leaned over and hit the END CALL button, silencing the line. She sighed, a hint of pity in her expression as she regarded him.

"Oh, Willy," she murmured, folding her hands primly. "I had such high hopes you'd work out. But you see," she leaned in, her tone clipped and brittle, "We must respect the well-defined security clearances in place."

She pressed a button Willy hadn't noticed under his desk.

Seconds later, two men in black suits entered. One of them drew a sleek, silenced pistol, leveling it at Willy's head. The man did not speak.

The other employees were working hard to keep their eyes glued to their screens, ignoring the scene. Lorraine's lips curled back into that unbreakable smile.

"Best to keep still, Willy," she whispered, her tone falsely gentle. Willy wondered if that had been part of the script.

A scream caught in Willy's throat as the cold muzzle pressed against his temple. The last thing he saw was Lorraine's smirk, dingy and unyielding as if etched into her very bones.

BENTALOU CRUSH

RAY VAN HORN, JR.

"I'M NOT SIGNING THIS INDEMNITY AFFIDAVIT, SCREW THAT!"

My client's breath reeks of fried onions and marbled ribeye. He'd been overly generous with his pepper shakes, like he'd been sucking face with a McCormick grinder.

I fucking hate onions.

I hate onions as much as I hate people. Those earning specific hatred include realtors, borrowers, sellers, investors, real estate attorneys and lending underwriters. In the mortgage title industry, this all-encompassing sentiment is shared among its foisted-upon workforce.

My twenty-three years' angst goes a step further, like fading Hollywood typecasts getting the shits of the same one-dimensional role. The money only carries your self-esteem so far. Enough becomes enough once you burn out or burn up.

Sometimes, then, you gotta let rage take over.

Stank Mouth is less generous with my time at the settlement table, considering I have a family sitting in the lobby, thirteen minutes past their scheduled appointment time of 2:00 p.m. The imposition is worsened considering I've been holding a raging piss for more than an hour with my fourth straight settlement on deck. Lunch has been speculative throughout the week. It'll likely become nonexistent, truth be told, since we've booked closings from morning through the times more fortunate folks are having their dessert and evening coffee.

It's Thursday, and I'd really had my heart set on some sesame chicken from Dragon's Fortune. Something to nullify the gurgling in my guts from the morning's Greek style cherry yogurt I must've let expire in my bachelor's fridge.

I've had to talk myself off the ledge vexing over the piling of emails and voice messages since I can see, much less hear our bubbly, single-mom receptionist, Trish, repeating my name to incoming callers. Even with the settlement room door closed, Jack Coville sounds satanic.

Fair enough, since there's been a few nights I've earned that tag.

Stank Mouth is Phil Singer, a notorious Baltimore real estate investor known for flipping the decaying city rowhomes he nabs for pennies on the dollar, and always under a single-member S Corp LLC that changes entity names every thirty transactions. Our monthly closing spreadsheets don't lie. It doesn't matter if it's a purchase or sale: Every thirty transactions, the pass-through changes to reduce Phil's individual taxation.

Today he's dumping a ratty three level on 2004 North Bentalou Street, one in an entire row of derelict garbage homes Phil owns on the block. In my world, "Bentalou" stands for *colossal risk*—potential insurance claim, if you want to get technical. Title insurance may be boring, but it's never dull. This joke is common in this incestuous business where everyone's been downsized together and then hired together elsewhere at least once in their careers.

Phil's problem child of the day is besmirched with a condemnation notice from the city and has been tagged with a code violation issued for property vacancy. Phil hasn't owned the slum rot long enough to do the rehab work and obtain a use-and-occupancy permit as should a civic-minded, real property buyer.

I have friends in sordid places who'd agree I should make it my civic duty to show Phil the error of his sketchy ways. Facilitators of waste removal, you might call them.

Phil's already chewed my ear off, grumping about the $493.42 water bill, pointing to a leaky pipe and the recent citations slapped upon him by the Environmental Control Board for trash, debris and illegal dumping totaling $350.00. Like many regional house hucksters, Phil bought the money pit two months ago, and he's selling the calamity "as-is." Boarded windows, graffiti, and leftover fire scorch marks, all dished for a mark-up profit sixty grand above his purchase price of $17,000.00.

I've asked the owner of Metropolitan Title & Escrow, Ari Bronstein, when we're going to stop dumpster diving for business. Ari always answers with a silent expression telling me the unemployment line is a far worse option.

"The unreleased mortgage against a prior owner from twelve years ago is hardly my problem, Jack," Phil snarls at me. "I pay you people your overinflated fees to make the bullshit go away. Seems like you shysters are torpedoing all my deals lately."

"I get you, Phil," I say, dropping phony sympathy as cover-up to my first thought of jamming the aqua-colored, Metropolitan Title pen into his fat-pocked eye, clicking it over and over into the cornea and sclera while humming a few bars of Hans Zimmer's *Gladiator* score.

I really wanted that goddamn sesame chicken.

Phil keeps every company pen he signs with. Cheap asses are cheap asses for a reason as he snorts through his derisive retort, "I highly doubt it, Jack, or you wouldn't be wasting my time like this, and don't bother quoting me the Maryland statutes. A Signet Bank mortgage from 1997 held against someone who hasn't owned the property in forever ought to be considered paid by default so we can move on without all this red-tape hogwash. I'm seriously thinking of moving my entire pipeline to Treadwell Title since they never give me a hard time like you guys do. They're cheaper, too."

"The prior owners never took title insurance," I respond patiently, wishing I had enough self-respect to stop the closing, open the settlement room door and swiftkick Phil's rotund ass on his way out. Instead, I remain calm. It's not my first rodeo with this blowhard. Nobody else in the office will deal with him—not even Ari. I also have it on good authority Phil's burned bridges with Treadwell Title. Incestuous business, like I said.

"Meh," Phil blurts. "This should've been a laydown."

"The fly-by-night title company who handled the property's last sale went out of business, as did Signet Bank, a long time ago. When we scheduled settlement, I mentioned the '97 mortgagor passing away and hit a dead end. I caught the underwriter in a good mood to get the exception, provided you sign their indemnity letter as the current owner. If you don't feel comfortable with it, Phil, I'm afraid—"

"Fuck it," Phil grumbles, scratching his name to the indemnity affidavit on behalf of the stupidly named Property Barons LLC, which used to be Singer Investments III LLC, and Great Bear Holdings LLC before that—it was thedownright tragically dubbed Hopscotch Properties LLC when Phil first brought his mucky business our way. Loyal customer though Phil may be, I've had enough of his badgering, bullying, and abusive conduct. Cutting off people midsentence has been as much his trademark as pushing for rushed turnarounds and breaks on title fees.

"That's a wrap, then," I say, fighting the urge to choke the life out of Phil, and not just for being the rude bastard he is. The settlement room suddenly reeks of anally discharged cheesesteak.

That does it. *Now* I'm in a killing mood. A slow and gristly cheese-grater facial kind of killing mood. A sinew-tearing gorefest that'd make *Terrifier* look pussy.

"Fine," Phil says, taking his pen and leaving me one of his usual sneers along with a drifting silent-but-deadly. "Scan and send my signed copies ASAP. When the buyer's hard money funds hit, call me—don't email."

Phil gives Trish a nod on his way out, barely covering his scowl.

I swear I want to kill him. Miserable pricks like Phil Singer need putting out of their misery like Starship's "We Built This City" had been buried

It's gonna happen. I can feel it like I can feel tomorrow will be an even bigger fuck fest.

The Schofields are next, and Trish gives them a *Price-is-Right* hand sweep from the reception desk indicating the settlement room. Her saccharine squeaks are as annoying as that geeky ghost Moaning Myrtle from those Harry Potter flicks I gnawed through when I was still married. *Trilling Trish,* I silently call our phone jockette. Her pipsqueak tweets to the Schofields spike my mounting desire to obliterate something.

I can see the couple's impatience through the settlement room's glass windows. They look more worn than excited buying a glitzy four-bed, two-and-a-half bath, brick Tudor down in Maxmillian Acres for $485,000.00. Their doldrums are exacerbated by the antics of two restless twin boys who've abandoned cell phones in exchange for more old-school shenanigans like swatting each other with rolled up lobby magazines. Right now it looks like they're battering each other with *Woman's Day* and *Vogue,* which Trilling Trish brings in every other month.

"Hello, Schofield family," I chirp at them with Ari bouncing through the front door from Mincha, his afternoon prayer session. "Please excuse me for a minute. I'm sorry for your wait."

"I thought the Schofields were our two o'clock," Ari natters at me as I blitz past all of them for the bathroom before my bladder explodes.

"Blame Phil," I tell Ari, stopping mid-motion and leaning toward his right ear. "Not only for his usual brawl tactics but for the olfactory gift he left behind. Stall the Schofields if you can. For their own sake."

"He did not just blow up my conference room again," Ari states instead of asks. He peels off his black suit jacket.

"Send grievances to Karl's Steaks."

"God in Heaven," Ari mutters, wringing his hands like an old lady while lifting his voice to greet the Schofields and buying me a moment to drain the lizard.

I cringe as, while zipping past my desk, I see the red message indicator on my phone console blink repeatedly, mocking me.

"Jack, Carla Haney's called for you three times," I hear to my right as my fellow title processor and settlement officer, Sarita Chaudhari, blasts toward me from her desk, sending her swivel chair into a one-eighty. Her left hand is outright and trembling as she hands me three sticky notes containing two different messages a pop. "These are all the people who wouldn't leave a message and expect a call back today. Except for one who said he has a proposal and you can call him back if you're interested, whatever that meant."

She's tapping with a mauve-painted fingernail at Gene Beckett from Crush It Enterprises.

"Where do these investors get their weird names?" she asks.

My adrenaline soars so high I nearly forget I need to unload.

I'll call Gene Beckett (not his real name) first. He's someone I want to speak to since it sounds like he's eager to set up a deal that has nothing to do with real estate.

You won't find Crush It Enterprises in the Maryland business registry or a Google search.

The dark web is the only place you'll find them: murder wholesalers.

"Carla wants a callback now," Sarita says, all but ordering me. "She needs the per diem interest corrected on 6218 Payson, closing tomorrow morning."

"I have another settlement, Sarita," I answer through wringing molars. I'm in such a state partially because I'm excited to call "Gene" back and partially because I'm going to stain my olive slacks if I don't get away from Sarita. "I've been in closings since 10:30. You know your way around a HUD1 as much as I do, just saying."

"I have my own closings, Jack!" Sarita shrieks back at me. If you've ever worked in a title company, interoffice hollering is just part of the daily-do.

To reiterate, sometimes you gotta let the rage take over.

"To Hell with Carla Haney!" I bellow loud enough to startle our college-aged post closer, Felicia Gibbs, and our funding manager, Joe Stack from their desks. They look as shattered as the rest of us, and now I've scared them shitless. Can't say I feel guilty about it.

AFTER WORK, I GET HOME AT 7:22, WHICH IS EARLIER THAN I expected, giving me enough time to charge myself up for an evening I'd expected to spend watching football in a drowse.

I'm a pet guy, but I have no pets. My little Corgi buddy Rippy went with my ex, Wendy. There's a price to be paid for working in the mortgage title industry, and the bill served me was an unjust alimony payment after Wendy couldn't hack my long evenings, weekend work, and overtime griping.

My temper may have played a hand in the divorce. Semantics.

I think of Rippy every time I write one of those goddamn alimony checks, triggering me to crunch or tear many of them into pieces. I've taken a lighter to two of them before cooling off to write new ones. My bank even called me about the odd sequencing of my check issues.

I miss Rippy's morning licks, and I longed for his evening skoodads that started whenever I'd get home. I long for Rippy's company —but not Wendy's. She could never be bothered to walk him but took him from me, nonetheless, to inflict the same vindictive pain I've been serving downtown Baltimore.

The sesame chicken is a long gone thought as I strain my muscles and crunch my abs. I'm tearing through reverse-lunge, straight-arm pulldowns on the Bowflex, one of the few things Wendy didn't contest. I pound out single-arm kickbacks and rows, tricep-extensions, and abdominal chops. I'm working out to my movie-score playlist. *Mad Max: Fury Road, Godzilla: Minus One, No Time to Die,* even throwback Eighties synth beats from the trash classic *Chopping Mall.*

I'm getting a boner from anticipation. I don't know if I'll crank one out before or after the main event tonight. Maybe both.

No, I don't want any food. I want to stay famished while pushing my muscles to failure so they're warmed, lubricated. I want to come hard and come savage, seeking satiation through blood.

Gene's offer tonight was delicious, and his confirming my prey's capture had me transferring the last of my savings to an offshore shell corporation called Limestone Funding, Inc.

I'll be taking the tax penalties—including the extra ten percent—to clean out my IRA after this, my fourth pay-to-play killing. It will be my last one because it has to be. Who can afford this kind of pleasure on a schmuck's salary? Ari may be generous, and his last three bonuses covered my alimony, but it *is* a schmuck's salary.

Worth it, though. I silence the music and towel off. This one will be extra special.

I could shower first, but I embrace the stench of my opened pores. I'm nowhere near as rank as Phil's butt bomb earlier today, though, and that makes me giggle openly and raucously, like a dam of restrained laughter had burst inside of me.

AN HOUR LATER, I'M PUSHING OPEN AN UNLOCKED DOOR AT 2008 Bentalou Street, two houses up from today's headache sale. Rival gangs have left their tags on the plywood covering the windows of the ramshackle row home.

I flick on my flashlight and flash the beam around an empty space with punch holes and mold scoring down the walls of a living room in better days when someone actually lived here—Freddie and Jolene Holliday. I remember these owners—the ones prior to Phil Singer—from our land-records search on the property. Those were the ones who'd neglected to buy title insurance and caused me a weeklong headache for some ingrate flipper who's closed his last deal in this town today. His last deal ever.

I swing the light toward the staircase on my left, hewn from once proud cherry wood now stained brown-black, blemished by dings and slashes. More spewed mold spans the higher tier of the foyer. Someone, possibly a squatter, has left crinkled hamburger wrappers, soda cans, an unfilled egg carton, and a torn bra of all things, along the steps. There's a teddy bear missing an eye and a drained fifth of Jameson.

The house smells gross—not only fusty but as if someone dropped a pile of shit in the kitchen.

I can tell the odor emanates from Phil Singer, whom my beam catches shaking, whimpering, and no doubt humiliated. He's been hogtied in his boxers, which are stained brown at his cumbersome ass. This is the same ass that's left an offensive wake in our office one too many times.

"How's it feel, Phil?" I ask, feeling my arms and legs inflate with epinephrine. They're pulsing, ready to do whatever I command. The hammer hanging from my right belt loop says it wants first dibs. The retractable utility knife with its pivot-point blade inside my left pocket makes its own case.

With his mouth industrial taped, Phil sounds like he's suffocating calling out my name.

"Ack!" he shrieks through his Uline vinyl muffle.

I also hear the drippage into what sounds like a sizable puddle in the basement. The cellar door is hanging off its hinges, opening a channel to the dribbling. 2008 Bentalou presents another case of neglectful assholes like Phil Singer purposefully overlooking the basics while stuffing their pockets with asking prices quadruple their worth.

"You deal in shit, you *become* shit," I say, smirking into Phil's face. He screams through the tape when I show him which weapon will get first crack.

ANOTHER TUESDAY AFTER
THE END OF THE WORLD

LYRA MEURER

The dripping ruin yawns before me, a throat into darkness. My flashlight struggles against the shadows. What I need is inside, not food, medicine, or books, but something more crucial, the key to life itself. As I step forward, a broken-nailed hand seizes my shoulder. A scream shreds my ears, the convulsive twisting of ruined lungs.

I wake up scrambling for my ringing phone, my heart shuddering. I glimpse the caller ID and groan. Sure enough, the moment I answer: "Hey, Casey can't make it in. I need you to cover for her."

"Lemme guess. She's sick but she's *sure* it has nothing to do with the weird date she had last week with the guy who wanted to bite her neck."

"What? She didn't say anything about that. She said she has a cold."

"Of course she did."

"Well, can you make it?"

"The threat level is up."

"It's only Threat Level C."

"Only? You know they changed the threat system, right? Threat

Level C is what Threat Level A used to be." I've explained this to him at least five times, but it never sticks."

"The map says it means 'Some activity, travel with protection.'"

"You know they changed the definitions, right? Even the colors are different."

"I'm sure they know what they're doing. Look, we need you today. With the threat level down it's going to be busy. You don't want Maura on checkout alone, do you? If you don't come in I'll have to issue a warning."

"Okay, okay. I'll try to show up on time and alive." I hang up. Hopefully that snark doesn't get me fired.

I DOUBLE-CHECK MYSELF BY THE FRONT DOOR. UNIFORM, phone, lunch, water, and a book in my backpack. Gloves, puffer jacket, and snow pants in mid-June, the bite holes re-stuffed and sewn up. Hood cinched tight around my head. Sunglasses and mask. Hunting knife at my hip, trusty shovel slung over my shoulder.

I tug open the curtains to peer out the window. No movement outside. I twist the doorknob all the way before easing the door open and poke my head out. The street is quiet. I slide the door shut, careful to not release the doorknob until it's entirely closed. My house key is in my hand, on a cord alone so it won't jingle.

I scan my surroundings, then hustle onto the sidewalk and down the street. Walking quickly, not running—what I called my gay speed walk in happier times. Glancing over my shoulders, peering at the spaces between houses, stopping at cross streets, alert to any movement.

The thirty-minute walk to work used to be nice, a time to enjoy dappled sunlight and lush greenery. I looked forward to the house where a rainbow of zinnias explodes over the fence, another where the lawn gnomes were always being moved into new arrangements.

These days, the gnomes hold their positions, toppled and fading, and I don't notice the zinnias because there's movement on the porch across the street.

I speed up, craning my neck as I pass. A figure stands in the shadows. Surely they'll wave at me. It's someone enjoying the weather, though how they can in times like—

The home's front door is open—not as if to let in a breeze, but slack like a corpse's jaw. And that shape is staggering toward the light, shoulders uneven—

It's best to walk away as fast as you can. If you get out of sight, they seem to forget you exist. The turn onto 6th Street is near. I bet I can make it there before this one hits the sidewalk.

I cut the corner at the turn, striding across someone's lawn, and my sigh of relief stops in my throat. A red Lexus idles at the intersection, doors open. I smell blood before I see it, splattered from asphalt to sidewalk. Someone was bitten and ran away.

BAM! The car rocks. Over the creaking suspension I hear a groan, the breathless rattle of one who no longer needs air.

My hesitation breaks. I'm running, hardly aware I'm running, worrying about that bitten stranger. Where are they now? Will they succumb, or emerge still human? Who will they bite if they don't make it?

Onto the bridge, past the line of trees that obfuscate the harbor. My head snaps left, right, as it does every time, checking—

Fuck.

White sails are angled toward the drawbridge.

I wave my arms at the operator in his safe, air-conditioned, concrete box, pointing down the street. Either he doesn't notice me or he thinks I'm crazy, because the bells shriek *dingdingdingding!*, the lights flash, and the crossing gates judder down.

As the two halves of the drawbridge lever upward, I see the tourists on the other side stopping, staring, laughing. Sunglasses, t-shirts, shorts, selfie sticks. No weapons.

No time to care. I run up to the barrier and turn around. A ragged shape staggers toward me, one arm curled before the empty crevasse of its torso, the other hanging by a thread. The shreds of cloth clinging to its body are black with purge fluid. Despite this damage, it's already made it to the base of the bridge.

The drawbridge clunks open. The sidewalk shudders underfoot. The boat must be sailing through behind me, but I can't look away. The afflicted can run if they want to. I've seen people die for forgetting that.

If the bridge closes soon, I can escape. Don't engage unless you have to—that's the rule. Any fight can kill you, even inhaled juices—

Voices on the wind. Those tourists are on the other side of the drawbridge, unprotected and unaware.

I want to scream, but rule number two is to never draw attention to yourself. Do I have to fight to protect *them*? The ones who sneered at me, who wouldn't help me in a fight because they came unprepared?

I imagine slimy teeth sinking into bare arms and thighs. It fills me with bloody satisfaction. But there must've been at least five tourists, and if all of them got bitten, statistically, at least one would succumb.

I grit my teeth. My enemy is twenty feet away. The heat of June has taken its toll; the stench of rot filters through my mask, sickly as overripe fruit and dark as earth. I'm rigid with indecision, transfixed by the details that once characterized this person: the glimmer of a necklace sinking into pudding-like flesh, the remaining nails still blue with polish, a stained mat of once-blonde hair.

Dingdingdingding!

The bell is like a starting gun. I run, my shovel raised, sharpened edge glinting. Only hard-earned discipline keeps me from shrieking a war-cry. I close the distance, hold my breath against the stench, and thrust.

Flesh and bone parts, soft as soil. My aim is perfect. Right through the neck, separating head and shoulders. The head falls back. The body sinks with a sigh and a thud. It's done.

I look around for movement. All is still. I inspect my clothes. No splatter. The shovel drips with dark fluids. I'll have to make sure no one touches it and rinse it as soon as possible.

As I turn, the drawbridge clunks back down, the barriers rise. The tourists stare at me wide-eyed as we approach each other and are silent as we pass. I'm too tired to say anything, to think of some pithy way to suggest they take care and stay alert. They wouldn't listen anyways.

Downtown is a bustle of short-sleeved pedestrians, all walking slowly and eating ice cream. They see me in my getup, shovel in hand, and swerve to avoid me—fine, so long as they're out of my way. I'm running late.

In front of a restaurant, a man lolls in his chair, his mouth open to the sky. Asleep, dehydrated, or dead and succumbing? I rush by, glancing over his bare legs and arms for bandages. No one else pays attention to him.

I arrive at the pharmacy two minutes late and panting. I reach for the door—and stop. What is this smear on the handle? Is it—?

BAM!

A bloody hand on the glass, a body bursting through. Cloudy eyes, fingers grappling with my shovel, a face still mobile enough to snarl.

The edge of my shovel finds flesh—once, twice. Thick blood splashes the bricks. The body collapses. It's no one I recognize. The door swings shut with a gasp of cold air.

I peer through the glass, searching for human shapes. Maura's head pokes above the counter, her eyes wide. I gingerly open the door, and say, "Was that the only one?"

"I think so," she stammers.

"Call the clean-up crew. I need to wash my shovel."

Behind the store, I run the hose, sluicing polluted water into the grate in the alley. For a moment, I let my guard down, closing my eyes and breathing out. A long day looms before me: the CZC van arriving to pick up the body, the barrage of questions designed to frame this as an accident unrelated to the ongoing apocalypse, the task of cleaning up the blood and disinfecting everything it touched, and, after this horror, a hundred customers buying bandages and popsicles. Then, after eight hours, I'll fight my way home to enjoy the remaining shreds of my "day off."

In short, it's just another fucking Tuesday.

CUTTING ROOM

NJ GALLEGOS AND NATHANIEL J. DARKISH

Ellibeth leaned against the counter and thumbed through the latest *Rolling Stone*, occasionally glancing up, keeping tabs on the store. She *hated* being caught unaware at the register gawking at photo spreads of Gwen Stefani. Through heavily lined lids, she surveyed her domain: Video Castle.

Over in New Releases, Mikey restocked shelves, their chunky highlights bobbed with the music overhead: The Cardigans *Lovefool*.

Carter—in typical fashion—was nowhere to be found despite his having somehow earned the title of "Assistant Manager." A few customers lingered in the horror and comedy sections while a kid agonized over his video game selection—*Resident Evil* or *GoldenEye 007*? Wes languished in Rewinding Hell, lamenting over the evils of people who opposed the *Be Kind, Rewind* Golden Rule.

Carter reappeared, lugging a bin of clam shelled tapes.

"If those aren't rewound, Wes might snap. You realize that, right?" Ellibeth said.

Carter shrugged and set the bin down. "It's bound to happen one of these days."

"That's the spirit."

The bell over the door jangled and Carter—not bothering to look up from sorting tapes—reflexively said, "Welcome to Video Castle, home of the Rewind Rewards program."

"Oh hey!" Ellibeth called out. "She returns!"

"What?" Carter glanced up, then broke into a grin. "Parker, you're back! How was... Greece, right?"

Parker slid her honey-blonde ponytail into the back of her green uniform cap—Video Castle logo stitched in gold—and pulled it on. "Oh, hi, Carter," she replied. "Yeah, Greece. And parts of Italy." Parker's face brightened as she waved. "Hey, Ell! Long time no see!"

"Hey—" Ellibeth started.

Carter cut her off, "Italy, too? Wow. I bet it was beautiful. Food? I want to hear all about it."

Parker kept her gaze glued to the floor and muttered, "Chickpeas and pasta as far as the eye could see."

"Well, hey, I was hoping for a phone call. I got you that international calling card and everything." Carter poked out his bottom lip, reminding Ellibeth of petulant children denied their favorite candy at the register.

"Yeah, I lost it. Went to call and... it must have fallen out of my wallet. Sorry about that." She clocked in by mashing her employee ID number at the register before adding, "I wanted to call. Really, I did."

Carter rolled his eyes. "Sure." He plucked a tape from the bin. "This isn't one of our cases," he remarked, handing it to Ellibeth.

"No, it isn't," she agreed. Black rather than their standard clear. "No label, either."

Wes trudged to Mikey with an armful of newly rewound tapes, then swung by the desk. "Those all better be rewound, or I swear to God—" he froze. "Wait, what's that?" He snatched the black case from Ellibeth's hands and inspected it. "Huh. A mystery tape." A sly grin spread across Wes' face. "We have to watch this."

"No shit, Sherlock," Ellibeth replied.

AT TEN O'CLOCK ON THE DOT, THE LAST CUSTOMER HAD LEFT, and Carter locked the door after them.

Holding the tape and a bucket of freshly buttered popcorn—by far the best perk of working in a video store—Ellibeth called out, "Showtime, folks!"

Like obedient ducklings, the staff gathered around.

"This popcorn for me?" Mikey asked, already fist-deep in the bucket.

"Um... sure," Ellibeth replied, popping the unmarked tape out of the black case. "What's this?" she asked, noticing embossed white letters on the top-right corner. She held it up for everybody to see the text: 01 CUTTING ROOM

"I bet it's homemade porn," Wes remarked brightly.

Ellibeth rolled her eyes. "You wish. It's probably back episodes of *Jenny Jones* or a home video of Christmas morning or some stupid crap." She popped the tape into the VCR.

The speakers gave a sharp whine and the screen flickered.

Black/white/gray.

A face materialized, and Mikey yelped, sloshing Pepsi on the counter.

"Chill out, it's just a mask," Carter said, lip curling. "Be a *man* about it, why don't you?"

Mikey wasn't a fan of horror or thrillers, abhorring jump scares—hence their preference for indie films or romance. Carter took any opportunity to be a total dick to Mikey, or as he sometimes called them—out of Mikey's earshot, of course—Video Castle's Resident Queer.

"Don't start with your phobic shit," Ellibeth said, shooting Carter a poisonous glare.

Ignoring her, Carter scratched his stubbled chin and peered closer. "I've seen that mask before..."

"Kinda looks like The Haunted Mask," Wes said. "You know, from *Goosebumps*."

Carter shot him a look. "Isn't that little kid garbage?"

Wes gestured toward the screen. "Does *this* look like kiddy garbage?"

The craggy, green-tinted face drew closer to the camera. Latex-gloved hands reached out. The screen shook as the masked figure grabbed the camera, giving the clustered coworkers a momentary view of white-checkered ceilings studded with those bright fluorescent lights often seen in dentists' offices or on *ER*.

"Did you see the eyes?" Ellibeth said. "They're wearing yellow contacts, really getting into character."

Shakiness ceased and the camera zoomed in on pale pink skin—a stomach, based on the belly button.

Parker moved towards the VCR. "Guys... we shouldn't watch this. Let's shut it—"

Wes cut her off and triumphantly exclaimed, "Told you it's porn!" He fist pumped. "Fuck yeah! Porn!"

"Even more reason to shut it off—" Parker protested, finger inches from the eject button.

Ellibeth brushed Parker's hand away. "Don't be a buzzkill, Parker. Lighten up."

A thundercloud settled over Parker's face, but she said nothing.

Tonight, something felt... off. Parker was usually game for anything.

"Um... what's that?" Mikey asked, voice cracking.

A masked minion popped into frame, revealing the rest of their outfit: mint green scrubs topped with a white plastic apron, paired with glossy black booties. They gestured to someone off-screen, brandishing a gleaming scalpel in their right hand.

"Oh shit," Ellibeth whispered.

The camera zoomed out, revealing a naked woman from the neck down. Her chest rose, filling with air—the only hints of life, as everything else about her was deathly still.

"Was—was that... a scalpel?" Mikey whispered.

No one replied.

Without preamble, the scalpel kissed the woman's skin—starting at the right shoulder, unzippering flesh. Sweeping the blade with flourish, the masked fiend created a Y-shaped incision extending from shoulder to shoulder down to the pelvis. Fat globules in the subcutaneous tissues gleamed under the lights.

"What the fuck?" Carter said, verbalizing everyone's thoughts.

Wes whispered, "Holy *shit*, is this like a new *Faces of Death*? I thought they stopped making those." He leaned in and wrung his hands with utter delight.

Bright red blood bubbled up as deft fingers hooked underneath the sliced skin and pulled back, displaying pearly bones: sternum, ribs, and clavicles. Intercostal muscles bulged and contracted with each breath. Steady. Regular. In. Out.

"This can't be real..." Ellibeth said, doubt coloring the words. Her stomach rolled.

Off screen, a machine whirred to life, sounding like the table saws in Mr. Jones' mandatory shop class. The tool came into view: a hand-held circular saw spinning, the blade blurring.

Someone in Video Castle moaned aloud—Mikey, if Ellibeth had to guess, but she couldn't wrench her gaze away from the screen to verify.

The saw paused mere centimeters above the sternum, as if wondering, *Should I?* before answering its own question and plunging down, cutting through bone as easily as a knife through softened butter. White flecks shot up and out, coating nearby tissues with a thin dusting of macabre snow. Blood droplets splattered, crimson gumdrops sticking wherever they landed.

Wes whistled in appreciation.

Bzzzzt!

Bzzzt!

Bzzt!

"Disgusting," Parker remarked under her breath.

Ellibeth shifted in her Doc Martens and peered quizzically at Parker, who'd turned from the screen and had scrunched her eyes shut, a deep line furrowing her brow Parker's *I'm-nervous* tell. The same stricken look she had the morning she took her SAT... and come to think of it, the same she'd worn after a few of her and Carter's spats. Normally, Parker couldn't get enough of the nasty stuff, gravitating towards the *Hellraiser* franchise due to the gratuitous gore—her favorite movie, per her new-hire questionnaire.

After the saw's movement ceased, gloved hands—streaked with gore—removed the chest plate, revealing vital organs underneath. Having taken Mrs. Ruth's biology course—suffering through frog and fetal pig dissections plus countless exams—Ellibeth knew what to expect: a fist-sized heart, spongy lungs, and a network of blood vessels.

All were accounted for.

But not for long.

Scalpel hacked, the woman's arms jerked and twitched.

RIIPPPPPP—heart tore free, still beating. Diaphragm hitched.

The mad surgeon tossed it over his shoulder.

Whooooooooh—lungs followed, tiny air sacs expelling precious oxygen.

Aorta went next. The body spasmed, shook, then stiffened.

Blood spilled out. So much blood.

"What the actual fuck?" Wes cried out, voice high-pitched with sick glee.

Someone handed the masked figure a bucket filled with tubular writhing... *masses*.

The Video Castle crew watched—mouths gaping—as the masses lost shape and uncoiled, revealing their true forms: Worms.

Several heads swiveled towards the lens—beady yellow eyes and razor-sharp teeth smiling an ungodly grin. Teeth gnashed and the creatures let out a chitter almost in harmony: *Eeeeckeckeck!*

Parker surreptitiously wiped away a tear, an act seen only by Ellibeth.

Ellibeth's eyes ping ponged back and forth—video, Parker, video, Parker. What was going on here?

The bucket overturned unceremoniously into the chest cavity, the creatures molding themselves into parts roughly resembling heart and lungs, only as though envisioned by a madman or LSD-driven artist. Once in place, they secreted a thick mucus—the green snot of a nasty sinus infection—anchoring themselves into place.

Ellibeth's skin tightened and a chill shot through her.

Mikey moaned, "Shit." Beads of sweat covered sallow skin.

"Mikey are you—?" Ellibeth started.

Mikey bolted, pushing her aside. Footsteps pounded down the hallway, and a door slammed open, followed by violent retching. Vomit splattered against porcelain.

And if *that* triggered Mikey's gag reflex, what came next would have put them in a body bag.

Plucking a creature from the chest cavity, the sick surgeon brought it up to their non-functional latexed mouth—except... its lips broke open, slurping the worm up like fettuccine coated in fluorescent phlegm instead of alfredo sauce.

"Okay, *that* was fucking gross and unnecessary," Ellibeth commented, looking at her remaining coworkers.

Wes's eyes were saucers. Carter looked grim. Parker averted her gaze, intently studying her scuffed Skechers.

The camera panned down to the body's pelvis. More chittering undulating worms—they'd multiplied into a horde. Some were no thicker than spaghetti noodles, while others had the girth of ballpark franks. A faint, pink tattoo—a rose—adorned the hip left unblemished by scalpel.

Carter leaned in until his nose nearly touched the screen.

What was this video? A joke? Something else? A nugget of unease nibbled. That tattoo...

Eeeeckeckeck! came screeches in horrible harmony.

The gloves plunged between ruined ribs and gripped the creatures, violently ripping some from their home. A terrible keening commenced, and green lifeblood spurted from their stumps, sending up sickly smoke, obscuring the scene.

Seconds passed, filled with trepidation.

What would they see?

Miasma cleared and dissipated.

"Okay, what the fuck?" Ellibeth murmured.

The body—the woman—had vanished, leaving a vacant steel table.

No blood.

No green goo.

Nothing.

Tape flickered.

Wes echoed Ellibeth's sentiment: "Fucking hell."

Parker's eyes were vacant and faraway.

The tape caught and stuttered, freezing in time.

They all sat in stunned silence, grasping for what to say—what to think.

A clock ticked, and through plate glass a dog's bark could be heard somewhere down the street.

Ellibeth's heart pounded in her ears—*thud, thud, thud*—and she wondered if the others heard it too.

Wes—naturally—broke the silence: "That was a perversion of everything sane and holy." A manic grin stretched his face. "A goddamn masterpiece!"

Carter and Ellibeth wrenched their gazes away from the frozen screen and turned toward Wes wearing identical looks of shock. Ellibeth stared at the sci-fi nerd—his lips curled into a fond smile as he studied the lingering image on the small television like a teenager discovering his father's *Playboy*.

Initially rendered speechless, she managed a response: "Um... what the *fuck*, Wes?"

He seemed startled by their aghast looks. "Are you kidding me? That was some of the best practical effects work I've seen in my life, and it's on somebody's bootleg tape. I just want to know who the hell shoved this—this *art*—down our return chute." Leaning towards the VCR, he proclaimed, "Let's play it again," and mashed the stop and rewind buttons in a fluid motion.

A small, white, rewind icon appeared in the upper-left corner of the screen and the tape wound backwards, distorting its images.

Empty table.

Worms.

Naked woman.

Carter stood and blocked Wes from further VCR machinations. "We are not watching it again."

"Are you okay?" Ellibeth asked, noting Parker's pallor—any tan acquired on vacation had left the building.

Tears stood out in Parker's eyes, but her expression was one of pure rage. "What. The. Fuck. Was. That?" she spat, glaring at each coworker.

"What?" Ellibeth asked.

"Was-a-matter?" Mikey asked, risen from the dead. They swiped a hand across their mouth and grimaced. "Yuck."

Carter raised his hands defensively. "Park... I think *you're* the one who needs to tell us what's going on."

Parker shakily rose to her feet, closing the distance between herself and Carter. Her lips curled into a snarl. "Was it you? Did you make this? Is this some sort of sick joke, something to make you feel better because I was gone all summer?"

Ellibeth tried to wedge herself between them, a difficult feat in such a confined space. "Whoa, let's not start blaming anybody for anything here. All we know is we just saw something deeply fucked-up, right?"

Carter glared at Parker. "Sure, if by 'fucked-up' you mean Parker exposed herself to the camera for all to see."

That was it! The rose. She *knew* she'd seen it before.

Parker's first tattoo.

Parker launched herself at Carter through Ellibeth. "What are you saying, you prick?"

Ellibeth held Parker in a tight bear hug, feeling her body shake as Parker continued shouting: "Are you saying I made an amateur porno, flashing my tits to make you jealous? Who do you think I am?"

"Hey," Carter said. "All I know is we all got a good look."

Ellibeth released Parker and pivoted toward Carter, shoving an angry finger in his face.

"We don't know shit. We saw some girl's boobs, but we also saw a lot more than that. Guts. Insides. Some messed up surgery—a dissection really. Worms... or whatever those were. How do you see something like that and think, *Hey, Parker did a nude scene?* Whoever the girl was in the video, she's dead. Making it look like Parker was..."

Ellibeth glanced at Wes with a pleading look. "What would you call it? Clever camera work?"

Wes frowned. "I'd have to watch it again to figure out how they did their effects. So how about it, Mr. *Assistant-Manager?* Can I see how they made movie magic happen?" He crossed his arms and glared at Carter.

"No damn way. We are not watching it again." Carter didn't bother to conceal his contempt. It positively oozed out of his pores.

Wes sighed, muttering, "Fuck you, too."

Parker turned away. "Yeah, I also don't think we should watch it again." After a long pause, she added, "It's too... violating."

Violating? Ellibeth thought. *What?* "What do you mean, *too violating?* That's not actually you in the video—right? So, why do you care about the tape showing somebody's boobs, unless they *are* yours?" Ellibeth asked.

Wes chimed in, a stupid grin on his face: "Well, I know one way to check! C'mon, Parker, go *Girls Gone Wild!*"

Carter lunged and punched him in the gut.

Wes released a comical *oof!* Pain in his voice, Wes added, "You know, to show that you're *not* some kind of slut." Then—to Carter—he muttered, "Asshole."

Ellibeth gently rested a hand on Parker's shoulder. "As stupid as it sounds, Wes isn't totally wrong."

Parker recoiled from her touch and Ellibeth hastily added, "I'm not saying whip out the girls. I'm just saying—" She turned around and looked at Wes. "Can you think of *any* way somebody could do those effects?"

He shrugged. "Sure, if you had a thirty-million-dollar budget feature film. But let's be fair: there are scenes in *Alien* that look rougher around the edges than this flick did... and that's goddamn *Alien*. Could a special effects master do this dicking around their workshop? No, not unless some absolute titan of low-budget VFX has escaped my notice." He gestured toward the black screen. "Did you see how perfect the organs looked? The skin pulling back? Not to mention the mask coming to life! And the fucking worms!" His voice unexpectedly broke and he shook his head. "The more I talk about it, the more I'm convinced that tape is legit."

Carter let out an annoyed grunt. "Are you kidding me? When did you become the supreme guru of how movies are made, Wes? And what are you even suggesting? That some—what—rogue government agent slipped this into the return slot next to copies of *Baby's Day Out* and *Die Harder*? Honestly, Elli, you know better than to feed into this idiot's fantasies. You and Michelle always fall for his bullshit."

Ellibeth gritted her teeth. "That's not their name, and you know it, you asshat. *It's Mikey.*"

Wes added, "And I'll have you know I *actually* know my shit, thank you very much. If you ever actually bothered to have a conversation about a goddamn movie more complex than *Hoosiers*, you'd know."

Ellibeth held her hands up. "That's enough! Listen, Parker. If you want to prove yourself, show us. If someone sliced and diced Parker up, she'd have scars... right?"

Wes enthusiastically nodded his head and Carter scowled.

Parker let out a gusty exhalation. "Fine. But I'm not showing... *them.*"

"C'mon then," Ellibeth said, gently grasping Parker's hand. She pulled Parker down the hallway and swung into the supply room. She shut the door.

"Parker—" she started.

Parker pulled away, tears streaking her face. "You want to see the scars, do you?"

"I—"

"Here! Here they are!" Parker pushed her long sleeves up and thrust her wrists in Ellibeth's face. Two jagged, puffy scars extended from thumb to mid-forearm. "Happy now?"

Ellibeth stared and gently reached out, running her thumb over a raised ridge of flesh: a thin silvery scar over a throbbing artery. "Parker... did you... hurt yourself?"

Parker's shoulders sagged. "I didn't go to Greece or Italy this summer, Ellibeth. My parents sent me away to a psych hospital." She shook her head. "I don't really remember much though. They kept me hopped up on meds." Parker gave a rueful laugh. An unreadable expression flitted across her face. "You can't begin to understand what—"

"You girls done lezzing out?" Wes called out from the other side of the closed door, making Ellibeth jump.

"Dammit, Wes!" Ellibeth shouted. Her gaze lingered on Parker; she hadn't exactly disproven the whole it's-Parker-on-the-video theory.

It couldn't be her though—right?

Right.

Ellibeth threw the door open and caught sight of Wes and Carter's curious faces. The unanswered question hung heavily in the air.

"It wasn't Parker on the tape," Ellibeth said, shaking her head. "And we didn't lez out, Wes. Parker isn't my type."

"Not goth enough for you, huh?" Wes asked smugly.

Parker pushed past Ellibeth and started down the hall. Carter's hand shot out and latched onto her bicep. "I don't believe you. I know that tattoo... I've seen it with my own eyes."

"Get your hands off of me!" Parker yelled.

Carter sneered and replied, "Make me." His eyes glinted dangerously. "You sure didn't mind me touching you before you left on vacation, *Parker*."

Viper-fast, Carter shoved Parker against the wall. A whoosh of breath escaped her lungs.

"Carter, what the fuck?" Ellibeth screamed and jumped forward, trying to pry Carter off the poor girl. Wes followed suit, but Carter had fifty pounds on him.

"Let her go!" Ellibeth demanded, punching Carter's neck and arms.

The point of Carter's elbow rocketed back and caught Wes in the throat. He made a strangled noise and fell woodenly to the ground.

Despite Ellibeth's best efforts, she couldn't stop the crazed Assistant Manager. Carter's cruel hand dipped down, plunging into Parker's waistband.

"We'll see what you got underneath here, you slut," Carter said, panting. A manic glee made his eyes bright. His fingers hooked and he started ripping Parker's shirt up—

"Let her go, you prick!" came a shout.

Carter flailed back, catching Ellibeth's temple. Stars bloomed in her vision, and she fell, catching herself on the opposite wall. A searing pain ripped through her head but even through the agony, Ellibeth saw with startling clarity what came next.

A heavy, steel Video Castle sign sliced through the air and met Carter's skull with a sickening *crunch*, sending up blood spatter that decorated the walls with garish flare. Carter's eyes rolled back, and he collapsed in a heap at the feet of his attacker.

Mikey: Video Castle's knight in shining armor.

Their chest heaved, and they glanced at Carter's crumpled form with a dazed expression. "Are—you—okay?" they asked Parker, breathing hard.

Parker's hair had come loose from her ponytail, and her cheeks were flushed. She nodded and quickly gathered her shirt—giving Ellibeth a momentary glimpse at the pale skin of her stomach—tucking it back into her jeans. "Yeah... Thanks, Mikey." She gave them a look of gratitude.

Mikey shrugged. "No problem. I don't know what that was all about, but... Carter deserved it. Such an asshole."

"You said it," Parker agreed.

Wes got to his feet, still holding his throat. "Did he—hurt—you?" he sputtered, his voice hoarse.

"Not this time," Parker answered.

Everything blurred together after that.

LESLIE—THE *ACTUAL* MANAGER—SOON SHOWED UP, AND flashing lights colored the parking lot. Medics assessed a blood-soaked Carter, applying bandages to the gash in his head while hauling him out on a stretcher with cuffs adorning his wrists. The remaining Video Castle employees gave statements to a bored officer.

No one mentioned the tape.

Once granted permission to leave, Ellibeth slid into her car and instead of starting it, stared blankly at the wheel, and turned something over and over in her mind.

Parker...

Knock-knock.

Ellibeth yelped and Parker's face appeared at the window. "Hey... listen. I just wanted to say—thank you."

"For what?" Ellibeth asked. "Mikey's the hero."

"For not saying anything," Parker answered. She giggled.

"And don't worry, I'm taking Mikey out to the all-night diner—as a thank-you for saving us." She pointed with her chin.

Mikey—wearing a Cheshire cat grin—waved from the passenger seat.

Ellibeth replied, "They'll love that." She knew Mikey had been crushing on Parker for years, long before coming out as transsexual.

"So will I," Parker answered with a smirk. "See ya around."

"Bye," Ellibeth said to Parker's retreating back. Rather than driving off, Ellibeth's mind whirled, pondering what she'd seen, right before Mikey clobbered the hell out of Carter: Healed incisions decorating Parker's stomach.

Parker's car roared to life, wrenching Ellibeth from her racing thoughts. She glanced up and caught sight of Parker through the windshield. Mikey stared out the passenger window, stars dancing in their eyes, not paying their date the slightest bit of attention.

"Oh no..."

Parker, a rictus grin on her face, held up the mask from the video for Ellibeth to see. Her mouth opened and her tongue—no... a yellow-eyed worm—darted its head out and back. Ellibeth heard the horrible worm noise from the tape loudly in her mind.

Eeeeckeckeck!

Manic eyes widened, and Parker brought her index finger to pursed lips.

Shhhhhhhhhhhhh.

CONTENT DISCLAIMERS
POTENTIAL SPOILERS AHEAD

For those ISO "trigger warnings," you've found them.

If you don't want anything that might spoil stories, please direct your eyes elsewhere at this time.

I'll wait...

Okay! Here we go, story by story. Please forgive us if we've missed something. We're doing our level best to help our readers make informed choices about what they read.

I. Corporate Terror

"Why You Should Always Bring Pizza to Meetings" contains foul language, fowl language, and references to off-screen deaths of children.

"The Ghouls" contains references to school shootings / mass acts of violence.

"Cute Aggression" contains hallucinations, night terrors, and imagined dismemberment of a stuffed (but alive?) animal.

"Say My Name" contains references to off-screen workplace sexual harassment.

"Outside In" plays on a sense of office-based claustrophobia and implied depression.

"Wade vs. Roe" contains graphic depictions of nausea and some mild body horror imagery.

"Hemogeny Orientation" contains physical violence and some gore.

"Closed for Maintenance" contains gross toilet descriptions (including references to fecal matter) and some light gore.

"In the Style of Meg Lift" contains no significant content triggers, in the editor's judgment.

"Lost in Can't Remember" contains a pervading sense of confusion, despair, and the other existential-dread vibes of a Kafkaesque maze of business-type hallways and offices.

"Mortal Decay" contains post-apocalyptic imagery as well as mild on-screen body horror (decay, bones, and icky skin).

"Ooh That Smell" contains icky, icky food.

"Mondays, Am I Right?" contains implied cannibalism—but nothing of that sort explicitly depicted.

"The Statement" contains off-screen self-harm / suicide.

"The Dead Are Always Such Trouble" contains a reference to an off-screen bungee-jumping death and is deeply imbedded in the horrors of the pension industry.

"Workforce"contains grievous bodily harm and violence (police / military), coercion (drugs), and employee subjugation.

"Such a Catch" contains on-screen employee subjugation and mild body horror as well as more explicit violence and gore / death.

II. Meet Work In the Future

"Second Amendment" contains a mass shooting event.

"The Sound the Ocean Makes" contains warehouse deaths.

"Alignment" contains off-screen suicide.

"Koschei's Thread" contains character grief & depression, as well as somewhat graphic details of decapitation, surgical procedures, and medical conditions. This story also contains references to gambling addiction and debt and a general sense of nihilism.

"You're Family" contains gaslighting, mental illness, and body horror.

III. Institutional Terrors

"The Devil's Playground" contains implied references to domestic / spousal abuse and incest. It contains more direct depictions of the commodification of sex and of poverty. It contains graphic depictions of violent murder, bodily mutilation, and gore.

"Slacker" contains drug references.

"Where's My Meds?" contains content related to chemical withdrawal. It also depicts on-screen gore, lycanthropic body changes, blood and guts, and beast-mauling.

"Raising an Elder God Isn't Hard" contains mentions of drug use, physical violence, and blood.

"The Seed" contains descriptions of physical violence.

IV. Retail Hell

"When Darkness Comes" contains a war-torn setting, descriptions of war violence, and the destruction of books.

"Become the New You" contains mild body horror.

"Chef Luciano's Monster" contains body horror in the form of mild eye trauma and strangulation and contains non-explicit blunt force injury descriptions and monster-on-human ouchies.

"Sprinkles" contains no significant content triggers, in the editor's judgment.

"Stick to the Script" contains off-screen / implied employee murder.

"Bentalou Crush" contains implied violence / torture but contains no explicit depictions thereof.

"Another Tuesday After the End of the World" contains violence, death, and pandemic imagery.

"Cutting Room" is a bit of a doozy and contains graphic on-screen surgery, parasites, masks, physical assault / violence, blood, gore, self-harm, and explicit transphobia.

CONTRIBUTING AUTHORS

Xochilt Avila (they/them) is a queer, non-binary, and multiracial author who currently resides in Maryland, USA. Their experience living outside of binary labels has fostered their appreciation for the uncomfortable, the uneasily defined, and the unloved. Outside of horror, they love playing video games and tabletop RPGs, getting lost in the woods, and fulfilling the whims of their cats. Follow them on Instagram @xochiltavilawrites and Bluesky @xavilawrites.

Robert Bagnall was born in Bedford, England, in 1970, and stood for parliament for the Green Party in 2024. He has written for the BBC, national newspapers, and government ministers. Five of his stories have been selected for the annual Best of British Science Fiction anthologies. He is the author of sci-fi thriller *2084: The Meschera Bandwidth* and two anthologies, each of which collects twenty-four of his ninety-odd published stories. He can be contacted via his blog at meschera.blogspot.com.

Tim Boiteau is a Writers of the Future winner and author of *The Nilwere* (Grendel Press). His fiction has appeared in venues such as *Deep Magic*, *Daily Science Fiction*, *Kaleidotrope*, and *The NoSleep Podcast*. His micro fiction, "Cherry Blossom," was awarded 2022's Story of the Year at *50-Word Stories*.

Samantha Bryant (HWA, WFWA) writes superhero and horror stories—which one depends on whether she wants to save the world today or burn it down. She is best known for her Menopausal Super-hero series of novels through Falstaff Books, winner of a Jacquis Award for feminist writing. (Well, that and her banana bread—the secret is sour cream).

P.W. Interrobang (Virgo, entrepreneur, mysterious mortal) has collaborated on several poems, short stories, and novellas with their peers. An avid horror enthusiast and fantasy world building fanatic, P.W. can often be found on their back porch, rereading their favorite Clive Barker paperbacks.

Barry Charman is a writer living in North London. He has been published in various magazines, sites and anthologies, including *Ambit, Griffith Review, The Ghastling* and *Popshot Quarterly. Doom Warnings,* his self-published collection of strange and speculative short stories is available in paperback on Amazon and as a PDF at https://www.blurb.co.uk/b/12079076.

Camsyn Clair (they) is a Black, queer therapist, artist, and horse lover from Maryland whose stories have been published by *Elegant Literature* and *Globe Soup.* When not writing, Cam can be found bonding with their Mustang horse, Zen, drawing, or causing chaos in tabletop role-playing games.

Ron J. Cruz breathes and pens fiction in the haunting shadows of the Sierra Mountains in the foothills of California. He teaches English Composition at Folsom Lake College, takes pictures of things that amuse him, and competitively throws darts erratically at a board.

Madeline Daniel writes marketing copy, horror fiction, and a lot of other things in between. Her work has appeared on the podcast *Thirteen,* and she is perpetually at work on a novel. When she's not writing, Madeline enjoys dancing, petting dogs, and using books as a coping mechanism. She lives in Ohio.

Nathaniel J. Darkish, is a horror writer and the co-host of the podcast *Scream Kings*. He has a degree in creative writing from Utah State University and works as a high school English and creative writing teacher. He lives in northern Utah with his wife and two children. He loves board games, ska music, and reading hundreds of books each year.

Eóin Dooley (he/him) is a writer from central Ireland. Having completed a master's degree in cognitive science and philosophy, he turned to creative fiction, primarily to stave off a PhD. This appears to be working. His previous work can be found in *Orion's Belt*, *Red Futures*, *Solar Press*, and elsewhere. His debut novella is *No Sympathy*, a literary urban fantasy published by Android Press. Find him on Bluesky: @eoindooley.bsky.social.

Allan Dyen-Shapiro is a Ph.D. biochemist currently working as an educator. He has sold short fiction to venues including *Flash Fiction Online* (where he is now a First Reader), *Dark Matter Magazine*, and *Small Wonders*. He also co-edited an anthology of science fiction, fantasy, and horror set in the Middle East. He is an active member of SFWA and Codex.

Neil A. Edwards attended film school at Bournemouth and Farnham in the UK, before earning his Master's degree in Writing for Stage and Broadcast Media from London's Royal Central School of Speech and Drama. Since 2014, he has been an Associate Artist for Shooting Fish Theatre Company, for whom he has written twenty productions, including: *The Murderess* (2019), *Cuttlefish* (2022) and *Newtopia* (2024). His latest play, *The Spy Network*, about Mary, Queen of Scots, and the failed plot that led to her execution, opened in Gainsborough in May 2025.

Emily Flynn-Jones (she/they) is an award-winning multimedia storyteller. Equipped with a PhD on death, Emily draws together horror, magical realism, romance, and science fiction as she peers into the darker recesses of our cultural landscape. She is known for her critically lauded game, CURSES, a semi-autobiographical tale of witchcraft and womanhood and the dark short story collection, *Is It Enough Yet?*, featuring twisted tales inspired by millennial music. Her work has most recently appeared in the feminine rage charity anthology, *Your Body, My Rage*. Proudly Welsh, she is a settler in Canada where she lives with a terrible cat.

N.J. Gallegos is an ER doctor by day, horror author by night, and co-hosts the Scream Kings podcast. She's written two novels: *The Broken Heart* and *The Fatal Mind*. Her novellas include *It's Me, Hi, I'm the Zombie, It's Me*; *Only You Can Prevent Forest Fires*; and *Just Desserts*; the latter which won an American Legacy Book Award in the Psychological Horror category. N.J. lives with her wife and three cats, enjoys craft beer, reality TV, running, and EDM.

Mallory Glass is an author who likes to create worlds within worlds for her characters to explore. She writes for those who love to embrace a little escape from reality. She spends her time planning her next big adventure and contemplating the vast cosmos. When she's not writing, Mallory loves stargazing and reading. Her first novella, *Stone Heart*, released in April 2025 from Sloth & Envy Press. Her work has appeared in *Toad Shade Zine* and *Humour Me* Magazine UK under a pen name. Find her on Bluesky @mglaz.bsky.social.

Cat Isidore lives in Toronto with two roommates and an orange cat. Her work has appeared in *On Spec Magazine* and *Shooter Literary Magazine*. She is currently taking courses towards a Certificate in Creative Writing at the U of T[oronto] School of Continuing Studies.

M. Kelleher is a speculative fiction writer and theater artist currently living in New Orleans, LA. She has over fifteen years of experience helping to tell stories as a Stage Manager and Lighting Designer in New York (where she's from) and New Orleans (where she lives with her wife.) Her work has been published in *Cosmic Horror Monthly*, and she is a board member and Director of Events for the non-profit writing collective Third Lantern Lit. Look for her upcoming short story collection *Super Shorts: Toxic Ruminations* with Stanchion Books in 2026!

Jordan King-Lacroix is a Jewish writer from the Blue Mountains, just outside Sydney, Australia. His first book, the non-fiction *Ugly: A Bikie's Life*, was published by Penguin-Random House in 2021, and his short story, "The Last Chosen", in the Jewish Futures anthology (Fantastic Books, 2023), was well-received by critics. When not writing, he can be seen gigging around Sydney in his punk band, The Limited.

Bénédicte Kusendila is a Belgian poet and writer whose haiku, senryu, and tanka have appeared in newspapers and journals including *Asahi Shimbun*, *Presence* and *Maintenant*. A former member of South Africa's Afrikaanse Skrywersvereniging, she has performed in Europe, the U.S., and South Africa. She was Artist in Residence at Olympic National Park (2023) and a Bridport Prize for Poetry finalist (2024). Her work often bridges literature and activism, with poems featured in campaigns against online hate and in pandemic-related or peace-building art projects.

C.R. Langille spent many a Saturday afternoon watching monster movies with her mom. It wasn't long before she started crafting nightmares to share with her readers. She is a retired, disabled veteran with a deep love for weird and creepy tales. This prompted her to form Timber Ghost Press in January of 2021. She is an award-winning author, affiliate member of the Horror Writers Association, the DEI Chair for the League of Utah Writers, earned her MFA: Writing Popular Fiction from Seton Hill University in 2014, and was named Editor of the Year by the League of Utah Writers in 2024.

Andrew Lenoir is a former speechwriter turned bookseller based in New York. With the help of his lovely and talented wife Charlotte Anderson, he owns and operates Ellipsis Rare Books. His nonfiction writing has appeared in outlets like *The Brown Journal of History, Fine Books and Collections Magazine, America Magazine, Atlas Obscura, All That's Interesting, Mental Floss,* and *The Revealer.*

John Mahoney is an aspiring author, mediocre sketch artist and recently released convict, determined to blight society with writing instead of misdeeds. He is a graduate of the Institute For Writers. Three of his short stories were published by *The Yard: Crime Blog.* Another was published by Pinky Thinker Press, and another in a horror anthology titled *That Is SO Wrong!* Two more short stories of his were published by *Etched Onyx Magazine.* His first publication was in *Highlights Magazine,* which saw fit to print a joke John wrote before he knew Santa Claus wasn't real. It counts!

David McLachlan is a disabled-veteran writer who lives and works in Northern California. His stories and poems have been published or are forthcoming with Timber Ghost Press and in *Witch House Magazine,* among others. You can connect with him at David-McLachlanWriter.com or on Bluesky: @davidmclachlan.bsky.social.

Lyra Meurer is a sentient muscle spasm with a restless hunger for writing. They live in Colorado with their husband, board games, and ever-growing stacks of journals and books. Their short fiction can be found in *Trollbreath Magazine, Heartlines Spec, Cosmic Horror Monthly,* and several anthologies. Lyra's contemplations on international music, early 2000s television, worldbuilding, and other bizarre phenomena, along with pictures of their doodles, can be found at https://lyrameurer.blogspot.com/.

Lisa Morton is a screenwriter, author of non-fiction books, and prose writer whose work was described by the American Library Association's Readers' Advisory Guide to Horror as "consistently dark, unsettling, and frightening." She is the author of four novels and 200 short stories and is a world-class Halloween and paranormal expert. Her recent releases include the novella *Placerita* (co-authored with John Palisano), *Calling the Spirits: A History of Seances* and the Rondo Hatton Award-winning *The Art of the Zombie Movie*. Recent short stories appeared in *Best American Mystery Stories 2020*, *Final Cuts: New Tales of Hollywood Horror and Other Spectacles*, and *Classic Monsters Unleashed*. She has appeared on such popular shows and podcasts as *Shock Docs*, *Coast to Coast AM*, NPR's *Throughline*, CNN'S *Margins of Error*, and *Chinwag* with Paul Giamatti and Stephen Asma. She is also the host of the weekly *Ghost Report* podcast. A six-time winner of the Bram Stoker Award, Lisa lives in Los Angeles and online at www.lisamorton.com.

Chiya Parvizpur is a Kurdish writer and translator from Sanandaj, Kurdistan, who writes novels and short stories in Kurdish and English. His debut novel, *The Smell of Wet Bricks*, was published in English by Transnational Press London and later in Kurdish. His second novel, *Twenty-four Seconds of Shehin's Life*, written in Kurdish, won the prestigious Kal Literary Prize in Kurdistan. He writes against colonialism in Kurdistan, using words to preserve memory. His fiction is inspired by Kurdish music, and he plays the Tembur, a unifying force for Kurds. Parvizpur has also translated influential Kurdish novels into English by renowned Kurdish authors. Four of his translations are scheduled for publication in 2025 and 2026, further solidifying his role in bridging Kurdish literature with global audiences.

Gevera Bert Piedmont is a neurodivergent cyborg swamp witch living on the edge of a frog pond in Connecticut with her spouse, cats, and an impressive collection of rubber lizards. An author and editor; her books include: *The Maw and Other Time-Traveling Lizard Tales*, the Mickey Crow paranormal series, *Necronomi-RomCom* Cthulhu Mythos duology, *Horror Over the Handlebars* (anthology of Connecticut horror), *Atlas of Deep Ones*, and *Fat Monster* (Nightmare Press). Her story "Toad in the Hole" (Wicked Sick) has been recommended by Ellen Datlow. Bert has an MFA in creative writing and belongs to HWA and New England Horror Writers. Connect at https://linktr.ee/bybertabird

Andrew J. Pixton of Salt Lake is the author of several acclaimed dark fantasy and horror novels—*Fables From Nevermore* is his latest release. Known for exploring unusual worlds and unconventional philosophies, he's now branching into new genres. When he's not crafting tales of the surreal and sinister, Andrew sustains a career in social work and enjoys traveling, practicing martial arts, and indulging his love for ice cream.

Jonathan Reddoch is co-owner of Collective Tales Publishing. He is a father, writer, editor, and publisher. He writes sci-fi, fantasy, romance, and especially horror. He's a prolific flash fiction author, but also writes poetry and short stories. He's from southern California but lives in Salt Lake City.

Adam Rotstein has been writing TV, or whatever we call the multi-headed beast that is TV today, for a long while. It's where he found people were willing to pay him, but it was never his first love. He's wanted to write stories and books ever since he could hold a crayon without putting it up his nose. A few of his stories have made it out into the world in publications like *First Line* and the *Rappahannock Review*. He is a member of the Writer's Guild of Canada.

Richard Shifman is an author and a market research contractor who worked for a dozen years at a Fortune 50 company, so he is intimately familiar with the horrors of corporate life. He lives with his wife near Doylestown, Pennsylvania. His weird fiction, corporate horror story, "Mayo Monday," headlined the October 2023 issue of *Cosmic Horror Monthly*. His ghost-adjacent, YA historical fiction novel, *Paper Airplane, Broken Bones*, was published in March 2025. Richard is an affiliate member of the HWA.

Rose Skye lives on an island in British Columbia and writes speculative fiction while sipping tea with a cat on her lap. Some of her other short stories can be found in the *Nonbinary Review*, *Cosmic Horror Monthly*, and the anthology *We Are All Thieves Of Somebody's Future*. She also writes tabletop roleplaying games, which can be found at vorpalcoil.itch.io.

Elizabeth Suggs is the co-owner of the indie publisher Collective Tales Publishing, owner of Editing Mee, president of the Utah Chapter of the Horror Writers Association, and is the author of a growing number of award-winning published stories, one of which titled—*Into the Dark*—part of the Collective Darkness anthology, was Amazon Bestseller. Another ("Technicolor Tears") was selected for second place in the Quills Short Story Contest. She is also a book reviewer (EditingMee.com), popular bookstagrammer, and cosplayer (@ElizabethSuggsAuthor). When she's not writing or reading, she's traveling the world or practicing yoga.

Ray Van Horn, Jr. is the author of Behind the Shadows, Revolution Calling and Coming of Rage. Ray spent sixteen years covering music and film for *Blabbermouth*, *AMP*, *Pit*, *Dee Snider's House of Hair*, *HorrorNews.net*, *Fangoria*, *Musick*, *Hails & Horns*, *Metal Maniacs*, *Noisecreep*, and many others. Ray was a runner-up finalist in *Alfred Hitchcock Mystery Magazine's* "Mysterious Photograph" contest. His work has appeared in *Rue Morgue*, *Eternal Haunted Summer*, *Punk Noir*, *Atomic Flyswatter*, *Horror Tree*, *Cyber Age Adventures*, *The Rubbertop Review*, and *New Noise*, plus the anthologies *Horror A-Z: X*, *Axes of Evil*, and *Axes of Evil II*.

Novelist, editor and poet, **Ruth E. Walker's** prize-winning fiction and poetry can be found in Canadian, U.S. and U.K. journals and magazines. Raised on fairy tales and fables, her broad literary appetite introduced her to Shakespeare, Isaac Asimov, and Margaret Atwood, among many others. Ruth's fiction and poetry appeared in *Science Creative Quarterly, On Spec, Eccentric Orbits Vol. 3, Utne Reader, Geist, Event,* and *Prairie Fire,* among others. She occasionally blogs at writescape.ca and her novels are represented by Ali McDonald at 5 Otter Literary. Contact: walkwrite@sympatico.ca

B. Zelkovich (she/they) writes Speculative Fiction, anything from dragon hunting and space whales to demon-dealing and ghost tales. She likes to explore human emotions in very inhuman situations. When she isn't escaping through her imagination, she escapes into the wonders of the Pacific Northwest with her spouse and their four-legged son, Simon. Their fiction is in the anthologies *Beyond & Within: Folk Horror Short Stories, Saltwater Sorrows,* and *Life Beyond Us,* as well as *Wyldblood Flash* and *Luna Station Quarterly.* She is a recent graduate of the Viable Paradise Workshop. Connect with her online at bzelkovich.com

ABOUT THE EDITOR

Steve Capone Jr., an award-winning Utah-based writer and editor, founded Whisper House Press in 2024. The indie horror publisher has released three anthologies so far and has plans for at least six releases in 2026.

Steve's latest espionage fiction novel, *Jimmy vs. Communism*, is currently under contract. His 2024 debut, *Max in the Capital of Spies*, earned him the League of Utah Writers Gold Quill Award for a top MA/YA novel.

Steve co-edited *Tricks & Treats: A Romance and Horror Microfiction Anthology* (2024) and contributed editorial consultation and work toward the Diamond Valley Writers Guild's debut anthology, *Managerie*. He curates WhisperHousePress.com, from which he draws stories for another yearly anthology series. His short fiction has appeared in numerous anthologies and literary magazines, including "Driving Angry Opens Doors" (*No Exit*, 2025), "Livelihood" (*Ghostlight Magazine*, 2025), and "Invitation to Eternity" (*Timber Ghost Press*, 2024). He also published his short story collection *That Was Weird: Three Short Stories* (2024).

Steve is also an accomplished, early-career screenwriter. His short screenplay, "Cure for Creativity," won Best Short Screenplay at the Bloody Mirror Film Festival in 2024 and was an official selection or finalist at festivals including Oregon Screams and the Chicago Horror Film Festival. His latest work, "Submission," is currently touring the festival circuit, where it has received selections, placed as a semi-finalist at HorrorFest International, and was a quarter-finalist at the Vancouver Horror Show Film Festival.

His award-winning nonfiction includes the Bronze Quill-winning essay "Teachers Need Guidance Re: Book Bans in Utah" (*Salt Lake Tribune*, 2024), movie and book reviews, and his *Education Week Magazine* article, "Dos and Don'ts of Hybrid Teaching" (2021). For his contributions to the arts, Steve received the Denis Diderot Grant, supporting his July 2025 residency at Chateau d'Orquevaux in France. He is committed to fostering literary communities throughout Utah, organizing events and serving as a proud member of the Horror Writers Association and the League of Utah Writers.

You can find Steve's incorporeal footprint at https://linktr.ee/stevecaponejr.

ACKNOWLEDGMENTS

I wish to thank the contributing authors, who have worked hard on their contributions.

I credit much of my success, such as it is, to the just-critical-enough-while-absolutely-supportive guidance offered by my Washington & Jefferson College professors. Namely, these are Arlan Hess, Lauryn Mayer, and Todd Verdun, among others inside and outside of the English Department at that institution.

I wish to acknowledge the ongoing support of local, independent bookstores in general, and in particular I want to call out The Printed Garden (Sandy, UT), Marissa's Bookstore (Millcreek, UT), Main Street Books (Cedar City, UT), The Book Garden (Bountiful, UT), Central Book Exchange (Salt Lake City, UT), and Winnie & Mo's (Idaho Falls, ID). Big Box stores like Barnes & Noble are getting in the act, too, and I've received support and kindness from those shops located in Murray, Park City, and Sugarhouse, Utah, in particular. Local bookshops are the lifeblood of our literary community, along with local libraries (thank you, Salt Lake County and Salt Lake City library systems!), and they ought to be acknowledged.

I thank Sal Profeta for introducing me to stories in general and in particular for showing me John Carpenter's *The Thing* at much too young an age.

One Mr. Ronald Cambest is a co-author of my continued survival in the face of ongoing personal challenges.

I owe an unpayable debt of gratitude to my wife Sara, our children, and our three dogs (Nova, Quinn, and Odin).

WHISPER HOUSE PRESS

Mundane Horror for the People.

Our mission: Whisper House Press publishes and promotes horror capturing life's mundane absurdities. We are committed to empowering and lifting diverse voices, to radical transparency and fairness, and to celebrating human creativity.

This is Whisper House Press's second publication. If you've read and enjoyed it, the publisher and contributing authors would be grateful for you spending a precious life moment to leave a positive review on the usual places and tell your local library and booksellers about us.

Writers, be on the lookout for submission calls for future anthologies. We anticipate the following themes will show up: *family squabbles, airports and train stations*, and whatever other terrifying minutia the editor-in-chief cooks up. Future calls will be posted in all the usual spooky places: HWA social media, HorrorTree, The Submission Grinder, Reddit, et al.

Please stay in touch by following along at www.whisperhousepress.com and subscribing to the editor's newsletter, which is linked from his linktr.ee @ www.linktr.ee/stevecaponejr.com.

Whisper House Press

Good luck out there.